I0550219

CODE NAME: JANE DOE

A Call to Action

Written by: Jane Darrcie

To sign up for sign up for my newsletter about upcoming books and free giveaways, please visit my website, http://www.JaneDarrcie.com

ISBN: 979-8-9858743-2-7

Fiction Disclaimer:

This is a work of fiction. Names, characters, businesses, events and incidents are solely the products of the author's imagination. Any resemblance to any actual persons, living or dead, or actual events is purely coincidental and nothing more. This story is just for fun and thrilling reading.

DEDICATIONS:

First and foremost, I dedicate this book to my son, Rian. Rian, you have been my light, my beacon of hope in what can be a very dark world sometimes. You have given me a reason to keep going even when it seemed like nothing was going my way, and the deck was stacked against me. You never gave up on me, and throughout every single difficult time, you brought light and love and laughter with you. You have no idea how much that meant to me. When you were little, I saved you from all the monsters under your bed, and now as a young man, you have saved me from all the monsters under mine. I cannot thank you enough. I cannot stress enough how incredibly proud of you I am. Over the years, we have grown up together, and I couldn't have done any of it without you. You are my inspiration. I love you, son...I love you to the moon and back!

L♥ve, Mom

I would also like to dedicate this book to my parents. Thank you for all that you have done for me over the years. Thank you for all that you have taught me. Throughout this book, you may read little nuggets that I wrote just for you. Those treasures are yours. I think you'll get a kick out of them. I love you!

L♥ve, J

I would like to thank all those who helped this book come to fruition. My graphics designer - Anonna, my #1 editor – Maryssa, and my friends who brought me support, inspiration and encouragement to finally get this out. So, Animal, Danielle, Tina, Mike, Miranda, Monica, Megan, Elida, Tara and Rachel... THANK YOU ALL!

L♥ve, J

I would also like to issue a special thanks to Rhonda Byrnes, the author of *The Secret.* That book and all who contributed to it and the other books in that series have truly made a solid impact on my life. Without reading that book back in 2014, I would have never had the courage to try to live out my dream of becoming an author. My superhero would have never come to life without understanding how the universe works first, and I owe that to you all. Thank you for writing that book. Thank you for sharing the tools that I and so many others need to truly change their lives and stars.

Sincerely, Jane Darrcie

Last but certainly not least, I would like to thank the author of *From Jobless to Amazon Bestseller,* Marc Reklau. Marc, Thank you for writing your book and for sharing the tools you have to help writers like me learn the tricks to self-publishing. It was so frustrating to need an agent that you can't get without a publisher and a publisher that you can't get without an agent. I wrote this book in 2020, and it is now 2022. Thanks to you and the tools you shared, I may finally be able to see my book in print and be able to share my fun imagination with tons of other readers. So, THANK YOU!

Sincerely, Jane Darrcie

TABLE OF CONTENTS

PROLOGUE:

My name is Jelena Prazich, and I am a sergeant in the United States Marine Corps. I have a foul mouth and a bit of a temper, but I am not a bad person...or at least I don't think I am. I am the daughter of two humble teachers, Charlotte and Radomir Prazich, who taught me all about the world, or at least I thought they did. My mother is a Native American, and my father is a Russian immigrant, so I got the best of both worlds. Don't think too hard about that strange combination...it'll just give you a headache.

Now, somewhere, someone thought I was pretty special, even though I didn't see it myself, and somehow, I ended up agreeing to help the Central Intelligence Agency. What I thought would be a short little assignment has changed my life forever, and regrettably, I can't say that it was for the better... yet.

What I was told would be "just like boot camp" turned into the most grueling four months of my life. I survived it, but barely...For now, I'll spare you the gory details. I met some great people along the way, and I still think highly of most of them, even though they did try to kill me a few times. I guess we all make mistakes.

On the other hand, I also met some really horrible people...Yep, they were real humdingers for sure. I try to keep my heart light and humble and not let their actions turn me too bitter, but it does tend to get harder and harder after so much time.

I am grateful, though, for all the lessons that my parents taught me...really for anything that anyone's taught me. Until this experience, I had no idea just how much my survival relied on their teachings. When I am going through something, no matter what it might be, my mind just sort of sifts through all of the memories, pulling out their lessons and wisdom. I can't count how many times their words brought clarity to my thoughts and insight into my world.

Well, now I have been given a new objective...a new assignment. To be honest, I am scared to death that I am going to fail...or, worse yet, get myself or someone else killed. I feel like I am totally out of my element here. I don't really have much information about this new assignment. These guys are kinda paranoid about handing out too many details, so I really feel like I am walking in blind. I have no idea what to expect. All I know is that every time I turn around, there is always something there keeping me on my toes. It's like living in an eternal cliffhanger.

I'll do my best, though. You can count on me for at least that. I promise that I'll do my best to try not to let you down. I'll do my best to protect you. I'll do my best to keep you on your toes and hopefully make you proud. I guess I had better get going...wish me luck! ♥Jelena

CHAPTER 1: QUESTIONING

The blood in her mouth was of little concern, as the small area around her was filling with water.

She thought to herself, *Oh, shit! What did I get myself into? I can't believe that I was dumb enough to actually agree to this.* She scrolled through her brain like a video reel, scanning every bit of information she had learned through life and training in hopes of figuring out just how to survive this awful experience. The water kept rushing in as she clawed and pried at the edges of the box that she was confined to. It was wooden and much smaller than she stood tall, mirroring the effect of a coffin. There was one small two-inch hole that she could see out beyond her confines. Her eyes hadn't seen daylight in weeks, so looking out of that hole caused her eyes to water and burn as if she was looking directly at the sun.

"Burning eyes are still not the fucking priority here, dumbass. I'm gonna have to breathe here in a minute, and I ain't a goddammed goldfish!" she sarcastically reminded herself.

The water, still rising, was now at her chest, and she gasped for as many breaths as she could, nearly hyperventilating. She could feel the intense panic set in. "Don't panic. There is always a way out. I just have to be smarter than the morons who came up with this contraption of death. There has gotta be a way out," she sternly told herself. *They wouldn't have taken me if they thought I couldn't handle it...right?* she thought as she questioned her motives.

She continued feeling around the seams of the box, trying to feel for any small crack or space to squeeze her fingertips into. The pitch blackness of the box yielded zero visibility, so her success and survival were all based completely on feel. She pressed her knees into the bottom of the box and pressed her back up, fighting to get any kind of leverage at all. The way they had positioned her in the box removed any chance for her to use her body to try to escape this damned death trap. When the water reached her chin, she pressed her face and mouth as close to that hole as possible, knowing that her source of precious air would be gone in the very next moments to come. She continued searching and scanning every inch of her mind trying to come up with some way to pry her battered physique out of this tiny tomb.

The panic, however, was overwhelming. "How can they do this to me? I'm supposed to be on their side...They're supposed to be on MY team. Why is this necessary? What did I do? I'm gonna die in here!" she said. All rational thought had left her consciousness, and all that remained was a primal urge to live...to breathe. As the water splashed into her nose and mouth, she continued to spit it out violently and thrash around, trying to loosen the corners of what seemed to be her final resting place. "They won't let me die in here. Please, God, don't let them let me die in here," she begged.

As she took her final breath, thoughts of how she got into this predicament ran through her mind like a series of flashcards. Playing back every interaction, conversation, and event leading up to her current circumstance.

(Flashback)

"PRAZICH!" bellowed a large military police officer in a deep, strong voice. She stood from her seat in the hallway and headed into the small conference room within the old base administration building. As she walked in, she saw a small, rectangular, wooden table, similar to the ones you might see in a cafeteria. Around that table sat five older, highly decorated Marine Corps officers in their Alpha greens.

Recognizing the situation, she immediately stood at attention and snapped a salute. They each stood up, returned the salute to her, and sat back down in their seats. Three men and two women all shared the same clean and crisp appearance. In the corner were two more men and one woman, seated but wearing plain black suits and nothing else to distinguish them: not even the base mandated name tags for visitors. *Hmmm, what's with the suits?* she thought.

She knew she was coming in for an evaluation on her performance and conduct, but honestly, she had never seen so much heavy brass in one place before. She was enlisted, and in the Marine Corps, birds of a feather flock together and fraternization between officers and enlisted is more than frowned upon. Flying with pilots, you frequently see the lieutenants and captains and even the occasional major, but the brass here was a shit-ton heavier than those guys. It took a minute for her to realize that these people were not even from her unit. She was familiar with absolutely no one in that tiny little room. Never even heard of them. Right then, she knew this was going to go one of two ways; short, sweet and straight, or long, invasive, and drastically sideways.

She took a second to glance around. At best, the room was perhaps ten by twelve feet with one small rectangular window that you couldn't even see through. Some fog-like condensation had come between the panes of glass, creating an opaque, smoked-out look, with merely a few little streaks of daylight coming through here and there. The floor was the old USMC linoleum that was waxed weekly. The walls were large concrete brick, covered in some semi-gloss shiny battleship gray paint. Nothing else decorated the walls. No posters, no flyers, not even any pictures of the good ole' Commandant. Nothing. For a second, it almost felt like she was in for some sort of court-martial or something.

As the MP closed the heavy wooden door behind her, the highest-ranking officer in the room stood and said, "Sergeant Prazich. I am General Raines. Thank you for coming. Please have a seat, and we will get started."

General Raines was a stout man, easily in his mid-sixties, but he was incredibly physically fit. He had a high and tight faded haircut of salt and pepper hair, but truth be told, more salt than pepper. One could guess that a lifetime in the Marine Corps would do that to you. Considering he had four shiny silver stars on each shoulder, she knew that he had seen more than meets the eye. He had very masculine and chiseled facial features, which kept him quite attractive despite his folded leathery skin. Most noticeable was his strong jaw, but only second to that were eyes as blue as a glacial lake. When she looked into those eyes, it was truly mesmerizing for a moment, like staring into an abyss. She could feel his calm confidence, but the years of battle were undeniable, and the toll it had taken on his soul was quite evident.

She looked around the room for her chair. She sat in the only empty chair available, set in the opposite corner with all eyes on her. Feeling their awkward, penetrating gazes, like laser beams burning into her, she thought, *Ummm, okay, kinda feeling like a zoo animal here. I wonder if I should moo or roar like a tiger? Nawww, wrong crowd for sure. What in the hell is going on here? This is really getting weird. Somebody needs to say something, as long as it's not me.*

She sat down in the most formal manner possible. Her back was straight, and she was very erect. Her hands were palms down, resting on the tops of her thighs and her feet were flat on the shiny linoleum floor, just like they taught her in boot camp. As she sat, she snuck another second to re-check her uniform. *Boots glowing…check. Gig line straight…check. Creases crisp…check. Ribbons in order…check.*

She went over that list in her mind just one more time. For a girl of only twenty-one years, she was the picture-perfect United States Marine. In her short three years of service, she was already able to earn the non-commissioned officer's rank of sergeant. To most, this would seem a nearly impossible accomplishment. Why her? What made Jelena Prazich so special?

She had skills that most girls couldn't even begin to grasp and an affinity for violence. Not the kind of violence where she was a felon or anything of the sort, quite the contrary. She chose to use her power for good and was indeed fearless. Fighting the good fight was something she enjoyed passionately, always sticking up for the weaker kids…always challenging the bullies on the playground. She never shied away from a fight in her entire life, but she wasn't a bad person…or at least she didn't start out that way.

Most of her useful skills were imparted by her father, Radomir

Prazich, a Russian immigrant. Son of Mary Agnus-Irma and Stanislaus Prazich from a remote southern town on the Russia/Poland border. They immigrated to the land of opportunity, America, to flee the advances of Hitler and the SS when Rad was only a small boy. They settled in Pennsylvania, and Rad grew up on the rougher side of Philadelphia, where most immigrants lived. His parents worked in the factories there, and they didn't have the easiest lives, but they had something that they never had before...hope.

Radomir grew to be a stern man, with a round face and a chiseled jawline that was always covered with a beard. He was big and strong and was a prized boxer in his own time, but his deep brown eyes were always warm and welcoming. He was the first in his family to be formally educated and to attend college. He focused on the subject of History, but he also studied the arts of war and peace...culture and science...and he was absolutely Jelena's idol. In her eyes, even though he was incredibly hard on her at times, the sun rose and set on her father.

He taught her everything that she would need to know to survive just about anything. He taught her to fight, shoot, and handle edged weapons like knives and axes...He taught her that the 'bad guys' don't care if she was a girl or a boy, that they would hurt her just the same, and she needed to always remember to get up and keep fighting, no matter what. He taught her that pain exists in the mind and that pain could be controlled. He taught her not only how to dish out the hits but also how to take them and how important recovery and refocus were in winning a fight or living to fight another day. He taught her how to hunt, live off the land, and so many other things that would come to be quite useful. Between the strength and precision of her father and the grace and cunningness of her mother, she blossomed into what would be one of the most beautiful but lethal flowers the world would ever come to know.

"Sergeant Jelena Prazich," General Raines began. "In your short service, you have become one of the youngest and most decorated Marines on this base. Most Marines cannot accomplish what you have, and **that** is why **you** are here. Your sergeant major and your commanding officer have even recommended you for acceptance into the Annapolis Naval Academy. I have to say, to impress those two salty dogs, that is quite the feat in and of itself. Your tenacity, combat skills, strength, determination, and character have built you a reputation that precedes you. I realize that you may not know us, but we most definitely know you. We have followed you, your tours, your actions. We have been keeping quite close tabs on you, actually, just to be able to convene this panel and discuss your future and how we can help each other."

Jelena's eyes must have shot over to look at the folks in suits just as the general looked back at her. When she realized that he was looking at her, she did not look away. She looked directly into his eyes without any visible reaction. Stoicism was one of her favorite games to play with people. She preferred playing her hands quite close to the chest, especially regarding her emotions and reactions. She prided herself in being 'difficult to read.' She called it her undefeated poker face. It had a two-prong

affect, in that it worked well with playing poker as well as playing politics.

"Sergeant Prazich, these folks have a project that we believe you would be perfect for," General Raines said. "Colonel Jacobs, I think this is where you can start to lay out some groundwork for the young sergeant."

Colonel Wanda Jacobs also looked like she had had a challenging Marine Corps career. She was a shorter lady, perhaps measuring 5'5 in her USMC-issued patent leather pumps. She had a very petite build with long delicate-looking fingers. She was a lady in her fifties, with sandy blonde hair and visible roots of a different shade. Her hair was pulled back in a gentle bun, with a few wispy gray hairs mixed in on the sides. She had deep round brown eyes that were magnified behind the gray military reading glasses she wore. She had some folds to her skin, as well, and some worry lines that were proof of her own battles. Being a woman in the Marines is tough enough, but to climb the ranks as she had done over the years is a tall order to fill.

Colonel Jacobs began, "Certainly General Raines. Thank you. Sergeant Prazich, my name is Colonel Jacobs. We obviously have some extra folks here today, and I am sure you are curious. They are not Marines, but they *are* with a different governmental agency. Should we conclude this panel and determine that you are indeed a good fit for their...umm...project, then you would be able to retain your military rank and pay, be eligible for a promotion, as well as future promotions, and be able to receive pay from their agency too, making this quite the lucrative project for you...should you accept, that is."

Lieutenant Colonel Barrs, the other female officer, then interrupted, "Please understand, Sergeant Prazich, we value your service, and we would hate to see you go, but we are all on the same team here," she hesitated and glanced back at General Raines before reluctantly continuing, "...ultimately at least...and in the name of what is in the best interest of our great nation, we all agree, that you are one of our finest assets, and that your participation in this project would be of an even greater value to our country. "

Lieutenant Colonel Mary Barrs looked like she was the youngest of the bunch. Either she was in her late thirties, or she just had some incredible genes allowing her to be quite attractive. She was around 5'9 and slender. It honestly looked like she couldn't have done a pull-up even with help. However, by most standards, she could have easily been a model. Her skin was smooth and tan, and her hair was cut at an angled bob just below her ears. Her hair was so black that it nearly appeared a deep violet in the few beams of sunlight that broke through the cracks in the window. She had vividly green eyes, perfectly straight, white teeth, and spoke without much presence. Her lack of confidence and command made Jelena question how this meek female became the leader of a rowdy bunch of Jarheads. Just seemed a bit unlikely, but then again, we all have sides of ourselves that are not always on display.

Jelena carefully looked at each of the five USMC officers, studying every single face. All displayed similar stoicism to her own, except Lieutenant Colonel Barrs. Although it was obvious that she was trying to keep and maintain her bearing, it was blatant that she was not happy with the situation or whatever 'project' the black suits were proposing. Jelena glanced over at the black suits. They had a much different look, almost of glee, sort of like the cat that ate the canary. All they were missing were the little feathers sticking out of the crooks of their mouths. They merely looked right back at Jelena as if she were the winning horse they had all bet on.

Hmmm, weird, thought Jelena. *No briefcases, no papers, no name tags, no wedding rings...hmmm, nothing. Not even a damn pencil. Who comes to a meeting with nothing? Who in the hell are these people? And more to the point, what in the hell do they want with me? What is this project? I think it's time for some answers!*

"Sir, permission to speak freely?" Jelena asked.

"Within reason, granted," General Raines replied.

"Sirs and ma'ams, I have a few questions," Jelena continued.

"Certainly, we will answer them to the best of our ability," the general followed.

Jelena took a second to gather her thoughts and stood up to address the panel and the three black suits. She tried to prepare herself for whatever crazy notions these bureaucrats had stuffed up their sleeves. She didn't want to give them any facial reaction that they may or may not misinterpret, but she knew they wanted something from her. From the look on Lieutenant Colonel Barrs' face, it was not even remotely in the realm of good...it may have even been immoral and most likely ethically questionable.

"Thank you, sir," Jelena said. "My first question is, what agency are these folks with, and is that the agency that I would be serving?"

The room began to buzz with movement. It was quite plain to see how that one particular question made every single person in the room, other than Jelena, rather uncomfortable as they looked back and forth at each other and shifted a bit in their seats.

Boy, did I just publicly announce the few national secrets that I am privy to, or what? Jelena thought.

"Before we answer any questions, we just need you to sign this first," said General Raines.

"What is *this*?" asked Jelena.

"It is simply a non-disclosure statement. In military terms, it is a gag order," General Raines explained. "It just means that you cannot discuss anything that is discussed here in this room, during this meeting with anyone at all. Also, you have to understand that once we discuss these things with you, we will need an answer from you immediately, so we do want you to ask as many questions as you need to come to a timely decision."

He slid a form across the table for Jelena to sign. It had all her personal details, such as name, rank, social security number, etc., already filled into the appropriate places. He held out a pen for Jelena to take. As she peered into his icy blue eyes, she gently took the pen and signed the form without hesitation.

I mean…it's just a form saying that I won't blab right. No big deal. So here ya go. My John Hancock right. There, done, she thought as she braced herself for some intense declarations.

"Okay, Sergeant. So, to answer your question," General Raines began. "These folks are with the Central Intelligence Agency, and yes, that is the agency that you would be working for."

Jelena continued, "What is the 'project' that they need me for, and what does that entail exactly?"

General Raines looked over at the taller of the men in the black suits and said, "Perhaps you would be best to field that particular question."

The taller man stood from his seat. Tall indeed, he was an easy 6'6 with an athletic frame. He had a few ethnic features, which made him look slightly exotic. Dark hair, dark eyes, high cheekbones, no facial hair, but he had thick full lips and an olive tone to his skin. Italian, Indian or Israeli, perhaps. Though he spoke with no accent, his deep baritone voice was the one crooners dreamed of having. Jelena thought he probably got his way quite often since his voice could melt nearly any female heart within earshot...except perhaps hers. Jelena watched as even the female officers in the room were tuned in completely to his every word and mannerism. She refocused her attention onto him.

"Sergeant Prazich, we need a fresh female operative. We have located a particular person of interest with some extremely sensitive information in their possession. We need a female operative to develop a relationship with this man and recover the thumb drive with the information on it. Then just simply bring it back to us," the man said.

"And who are you?" Jelena asked.

"Who I am, is of no importance," the man replied

"Well, what kind of information?" Jelena asked.

"That is also none of your concern," the man replied. "When you work for us, you only get the information that you require to get the job done. Nothing more. Consider it classified beyond your security clearance level."

"Um, okay," Jelena mumbled. "How long is this project supposed to take?"

"However long it takes for you to earn his trust, learn where he keeps the drive, steal it and return with it. So however long it takes, is however long it takes. We will not reach out to you, but you will have a point of contact nearby and a handler, and you will be responsible for reaching out at least once a month, or more, to provide us with appropriate situational reports. Progress reports, if you will. You will be issued a new name with new credit/bank cards, identification, passport, and the lot. You will also be issued a code name. A name that only a very few assets will know. People that can help you in the field, when we cannot," the man explained.

"Alright. Do I come back to my unit once this 'project' is over?" Jelena asked.

"Yes," the man stated. "However, we may call on you in the future for other… 'projects.' It is very time consuming and costs quite a bit to get operatives trained and field ready. Once we have sound operatives, we contact them first when assignments come up. I am sure you understand."

"Absolutely," Jelena said. "I totally understand. What happens if I get caught?"

"My best suggestion is...don't. Don't get caught. Typically, if you get caught, we don't know you and we will deny all involvement with you. Your getting caught and us admitting that we know you could cause the next World War. Upper management will do everything possible to avoid that situation, and I do mean everything. There are extremely rare situations where we will try to help you to the best of our ability, but really it will come down to your prowess to get yourself out of those situations," the man explained. "But there are other assets out in the field, resources that you can contact for help if you get jammed up."

So, no guarantee on getting any help to get out of there, huh. Gotcha. I've always had my unit...I have never gone by myself before...totally rogue. I mean, this seems easy enough, and more money...just steal the drive and get the hell on out of there. I think I can do this. I can't believe that he basically said, 'You're on your own, kid,' Jelena thought.

Jelena was quiet for an extended moment, processing the information she was just told.

"So, I just have to go somewhere and meet some guy, pretend to be his girlfriend, steal some thumb drive, and then come back...right?" Jelena asked as respectfully as possible.

"Yes, basically," the man replied.

"Sergeant Prazich, do you have any other questions?" asked

General Raines.

"Yes, you mentioned getting field operatives trained and field ready. What exactly does that mean? I mean, what do I have to do in there?" Jelena asked.

The man explained, "We send you to a sort of boot camp training facility, not much more different than Field Combat Training. We will teach you how *we* do things and put you through various training scenarios. Once you have completed that successfully, we will send you on a very simple assignment with another asset...a more senior and experienced asset, to see how you do. We only have one shot at this guy, Sergeant, so we cannot afford to send you in if you are not one hundred percent ready and able to accomplish the goal of this assignment completely on your own."

"Alright, I understand," Jelena said. "If I say 'yes' that I will accept this assignment or project or whatever, when do I leave for this training?"

He responded curtly, "In less than twenty-four hours."

CHAPTER 2: NOT-SO-WARM WELCOME

"You have the next few hours to get your personal affairs in order. Then we'll have a team come and pick you up," the man in black explained.

"I am assuming that while in the field, I will not be able to contact my family. Am I allowed to say goodbye to them?" Jelena asked

"Not specifically, but what you *are* allowed to tell them is that you are being deployed for an indeterminate amount of time. You can tell them that you will reach out again once you return from that deployment. Please keep in mind, Sergeant, that we have been watching you and listening to you. We are always listening. Failure to follow our rules could only earn you time in Guantanamo if you catch my drift," he said.

"Yeah, I got it," Jelena replied dryly, knowing that a vacation in Guantanamo was not on her bucket list. For a split second, she wondered just how many spies have been spying on her this whole time and exactly how much did they know, but now was not the time to go down that rabbit hole. "What do I bring for this training?"

"Nothing. Your home will be secured and checked every so often to ensure it stays secure. Your identification and other things are not necessary, so find a safe place at home to stash them until you return. Once the assignment is over, you will come back here and resume your original life, keeping in mind our little 'Hush-Hush' agreement. After all, loose lips sink ships, right Sergeant?" the man said, chuckling.

Jelena's face remained stoic and emotionless. She sat back down and quietly pondered over this new opportunity. Was this a blessing or a curse? Jelena had received word, a few weeks back, that her mother was fighting breast cancer. Her family was under a bit of financial duress and could certainly use a little help paying some bills. She also had a younger brother, but he was still too young to contribute much. This opportunity may be the blessing her father had been praying for. Should she trust this man in black? His answers seemed so cold and manipulative. For some reason, Jelena's gut told her that there was wayyyy more to this assignment than what she was being led to believe. Was the risk worth it? That was the question. What would her parents do if she died? What if this 'person of interest' killed her? What then? So many questions, but undoubtedly questions that the men in black would refuse to answer or would answer with some schmoozy beat-around-the-bush bullshit that Jelena could see right through.

"I just have one more question, sir," Jelena said.

"And that would be?" the man said, now quite obviously losing his patience with this game of twenty questions.

"If I die...If I am killed out there...what would my family get? I mean, what would happen? How much money would they get?" Jelena asked.

"Well, we hope that will not happen, and with the intensive training that we provide, that should be unlikely. However, things do happen sometimes. If, for some unfortunate reason, you were to be killed, you would receive a military burial under your original name and rank. Your family would receive not only your military life insurance money of one hundred thousand dollars, but they would also receive what would amount to one year's worth of your new salary, which would be around one million US dollars. They, however, would **never** know the actual events leading to your death, just that you died honorably in the line of duty. No accessible records will be kept. Your CIA-life will have never existed," the man explained.

"Okay. May I have a moment to think about all this, please?" Jelena asked as she looked at General Raines.

"Certainly, Sergeant," he replied.

Jelena remained seated. Her position was still rather erect and straight. However, her eyes were slowly changing their focus between the beam of light coming through the crack in the window and the nearly invisible boot print left behind, by whatever Marine took the easy waxing option of Mop and Glo instead of regular floor wax. Mop and Glo was a quick, easy way to get the floors shiny in a hurry on a Friday night field day, but damned if you stepped in it, your boot print would be left like a time capsule.

Jelena had so much to think about...Not getting to say goodbye...Less than twenty-four hours...Could this even be real? Maybe she was just dreaming...but a quick zapping pinch to the skin between her pinky and ring fingers proved that she was quite awake. Her mother, in a battle for her life...Her father battling to pay the bills. If she lived, she could help them, and even if she died, she could still help them...right? So, maybe it really was a win-win situation.

The question she had to ask herself, is *could* she do it? Could she 'pretend' to be some stranger's girlfriend, along with all the intimate things she would have to do to be convincing? Could she live with herself after?

Hell, could she even get through the training? If it is only like boot camp, that's an easy answer. Bootcamp had its more challenging moments, but her father pretty much prepared her for most of what she had to do there. From the time she swore in, her parents were so incredibly proud of her and reminded her of that every time they spoke.

Jelena, on the other hand, never thought much of herself. Humility was one of the greatest of traits, according to her father, whereas ego never helped a soul. However, she never had nearly as much confidence inside compared to what people thought she had. She just did her best and hoped that she wouldn't let anyone down. Her mind kept circling the question, what made *her* so special? All she was doing was her job as a Marine. Why did the CIA of ALL agencies want *her* to be an operative?

FUCK! So many fuckin questions in my head and so very little time to answer them. I have to make a decision. I can feel their gazes once again, burning into my skin, waiting for a response. I wonder what would happen if I didn't agree…What would happen to me then? Would my military career be ruined? God, please help me make this decision! Jelena thought.

She closed her eyes, took a deep breath, and said, "General, I have made my decision."

The room started buzzing with movement again. Everyone straightened in their chairs as if they were on the edge of their seats, waiting to hear the winning lotto numbers.

As things quieted down, Jelena said, "I agree to become a field operative for the CIA. I agree to participate in this project and help you recover your stolen information. I want, in writing, what will happen should I be killed. I want in writing, what my family will receive financially, should I die. I want that before we all leave this room. Then I will quickly tie up my personal affairs and be ready when it's time. Okay?"

Before anyone could answer, two loud knocks came from the wooden door. Being the closest to the door, Lieutenant Colonel Barrs got up to answer it. On the other side was the colossal MP, who was charged with guarding the door and the hallway, preventing anyone from overhearing anything that might be said. He handed the Lieutenant Colonel a sealed manilla envelope.

"Thank you so much, Corporal," she said softly as she shut the door.

Lieutenant Colonel Barrs then handed the envelope to General Raines, who immediately slid a finger under the sealed edge to open it. "I believe this satisfies your request," he said as he handed it to Jelena to review.

HOLY SHIT! Jelena thought. *They really ARE listening to everything!*

Jelena slowly looked over the statement, which looked more like an insurance guarantee paper...all the numbers were there...even her parents' names and address were correct...

Radomir and Charlotte Prazich... 5646 Adrian Avenue, Lakewood, Florida 35416... In the event of the untimely demise of their only daughter, Sergeant Jelena Radomir Prazich, in the line of duty...blah blah blah...they are to receive the amount of one-point-one million USD within no more than thirty days of her reported (not confirmed) death, to be received from the US Treasury. This amount is exempt from any type of taxation and is free and clear to the listed beneficiaries above.

"Sergeant Prazich, Is that satisfactory?" General Raines asked.

"Yes, sir. Thank you. May I please have a copy of the signed document?" Jelena replied as she handed it back to him.

"Most certainly," General Raines said, as he signed the document and passed it along for the other four panel members to sign, as well as the three CIA officials.

Only mere minutes passed before there was a copy of that signed document in Jelena's hand. She looked at all the signatures and noticed immediately that three of them weren't even signatures at all, but instead alphanumeric combinations. The CIA officials only put some code indicating their identity. *Weird*, she thought, *these guys are uber paranoid.*

"Good. We are done here. We'll be in touch, Sergeant," said the tall mystery man as he and his comrades bustled past her through the door.

"Sergeant, thank you for your help and your dedication to our country. Good luck out there, and we'll see you when you get back," General Raines said as he smiled at her and extended his hand to shake hers. Jelena quietly shook his hand and nodded her head. She popped a salute to him and the higher ranks in the room, and once they returned the gesture, she began down the long, echoing hallway. The anticipation of what she just got herself into caused her ears to ring so bad that she could only hear her heartbeat in time with her boots hitting the floor. The anxiety she was feeling was a familiar friend who always showed up just before a deployment or a nighttime OP with the grunts.

On the way out, Jelena decided to stop by the base chapel. *Hey, a prayer or two or a good old blessing from a priest couldn't be a bad thing before you do something stupid, right?* Jelena thought.

She walked into the chapel and was greeted by Father Maggille. "Hello," he said. "How can I help you today, Sergeant?"

"Well, Father, I am being deployed. I'm a little nervous, and I was hoping you could maybe pray with me a bit...you know...put in a good word for me with the big guy upstairs, maybe? Or maybe throw in a few blessings or Hail Marys or whatever you guys do? I'm sorry, I don't know all of the fancy prayer words, my parents taught me that God knows what's in my heart, so I just kinda always just ran with that," Jelena confessed.

"He certainly does, my child. I would be happy to pray for and with you, for your safe and successful return," said the priest as he placed his hand on Jelena's shoulder and began to say some fancy-pants Latin prayer.

The only things she halfway recognized were the Hail Mary, the Lord's prayer, and that Psalm about the shadow of the valley of death and not fearing any evil...*Ahhh, that seems about right,* she thought.

"Thanks, Padre!" Jelena said softly once the priest finished praying.

"I would say peace be with you, but we both know that lies are not becoming. So, how about, umm...May the Lord's hand protect you throughout your journey," the priest replied.

"That works. Thanks again," she said as she headed toward the colorful stained-glass doors.

Jelena went home that afternoon and immediately began writing letters, three to be specific. One to her mother, one to her father, and even one to her much younger brother. Quietly she snuck around her own house, trying to figure out the best, most ingenious place to hide the insurance document as well as the letters. Her safety deposit box was way too obvious, and regardless, the bank was already closed.

If I am leaving in less than twenty-four hours, then the bank's out, she thought. She sat in her living room, racking her brain for the perfect little hiding spot. *Hmmm racking myyyy brainnnn...rackadoodle friggin dandy...rack'em stack'em robots...rack'em...crack'em...I got it,* she thought. Knowing that they were listening to her every move, she turned on some music to prevent any sounds that she made from providing any clues as to where she was hiding these documents.

Over her kitchen island was a hanging rack, where Jelena would hang her metal cooking utensils and pots and such. She pried open the ends of the utensils and tightly rolled each document into a tiny stick, which she shoved into the base of different utensils. She snapped back on the end caps and hung them right back where they were.

Jelena trusted her commanders, but only to a certain extent. She had been on enough, don't ask – don't tell missions, entailing the act of dropping men in black, armed to the teeth into tree lines around the world to know better than to trust them completely. She knew that good o'le Uncle Sam wasn't nearly as noble as he proclaimed to the public. Most importantly, she knew that she was just another tool, who could be disposed of just as quickly as they picked her up. In this line of work, you just never know what mission might be your last. She needed to leave letters and proof, where her father could find it. She did as she was told, and when she called her parents, she told them that she was being deployed for an indeterminate amount of time to an undisclosed location and would call again when she got back. Jelena and her father spoke for a good half an hour. She brought up the memory of how her grandma Agnus-Irma would always cook a meal in honor of people in her family who had died. She would always say, "Cook them an honorable meal and use the good cookware...hell...use ALL the good stuff...don't be stingy." Her father just laughed at such a funny memory of his mother.

Before Jelena hung up, the last thing she said to her father was, "Papa, If I don't make it back, please promise to come to my house and cook me an honorable meal...and don't forget to use the good cookware!"

"I promise, my girl. I love you, and I will do as you ask," Radomir replied. "Stay safe and remember your lessons."

"I will, Papa. I love you and Mama too. I will talk to you soon. Bye," Jelena said.

"Bye-bye now," he said, already missing her.

Jelena tidied up her small semi-rural two-bedroom home and made herself a sandwich, even though the nerves in her stomach indicated that eating might not be the best plan. She made herself eat the whole sandwich along with an apple and some water. Her stomach was still uncomfortable, and she just couldn't calm the waves of anxiety and nervousness.

Those shady bastards, she thought. *Listen to your instincts Jelena...telling you that it may be a long while before you get to eat again once they get their hooks into you. Simple job though, they'll come...I'll do their little training...I am at the top of my game. What am I worried about? I already run ten miles a day, and I'm strong. I'm a BEAST, haha. This is fine. I really am just freaking myself out over nothing. Get a grip Jelena! You are a Marine, for Christ's sake!*

She finished up her apple and chugged the last bit of her water before taking the trash out. She decided it was best to throw away the food in the fridge since she wasn't sure when she'd be back but figured the things in the freezer ought to be okay. She gathered the strings of the bag, tied them in a tight little knot, and headed outside. As she lifted the lid to the outside trash can, everything went black. She tumbled to the ground and immediately realized that someone had tackled her and put some bag over her head that reeked of bad breath and vomit. Before she could even begin to fight back, she was face down on the ground and could feel her hands and feet both being tied together.

"FUCK! HOLY SHIT! WHAT THE FUCK, MAN! LET ME GO!" Jelena screamed.

"Shut the fuck up. Nobody's talking to you, you fuckin bitch! So just shut the fuck up already!" a deeper unrecognizable voice whispered near her ear.

"WHO THE FUCK ARE YOU??? WHAT THE FUCK IS THIS??" Jelena screamed again.

Just then, Jelena felt a huge hand grab the hair on the back of her head, through the bag, and pull back violently with an equally unpleasant knee in the middle of her back... "Listen here, you salty bitch, if you know what's good for you, you will abso-fucking-lutely shut the fuck up right this second, or I will beat the life out of you until you do...am I clear?" he quietly demanded.

"Crystal," Jelena croaked.

Jelena felt the pressure of at least three guys lifting her, with the bag still on her head, and subsequently felt them throw her onto a hard surface. The first thing Jelena smelled was motor oil. She assumed that she was in some sort of vehicle, like a van, maybe. "Well, Jesus, I certainly didn't think being 'picked up at home' meant being fucking hog-tied and thrown face-first into a goddamned van. I am starting to have some serious second thoughts here about what exactly I have entered into. What the fuck have I done?" Jelena asked under her breath.

As she lay there, she remained quiet, just listening to the small, seemingly insignificant sounds that were going on around her in the van. Nobody else seemed to get in, and it wasn't running. They didn't even shut the side door, as she could still feel the moist, cool night air against the little bit of skin that was exposed. She listened. She heard the trash bag crinkle and the lid slam shut. She heard them open and shut her front door, and she was pretty sure that she heard them check that it was locked.

"That's good…let's go," she heard one of them say from a distance.

"Yeah, let's get this fuckin cunt to her destination…Christ, don't they have better shit for us to do? I'm not a fuckin Uber!" she heard another one snip.

"Now *you* need to shut the fuck up…she don't need to be hearing all this!" she heard the third one say.

"Damn…I guess this *is* my ride…Hmmph…Uber…now that guy's funny," she whispered.

"Get the fuck over," the second one yelled as he kicked her and shoved her body over to one side of the van with his boot.

Everything was so quiet for a long time. The only discernable sounds were the tires on the pavement. *There must be a hole in the floorboard somewhere*, she thought.

She was quite uncomfortable and tried to shift so that she could regain feeling in her feet and hands. As soon as she moved, she felt the heavy weight of asshole number two's boot pressing down on her.

"Where do you think you're fuckin goin'? Make yourself useful and take a fuckin' nap or something," he said.

Geez, this guy really needs my mom to wash his mouth out with some liquid soap or something, she thought.

The minutes turned into what seemed like hours. No music, no talking, no nothing…just the agonizing pain of contorted limbs and double zip ties. Jelena began to drift off...only to be awoken by the sharp pain in her limbs every now and then or when the driver hit a bump. As she drifted off, she began to dream-dive into memories of lessons her papa had taught her.

In her memory-dream, Jelena is about seven years old and has fallen from her bike. She has a scraped knee that was bleeding. Her father was down beside her wiping the tears from her face. He scooped her up and brought her inside to the kitchen sink. As he talked to her, he turned on the cold water from the tap and ran it over her knee. Jelena listened and watched as her blood washed down the drain, and he said, "Remember, Jelly, pain is only in your mind. It can be controlled, and you are the one with the controller. When something hurts, close your mind and wash the pain away like washing away a stain. In your mind's eye, pour the cleanest water over that pain and watch it flow right down the drain. You can do it, Jelly. Pain is not the end...It is only a reminder that you are still alive."

The screeching halt of the van put Jelena's body in motion, flying forward against the backside of the front seats, jarring her awake. She heard the van door slide open, and asshole number two spout, "Come on, fuck face...time to get this party started," he said, as he dragged her limp, numb body out of the van.

The pain was no more. Jelena had done what her father had taught her and washed the pain away...all that was left was the numbness of what had now become utterly useless limbs.

Jelena could still feel the three men carry her. She was still tied and still had a bag over her head. The pressure in her shoulder joints was heavy and prickly, and her head felt too heavy to even lift. They carried her for what felt like forever, but in reality, it was perhaps the distance of one football field before they dropped her again…face-first onto the hard, concrete ground.

Snip…snip…she heard, followed by the slamming and locking of a large metal door. They had cut the zip ties but had left the bag over her head. All she could do was lay there, helplessly, until she could mentally will her limbs back into a functioning state. As she lay there, remaining somewhat in cloaked darkness, waiting for the sensation to return to her limbs, Jelena continued to visit memories of her father's lessons. "That's right, Jelly. Your mind controls all. You simply must control your mind. You can do it, Jel! Don't give up!" she remembered him saying quite frequently.

Slowly, the feeling returned to Jelena's arms, hands, legs, and feet, inch by inch. She concentrated, cleared her mind, and guided the sensation back to her various appendages. It was a tediously slow process, but once the sensation had mostly returned, Jelena pushed herself into an upright sitting position, with her long legs extended in front of her. She was finally able to pull the bag off her head to see her new surroundings.

"Shit!" she gasped. "This is soooooo not good."

CHAPTER 3: TRAINING OR TORTURE

As Jelena regained feeling in her arms and legs, she pulled the dark bag from her head. She quickly realized that she had bitten off way more than she could ever chew and may have gotten herself into a situation that would test every limit that she possibly had. She looked around, and what she saw not only made her uneasy but extremely grateful that she made herself eat that damned sandwich.

"Yeah, I don't think brunch on the veranda is included in this little field trip," she quietly said to herself as she began to test her legs to see if they were ready to bear her weight.

Once she got to her feet and felt steady, she began to examine her surroundings more closely. The room was slightly bigger than the squadron's hanger conference room, which she had paced out to be approximately twelve feet by fourteen feet, but this room was empty. The floors were some hard-grated metal panels with some type of weird star pattern throughout. They sort of reminded her of those metal mud flaps you find on the ass end of semi-trucks. Three walls were flat, concrete, and painted an intense dark gray. One wall was a huge mirror, probably a two-way, with video and sound on the other side. The ceiling appeared to be a metal drop ceiling with some sort of vent, but that puppy had to be at least fifteen feet tall, and there was no way to get up there. Four bright lights shone down from the four corners of the ceiling, creating a reflection off the floor panels.

"Where's the damn door?" she whispered.

As Jelena could now fully feel her feet and legs, she began to walk the perimeter of the room, searching for the hidden door. She heard it slam earlier, so she knew it was there...somewhere. She felt the walls, searching up and down, rather methodically, for what could be the seam or opening of the hidden passageway. Hidden quite cleverly in plain sight, she discovered a seam at the edge of the two-way mirror that just had to be one side of the hidden door, but there was no way to open it. No handle, no lock, just a barely-there seam, hidden in the reflections of the mirror. She paused for a moment, knowing that this was one situation where her stoicism would benefit her. She didn't openly display any reaction to finding the door, and although she was pretty impressed with how cleverly it was hidden, she still didn't want to show how pleased she was with herself for finding it.

However, finding it didn't equate to opening it, and this, in and of itself, was rather disappointing. That feeling...that sinking feeling of disappointment, was so much harder to conceal. Under no circumstances did she want to give her captors any satisfaction in knowing the utter disappointment that she felt over the fact that even with her wit and field combat skills, she had no way on Earth of opening that damned door. But hell, they were probably watching her try to figure it all out anyways.

"Pricks and puzzles...What fun!" she said under her breath as she continued to look around. She took a long pause and a huge sigh before continuing, "Hmm...not even an electrical outlet...Damn!"

Jelena really did not like providing any kind of reaction, whatsoever, for other people to enjoy. She learned as a small child from her mother that sometimes people would do things just to get a reaction. If you take that reaction away, then eventually they leave you alone because it's no fun when the victimized person just stands there stoically looking at you like you're an idiot. For the longest time her emotional wall building skills may have gotten a bit too good, because even her beloved father thought she actually did not love him. Although that was not at all true in regard to him, when it came to strangers, she felt they simply did not deserve any type of reaction from her, good or bad. The less ammunition Jelena provided to others, the less that could be used against her. This was how she protected herself from emotional, psychological, and other types of manipulative attacks.

Once again, Jelena decided to remain stoic. She plopped down in a corner, propped herself up against the walls, and remained calm and quiet. At this point, she realized that getting upset would not make her captors hurry up to retrieve her. So, her best bet was to distract her mind to pass the time. They come when they come. Throughout her childhood and military journey, Jelena had learned the importance of meditation and could pretty much free her mind regardless of her location or even activity at times. So, she sat in that corner and silently meditated, taking the time to revisit many of her father's lessons that she learned while growing up. Sometimes this meditation would put Jelena in a dream-like trance, so around the time Jelena turned fifteen years old, she started calling the practice "dream diving."

One memory she dove into was when her father talked to her about introspection and the passing of time. The family had taken one of their traveling vacations up to the Grand Teton Mountains in southwestern Wyoming. There, they found a perfect camping spot, on the very edge of a glacial lake with water so calm and clear that it almost appeared invisible when looking straight down at the rocks below. The rest of the time, the water looked like glass, perfectly reflecting the image of the neighboring snow-capped mountains. As she was on her knees, looking into the water, her father came behind her and smacked the surface of the water with a stick.

"Ahhh haha, what can you see now?" he taunted her.

"Papa! Now I can't see anything! Why did you do that?" she scolded.

"No? You can't see anything now? Well, what could you see before, Jelly?" he asked.

"Well, Papa, I could see all the way down to the bottom. I could see all the little fish and all the rocks. The water was so clear," she explained.

"Okay. And why can't you see now?" he asked, trying to navigate the conversation in a certain direction.

"Because you messed it all up, Papa! You smacked it with a stick, and now I can't see anything," she huffed back at him.

"Oh, Jelly," he said as he sat next to her. "I did that on purpose. When the water is calm and still, you can see all the way to the bottom. You can see all the little details. But, when you disturb the water and that water becomes agitated and filled with movement, you can't see anything. Your little soul is very much like that. For you to see the details inside your mind and heart, you must learn to be still because when you are agitated or upset, you won't have any clarity, and you won't be able to see a single thing. We can choose to feel anxiety and fear when we sit still, or we can learn to harness the clarity that comes with those moments of calm."

He kissed Jelena on the top of her head as he got up and went back to setting up camp. He left her there to think about how important calm and stillness are sometimes. As she was thinking about what he had said, she noticed how amazingly colorful everything around her was. Green plants were growing, and colorful wildflowers were everywhere, and apart from the random summer breeze that would move them a little, most of those things remained pretty still. But eventually, she would always come back to the lakeshore. The water was so blue that it would mesmerize Jelena for hours. Perhaps that's why she had a thing for clear blue eyes. They were simply hypnotic to her.

Jelena and her father would sit on the edge of that lake and talk or sometimes just sit and admire all the good Lord had created for them.

Jelena was nine years old on this trip. She was tall for her age but slender. She wore a unicorn T-shirt, blue jeans torn at the knee, flip flops, and mostly wore her strawberry blonde hair up in a ponytail. She had quite the eclectic fashion sense and most definitely marched to her very own beat. She would ask the questions that most adults would not bother with, but to Jelena, those were the questions of her universe.

"Papa, what *is* time?" Jelena innocently asked as they sat skipping stones on the lake.

"Time is time, Jelena. There is no stopping it. It shall continue to pass no matter the efforts made to stop it. What *is* important, Jelly, is what you *do* with that time," Radomir responded.

"What do you mean, Papa? What I do with it? I don't understand," Jelena continued.

"Well, Jelly, if you were to sit in your room doing nothing for three days, or if you were to go to school and learn all of your lessons for three days, the same amount of time would have passed. Three days...right? The difference is that with one choice, you have accomplished nothing, and with the other choice, you have not only invested effort into yourself, but you have also accomplished the task of adding more knowledge, things that you didn't know before, to your mind. Your mind is like a sponge and can learn all kinds of things. Just like a sponge soaks up water, your mind can soak up all kinds of information. Right now, you are learning about time...and perhaps sponges..." he said with a chuckle. "One thing to be careful of, though, is when you are learning all of this knowledge, and your mind is soaking up all of this new information, it does not separate good information from bad information."

"What do you mean, Papa? Good information and bad information?" she asked.

"I mean that some people and sources will give you good information. Information that is correct and true and real. But there are other people and sources, Jelly, that will give you bad information that is not correct nor true nor real," he explained patiently.

"Well, how do I know the difference, Papa? How do I know what is good or bad information?" she asked as she piled some smooth river stones in front of her.

"You don't. You hear everybody out. Then you read and listen and read and listen some more to as many people and as many sources as you can, to find out for yourself what the correct and true and real information is. You MUST THINK...FOR...YOURSELF!" he said as he pointed at his head to emphasize his point.

"Jelena, you mustn't be lazy and just accept any information that you are given. It is sad, but there are many people who might try to mislead you and many others. Have the grace to hear them out tolerantly, but you also must have the smarts to go and research it for yourself. Only you can choose to be an independent thinker. Only you can choose to challenge what you are told and to pay attention to the little details. Only you can decide how to invest your time. Make the most of each minute, Jelly, because you won't get a wasted one back and always know, my girl, that you *are* worth the investment. You may be small now, but you can make choices that will lead you wherever you wish to go...to be whatever you wish to be," Radomir continued.

"Can I fly a spaceship, Papa?" Jelena asked excitedly.

"Haha, my wild girl...OF COURSE, you can!!" he roared. "But LOTS of lessons needed to do that."

Radomir jumped up and scooped up Jelena as they both laughed and spun around.

Just then, Jelena was pulled back into reality and jarred from her meditative state by a large blaring sound, almost like that of an obnoxious air horn, coming through the speakers of the containment room.

"FEMALE. In a few moments, I will come back on and give you an instruction," a large booming voice said over the loud hidden speakers.

"That's it? I get an instruction? Seriously?" Jelena said loudly, waiting for a response.

The room went back to its previous silent state. This was the type of silence that drove men to the brink of insanity. Silence so deafening that you would almost think your ears are ringing. The only occasional sound was the humming of the bright lights above. Jelena was beyond all of that. She had spent so many moments training herself to find comfort in the sound of her own synchronized breathing. In this silent room, she was not alone. Her memories of Radomir and Charlotte were so vivid in her mind that they were able to keep her good company during her wait for this...instruction. Minutes again turned into hours, and Jelena found herself inside a different memory. This time, with her mother, Charlotte.

Jelena was ten years old, and she and her mother were supposed to be heading out to see one of the local community's parades. Jelena was in a white-flowered dress that her grandmother had made for her, embroidered with pink tulips along the edge, and on her little feet were cute white sandals. Once again, her hair was pulled up out of her face into a messy ponytail. Jelena's mother was finishing up a task in the kitchen and wasn't quite ready to take Jelena to the parade yet.

"Maaaamaaaa HURRY UPPPPPP!" Jelena whined at her mother.

"Jelena, haven't you ever heard that patience is a virtue? Good things come to those who wait," Charlotte responded patiently.

"I am bored, Mama. I am ready to go. We will miss the parade if you don't hurry," Jelena continued.

"Jelly, what do I always say about boredom?" Charlotte asked.

"Yeah yeah, I know…" Jelena mocked as they said together, "Boredom exists only in the mind…" in some sing-songy tone.

"Jelena, seriously, perhaps you should go read a book until I am ready to go. The parade doesn't start for another hour and a half. You will be fine," Charlotte said, becoming a bit irritated with Jelena's mockery.

Jelena stomped off into her room to wait for her mother. She plopped down on her princess canopy bed, her face red with frustration. Jelena had quite the hot temper and could definitely throw one hell of a tantrum, a bad habit that her parents were trying to get her out of. She had so much emotion and passion that it would frequently get her into trouble. It was in these types of memories where Jelena realized that perhaps showing emotion wasn't always a good thing, and she needed to not only learn but master the art of controlling herself and only showing people certain emotions or reactions.

A few moments had passed when Charlotte entered Jelena's room and sat down next to her on her bed. She put her arm around Jelena and pulled her in close to hug her.

"Jelly, I love you so very much!" Charlotte began in a soft tone. "I know you can get a bit impatient and mad, but these are not good qualities,

JellyGirl. You have to learn to control your emotions. You will not always be able to control every situation, but the one thing you can always do is control your reaction to it. Even if you are right sometimes...you can still be wrong. And anger can only hurt the ones you love. We love you so much and are only trying to teach you the better way. Now, are you ready to go to the parade, girly?" Charlotte asked.

Before her memory even concluded, Jelena was abruptly brought back to the present when the invisible door of her chamber flew open and two men charged in at her. They were both larger men, wearing all black, to include black face and head covers, sort of like ski masks. All Jelena could see of these men were the anger and hatred in their eyes, and before she could even stand, they were on her.

The first man she locked eyes with didn't say a word but merely charged her and punched her square in the face with far more force than she was expecting, leaving her relatively disoriented and seeing stars. He grabbed her messy ponytail and dragged her out of the concrete enclosure, with the other man following closely behind. All she could do was grab the man's arm so that he wouldn't pull out her hair while dragging her weight.

He dragged her down a long concrete hallway. It was barely lit with small light bulbs, some of which didn't even work. The ceiling was lined with pipes of some sort, and the concrete beneath her felt damp. All she could figure was that perhaps it was some underground sewage control facility. Nonetheless, this was not a good situation at all. Could this possibly be the training they were talking about? She didn't remember ever being dragged by her hair at boot camp, that's for damn sure.

Finally, the pressure on her head ceased as the man came to a stop at another large metal door. He pulled out a key from his pocket, unlocked the metal door, and opened it. Once again, there was more pressure on her skull as he began to drag her into this even smaller and much darker room.

Jelena could feel the skin around her right eye begin to swell a bit. Not as much as when she was boxing and took a hit, but she could still feel the sting. The man nearly lifted her by her hair and threw her down into a corner. Again, before she could even compose herself, the other man grabbed her by her arm, hoisted her up, and threw her into a chair. As Jelena tried to balance herself, one of the men grabbed her by her throat and began to squeeze while the other man pulled out some silver tape. The two worked together to subdue and secure her to this chair, so she figured that any attempt to fight back would not only be futile but would probably incur an even worse beating than what was already in store for her. While one man wrapped the silver duct tape around the chair legs to each of her ankles, the other man let go of her throat and began to tape her forearms to the arms of the rough wooden chair.

As she was stretching her neck from his fresh release, she recognized that her situation was going from really bad to even worse and faster than she expected. "Aww FUCK! Yeahhhh, this is DEFINITELY NOT GOOD! I am stupid, stupid, how stooooopid am I? Why oh why didn't I just say no?" Jelena said under her breath. The man working on securing her arms paused, looked at her in frustration, and popped her good in the mouth with his elbow. Her head snapped back from the blow, and for a second, she thought he had even cut her lip.

He grabbed her face and quietly said, "Shut…up."

At this point, Jelena lost track of which man was which. To her, both of them were nothing but cowardly bastards that enjoy beating up a girl. She even found herself imaging the ridiculous social media employment advertisement. "Wanted: Two dickless bastards who enjoy hurting women. Will Train." Once they were finished securing her to the chair, one man went and shut and locked the door.

Jelena licked her lip from where the one man struck her with his elbow and smiled at them. "Yeah, hey fellas, this isn't exactly the kind of ménage et trois I was looking for if you don't mind," Jelena boldly but sarcastically said.

"So, she likes to talk…" one man said. "Well, we can fix that." And before Jelena could even get the follow-up quip out, she took another blow to the face, this time snapping her head back and splitting her lip wide open. She immediately tasted the bitter iron-flavored blood now floating around in her mouth and nose.

"Now…while you're feelin' the echo on that one…this may be a good time to shut your not-so-pretty little mouth and listen to how this is going to work. Got it?" the same man snipped.

Jelena nodded her head to indicate her understanding of the new rules of 'quiet time.'

The man continued, "I am going to ask you some questions, and you are going to give me the answers to those questions…"

Before the man could finish what he was saying, the willful Jelena piped up, temporarily forgetting the new 'quiet time' rules, and again sarcastically said, "But I didn't study…"

The second man, now quite annoyed at Jelena's arrogance, charged forward, pushing the first man out of the way and back-handed Jelena so hard that her chair fell over on its side. It was like being hit in the head with a damn skillet. Her ears were ringing, and she hit her head pretty hard on the concrete when she fell over, resulting in a decent-sized headache.

The second man grabbed the back of Jelena's chair and put her back in the upright position nearly in one motion.

DAMMMMMMMNNNNN! FOR FUCK SAKE! Jelena thought. *Now really feeling that right eye swell. I think my friggen teeth rattled on that one…okay, so definitely the wrong crowd for jokes…no good humor men in here. Got it!*

Jelena sat there quietly as her lip and nose continued to throb and drip blood onto her shirt and lap. She could feel her head throb and her neck ache horribly, probably from not only the hits but also the dragging. As she tried to look up, she realized that it felt like her head weighed a million pounds. *These guys are no joke. They are friggin psychotic!* she thought.

"Okay, so as I was saying before I was rudely interrupted by your little comment…I am going to ask you questions, and you ARE going to answer those questions. If you don't answer those questions or you don't give me the information that I need, then this will be one of life's more painful lessons, I promise you that. Oh, I should warn you though that this kind of engagement does make me a little tired these days. So, I encourage you to make things simple and answer my questions quickly because when I get tired, my friend here will take over for me, and he is neither as patient nor as lenient nor forgiving as I am. Annnnd I should probably mention...he does have a bit of an impulse control problem. Now, if you understand what I have just told you, then nod your head...mmmmkay?" the first man said.

Jelena nodded her head to show that she understood.

"Good girl. Now, when you were in the holding room, you were given an instruction. I need to know what that instruction was," the man asked.

Jelena's eye got big, and as much as she liked to play the stoic game, it was impossible to hide her panic. Was she meditating and didn't hear the actual instruction? Did they even give her an instruction? Surely, she would have heard that booming voice, and that would have brought her out of her meditative state.

" I...I...I don't know," Jelena whispered. "...I...ummm...wait wait wait..."

"And THAT is the wrong answer," the first man said as he released a blow directly into the center of Jelena's chest, this time knocking her chair over backward and suspending her ability to breathe.

CHAPTER 4: SHOCKING REVELATIONS

Jelena gasped and fought to get even a single breath. It was like all of the oxygen had been removed from the room as the intense pain radiated throughout her torso. She could feel the tears welling up in her eyes as she continued to struggle to breathe. She remembered the pain lesson her father had taught her and was trying to focus on that...she flashed through images of both her mother and father, hugging and loving her. She tried to reestablish control over her lungs and diaphragm, which were now spasming in protest.

She flashed to a memory of her father telling her, "Jelena, you must be able to recover from any blow. You will get hit, and the key to survival is recovery." Nevermore than in this very moment did that quick recovery seem to be absolutely impossible, and if she couldn't do that, how would she ever survive?

The second man, yet again, placed Jelena back in the upright position. He had to have been gargantuan, as it seemed like he picked her and her chair up with one hand and righted them, exerting no effort at all. He then walked to the back corner of the room, and as he did so, he lifted just the bottom part of his mask, exposing his lips. He lit up a cigarette and took a long and slow drag as he leaned up against the wall. She recognized something about this man now...his lips...he had very full lips, and even in the dim light, she could tell that either his chin was dirty, or he had a somewhat olive tone to his skin. He had not spoken a single word...yet, and she couldn't help but wonder why?

Could his voice be so recognizable that it was best for him to remain silent to conceal his identity? Was this the same official she had met earlier, during the initial meeting? The tall, dark mystery man? With her one open eye, she then looked at his eyes…dark…ominous…and nearly glowing as they reflected the burning ember of his cigarette.

Holy shit! she thought. *It's him. I know those lips. I know that is the same fucking guy. He knew this shit was not going to be anything like fucking boot camp. What a fucking liar! I swear to God, when I get out of this chair, I am going to kill him with my bare hands! I am going to rip his fucking lying tongue right out of this goddamn throat!*

She swore to herself inside her head. She continued to silently study him and plan his demise by her own hand until her own impulse control problem showed up. She spit the blood out of her mouth onto the floor and brazenly exclaimed, "Hey! Don't I know you? Yeah…You were there…"

At this moment, he seemed to realize that Jelena was not only studying him but had possibly recognized him as well. In a fraction of a second, before she could even finish, he threw down his cigarette, flipped his mask back down, and charged at Jelena, grabbing her by the throat. She could feel his large fingers pressing into her flesh, collapsing her carotid and jugular, and damn near crushing her trachea. It was still not easy to breathe from the previous blow to the chest. She squirmed, trying to loosen his grip around her neck, but with her hands still bound to the arms of the chair, she had no possible way to intervene. He refused to let go and gripped her harder.

Jelena began to feel faint and almost passed out before he let go. What was certainly seconds seemed like the longest minutes in history before he released her throat. Although she couldn't see very well and her ears were ringing louder than ever, she did hear herself gasping in relief. Breathing in every bit of air that she could possibly fill her lungs with. She wanted to pass out...to give up...even though she knew that would only prolong this shitty event. Everything was starting to hurt. The fatigue was setting in now, and her head still felt like it weighed a ton. It required so much effort just to pick it up to look at her captors. So, she stopped trying and just let her head hang low while she worked to catch her breath and regain a full level of consciousness. She still hoped to pass out just to get a break from the pain.

"Perhaps you don't understand what 'impulse control problem' means?" the first man calmly said.

"Yeah...I understand...I have a bit of a problem with that myself," Jelena snarked back at him, still a bit out of breath.

"Obviously..." he replied, sounding rather annoyed. "Listen, I really don't want this to continue. I *am* getting rather tired, and that has no good outcome for you, dear, so please, just tell me what I want to know. What was the instruction you were given?" he demanded.

"Listen, Jack, I...really...don't...know...I..." Jelena began, but her response was stifled when once again, she was grabbed by the throat by the second vicious man. "Noooo!" she gasped as he squeezed her, applying pressure to the very same spots around her neck. She could feel the small capillaries in her eyes begin to burst.

The first man tapped him on the shoulder. "Let her finish," he quietly said.

The second man released her throat, and she continued, "No, I wasn't given any instruction. I was told I would, but I swear...the guy...he never came back on...he didn't tell me anything. I swear he didn't!" Jelena screamed.

"Well, sweetheart," the first man began, "I truly wish that I could believe you...but I don't..."

"No...you HAVE to believe me!" Jelena interjected. "I am telling the truth! I wasn't given any instruction."

Both men looked at each other in some sort of silent agreement when the first continued, "Well then...a painful lesson it shall be."

He had no sooner finished his sentence that Jelena felt a sharp sting in her upper arm, realizing in nearly slow motion that the second man had retrieved a baseball bat and released another blow onto her arm hard enough to once again knock her chair right over. The pain was so bad that she was certain he had broken her arm. He began to repeatedly jab and swing at her with the bat, apparently considering no part of her body to be off-limits. He ran the bat up in between her legs, thrusting it into her crotch area as if he was going to rape her. *How long is this shit gonna last? Why can't I die already?* she thought as she continued to endure his blows...This fucker continued to beat the ever-loving shit out of her like he was at the spring try-outs at Yankees Stadium...to her legs, arms, stomach...until...CRACK!

The last sound Jelena heard before everything went black was the crack of the bat against her skull. It was a hollow sound. Normally she could trick her mind into escaping anything by dream diving, but this time she didn't...she couldn't. She had no idea how much time had elapsed. She woke up still taped to the chair, lying on her side, covered and wet with sweat, blood, and most likely her own urine. She could no longer see out of her right eye, and every inch of her body screamed in pain.

"Well, looky looky, who's awake?" the first man said snidely. "Are you ready to cooperate now, darling? Get her up!"

The second man set her upright...again. Right then, Jelena felt this intense, primal rage and savagery rise within her.

If they know what's good for them, they had better NEVER let me out of this fuckin chair! Jelena thought.

"Now, what was the instruction you were given?" the first man asked again.

"FUCK...YOU! Even if I did know, I sure as fuck wouldn't tell you, you fucking pansy ass little bitch! You wanna beat me???? Then why don't you shut the fuck up and just do it already!" Jelena hissed. "I'm awake. Why don't you kill me this time? Better yet...Why don't you cut me loose, and we can go a few rounds? Me tied up kinda takes the sport out of it, don't ya think???" she dared.

The beatings continued for what seemed like an eternity. Jelena's body absorbed every blow that these two bastards were dishing out. She prayed for one of them to just knock her unconscious or kill her already, just so that she could escape this torture. The sad truth is that, in reality, she never did receive any further instruction, and this was merely another cruel lesson just to see how much she could endure. Finally, the black darkness returned as Jelena was knocked unconscious again and temporarily freed from her agony.

Though, this time she was able to dream-dive as her mind entered into a different state, she was at home, with her mother and her father. She could hear them laughing and joking. She could feel the warmth and love in her home. She could feel the soft velvety tongue of the family dog licking her face. Sassafrass. Sassy was such a good dog, a mutt, about sixty pounds that they had rescued from the pound one summer. Jelena's mother said that she named the dog after her since Jelena was so sassy and rather smart-mouthed all the time. Jelena didn't mind. Sometimes she was quite sassy and on purpose too. One could guess that was just part of her unique charm. Jelena was never one to allow herself to be bullied and never seemed afraid to speak her mind quite freely, even though it would get her into trouble from time to time.

Jelena's mind had taken her far away from her current situation. She was at a family barbeque, and her father was grilling salmon steaks and baked potatoes, which was easily one of Jelena's favorites. They had a little pool set up that summer, and Jelena's memory was so incredibly real and vivid that it was allowing her to feel the cool refreshing water on her skin...or so she thought. Nevertheless, it was so soothing and refreshing. Sometimes her dreams would help her get through really hard and difficult times, but other times...other times, it would seem to be just another cruel joke played upon her by her own mind.

"AHHHHHHH!" Jelena screamed as she was given a violent shove back into the realm of reality. She realized that she had been removed from her chair and stripped of all her clothing and was now hanging by her wrists from a chain that stretched up over her head. Her shoulders and arms grossly protested this new position, and Jelena felt incredibly vulnerable, hanging there naked and helpless. As the hose came on, the painful sting of the water spraying her felt like millions of little needles, all piercing her battered body.

"JUST FUCKING KILL ME ALREADY!" Jelena screamed as loud as she could.

"Well, that wouldn't be any fun, now would it, darlin? We decided that you stunk...all covered in your own piss and vomit...so we decided that you needed a bath...you know...to freshen you up a bit," the first man snarled. "What the fuck did you eat anyways? Some kind of sandwich? Jesus girl!"

Jelena was in and out of consciousness. Every time he sprayed her in the face, her wounds just rang out in pain. Every time she tried to breathe, she just ended up sucking in water, literally like she was drowning on dry ground. It hurt so bad that she no longer possessed the lucidity to recognize that she was hanging there stark naked, like some dead fish on a hook.

Her mind carried her away again. She felt the warmth and comfort of her own bed. It was so soft, and the quilt that her mama made for her had weight to it, like a warm, soothing hug. She saw her father's face. "Jelly, pain is not the end. It is only a reminder that you are still alive. You are Jelly.

You ARE still alive. This is not your end. This is **not** where your story ends. You have to keep writing your story," her father said in her dream.

She thought that she could feel her father brushing the hair away from her face, but she could also feel the pain as she was coming to.

"Papa?" Jelena faintly whispered. "Papa, is that you?"

"No, I'm Adam," a strange voice said to her, bringing her out of the darkness.

Jelena continued to regain her clear-mindedness one level at a time as she opened her eye and looked around. Someone had dressed her in only a bra and panties on and she was lying on a small cot. She realized that she was in some kind of cage made of razor wire and barbed wire components. There was only a small light to illuminate her little space. She looked up and saw a man that she did not recognize.

He was crouched down beside her, pulling her matted hair out of her open facial lacerations. He was dabbing a cool cloth onto her face as she winced in pain. He was a Caucasian man with an athletic but albeit battered physique. He was dirty but quite attractive with blond hair and kind, deep blue eyes, wearing only his boxers and the evidence of a not-so-warm welcome.

"Hi. My name is Adam," he whispered.

"Ummm, hi. I'm Jelena," she whispered back. "Where are we? Why are they doing this to us?" she asked as her voice got a little louder. She could feel her throat burn from the screaming and the vomit, and it felt like she had nearly lost her voice completely.

"Shhhhhh," Adam pleaded. "Not too loud, the guards aren't too far away, and we are not supposed to be talking," he continued. "I think this must be the farm...the CIA training facility. My buddy told me about it just before I was... um picked up. I volunteered for some shady espionage project and then I wake up here. When did you get here?"

"I don't know..." she whispered. "I was taking out my trash, then I got attacked with a bag over my head, and then something about some goddamn instruction that I never got...umm got the shit beat out of me and tortured with a fuckin fire hose or something...maybe a few days I guess."

"I think we both came in around the same time then...I'm guessing that we have been here for maybe four days...here, eat this protein bar and drink this," he said as he handed her the bar and a small metal cup with some water in it. "Slowly...you have been unconscious for about twenty-four hours or so...they gave that to me, to give to you when you woke up."

"Twenty-four hours??? I have lost twenty-four hours?? How can you tell?" she asked as she woofed down the protein bar.

"You see those wooden boards on the wall just over the guard's head? I think that's a window...early in the morning, a small light shines through the cracks. It is the only way I have come up with for telling time. I have been giving you a little water every so often. When was the last time you ate anything?" he asked.

"I ate a sandwich and an apple right before I took out my trash, but I am pretty sure that ended up all over the floor somewhere after the bat man got ahold of me," Jelena confessed sarcastically.

"Yeah, that fucker really does love that goddamn bat!" Adam replied.

"So, is Adam your real name or your code name or whatever?" she asked.

"Ha, code name...no, it's my real name. Lieutenant Colonel Adam Burke, USMC, at your service."

"Sergeant Jelena Prazich, also USMC, it's nice to meet you, sir," she said, now realizing just how exposed she was.

"Please don't call me sir," he started. "We're both equals here in this pit, and from the looks of it, you took a much worse beating than I ever could have endured. So, no sirs, please...okay?"

"Okay, I can do that, so how does Adam and Jelena sound?" she asked.

"Perfect!" he said with a smile showing his nice white teeth.

"HEY, SHITBAGS!!! SHUT THE FUCK UP!!! NO TALKING!!!" the guard yelled.

"Here, Adam," she barely whispered, nearly mouthing the words, "you can share my cot." She scootched over and both of their beaten, bruised bodies intertwined together on the tiny cot.

"Goodnight, Adam, it is nice to meet you," she whispered.

"Goodnight, Jelena. Nice to meet you too," he whispered back.

It felt like she had only been asleep for a few minutes when they both jumped from the sound of the baseball bat banging on the neighboring cages.

"WAKEY WAKEY EGGS AND BAKEY, YA FUCKIN PIGS!" a new voice screamed out. "Well, look who's getting all cozy up in this bitch?! Is she putting out there for ya big guy? Or are you just takin a serving out of that ass?"

Jelena was so startled that she jumped up and tried to stand, cutting herself on the razor wire lining the top of the cage. "Ow," she cried.

"You can't stand up in these cages..." Adam said under his breath.

BAM! (the bat cracked into the cage support). "I think the two of you have had enough make-out time for today...how about a trial separation?" He snapped as he reached into the cage and pulled Adam out by his hair.

"ADAM!" Jelena yelled as the guard pulled him down, dragging him onto his knees.

"And this little piggy is comin' with me," the guard snarled as he slammed and locked the door.

Within seconds Jelena lost sight of Adam. All she could do was pray that he could stay alive in this place and endure whatever bullshit torture they were going to get him with today. She was so focused on the guard dragging Adam that she didn't see 'the bat man' coming back for her.

"Yooo-whooo..." he sang.

Jelena whipped around to face him. She was so scared that she fell back onto her rear-end and backed as far as she could into her little cage. As he unlocked the door, she pressed her back into the barbed wire until she could feel the sharp barbs puncturing her skin. He reached into her cage, and she did her best to pull her legs in tight in hopes that he couldn't reach her. He shot her a look that could have burned through steel as he reached further and got a firm hold of one of her ankles.

"FUCK!" she yelled as she felt herself being dragged out of her cage and down the hall in the opposite direction of Adam.

The 'bat man,' still dressed in black and fully masked, continued to drag her down the hallway and into another different room. He finally let go of her foot and said in a deep but familiar voice, "Get up and get onto the table." Jelena got up and propped herself up onto the table as ordered.

She took a second to scan this room to try to determine exactly what she was in for. It was so dark in there that she began to wonder if she would ever see the light of day again.

Damn, what are these fuckin guys?? Vampires? she thought.

She continued to scan and saw that the walls were a combination of brick and wood, stained with things Jelena had zero interest in knowing about. It had one light bulb hanging from a string. In the middle of the room, she was now sitting on some weird table chair thing that looked like something you would find in a doctor's office, with wide leather-looking straps. Suddenly she realized that she was perched rather precariously on what she would now call 'the table of doom.'

The 'bat man' put down his bat and prepared to tether Jelena's excruciatingly sore hands and feet to the table with the wide leather straps. At this moment, she discovered that when they ripped off the duct tape, they also took most of the skin. Jelena pulled her hands away in an attempt to not allow herself to be bound again. "Please...no more," she begged.

The bat man looked at her and snatched up her hands in one fierce movement. As he squeezed them together, he moved closer to her face and quietly said, "No is not an option here." He grabbed one wrist as she winced in pain and reached for the leather strap with his other hand. As he was tethering her, she made a move to get ahold of the bat, but she wasn't quite fast enough. He managed to grab her arm and remind her that she was in no condition to win any hand-to-hand fight with him.

"You really want to do that? Do you really think that in your condition that you can win against me? I *will* get your other hand. I *will* get your feet. I *will* tie your whole fucking body down if I have to. You can choose to start this off the easy way or the hard way. Either way, it's gonna suck, but you need to understand that the more you fight me, the worse it will be for you. So, you decide how much you want to take today. No matter what you choose, though, I promise, you'll wish you were dead," he explained.

Jelena thought for a second, and against every thread of sense in her body, she held out her hand. He pushed her shoulders back to force her to lay on her back, and as he tethered her other wrist, she couldn't fight off the feeling that submitting to this man was a big mistake. She didn't like not being allowed to fight back. She continued to look around the room when she noticed something she hadn't before...a small table in the corner. With her good eye, she strained to see what was on that table, and for a second, all she could discern were various cables and unidentifiable tools. She finally recognized what was on the table...

Once she realized what it was, she exclaimed in a raspy but panicked voice, "Sweet baby Jesus! Is that a fuckin car battery?"

"Yep," he growled.

CHAPTER 5: TRUTH OR DARE

Jelena began to panic immediately, realizing that an intimate relationship with a car battery was in her very near future, and found herself questioning her "easy way" choice. At this point, she was positive that she had made a tremendous mistake, and the only one with an easier way was HIM! Never before had she regretted a choice she had made, as much as she regretted this one at this moment.

"Listen, bat man. I swear to you that I have abso-fucking-lutely no idea what it is that you people want. I was never given any goddamn instruction. Is this just some...some...sort of fucking twisted torture game? If it is...then...You win...man...okay, you win! You fucking win!" she pleaded with her captor as she wrestled with her restraints, causing her wrists and ankles to scream in pain from where there was no skin.

He looked her over and paused for a moment as if he was taking in the view. However, as he stood there, she remembered that she was now laying there, strapped to a table, in just a thin bra and panties. A sense of sheer vulnerability and fear washed over her, and her heart started to race. Seeing the look in his eyes, she now felt like electroshock therapy may not be the only goal on this asshole's mind. All she could do was lay there...helpless. He came in close to her. She shuddered as he ran his bare hand up her leg, continuing up her thigh, only to stop and rest his hand on the warmth of her essence. He rubbed the desired area a few times softly, not to seduce her, not to entice her either...only to remind her that he was in complete control of her body and he could do anything he wanted to her at any given instant. She could see in his eyes that he was considering more than her electrocution, but her prayers were answered, and he continued to move his hand upward and softly over her stomach in the direction of her breast. His fingers circled the bruises and marks he left on her skin the day prior. He was circling a particular bruise on her sternum when his fingers went on top of the thin fabric covering her breast and outlined her nipple. This time he did not restrain himself. His fingers followed the line of the fabric before slipping his hand underneath to completely cup her bare breast and stroke her nipple between his index and middle fingertips. Jelena gritted her teeth, and every muscle in her body tensed up in protest.

"Be careful, big boy..." she whispered. "Remember, you gotta cut me loose eventually, and I have an insanely vivid memory...and after all...I'm in here for a reason, and we wouldn't want to do anything that can't be undone or forgiven."

Without a word, he stopped. He locked eyes with her as he ran his hand up to her neck, where he grabbed her throat tight. He got his face very close to hers, and as Jelena flinched in anticipation of another blow, he lifted his mask to pull it off his head.

"Holy shit! I KNEW it was you!" she squeaked with the little bit of air that he allowed into her lungs.

"Shut...up..." he whispered in her ear. "I am going to do the talking now, and *you* are going to play the quiet game. Understand?"

Jelena nodded rapidly, and he released his grip from around her neck.

"This is the farm. The CIA training facility. If you expected a warm welcome, consider yourself foolish. If you expected this to be another easy military training site, consider yourself ignorant. And if you expected me to go 'easy' on you, consider yourself naïve. This is your training, and I am your trainer. I will also be your handler for at least the next year of your CIA employment. Since you have already dubbed me 'the bat man,' you can call me Bruce from here on out. This training is specifically designed to push you far beyond anything you have ever tolerated before, to push and expand your limits of pain tolerance, psychological torture tolerance, food and water deprivation, sleep deprivation, etcetera. Don't worry about the lacs on your face. We have a plastic surgeon on staff that will pretty you right up once your training is complete. But understand this: you will bleed... you will scream... you will think that you are gonna die, and I will break you. You see, I have to break you so that I can build you into the operative you need to be in order to survive. You, Jelena, are about to be educated," Bruce explained.

He walked away from Jelena and toward the small table with the battery and tools. He grabbed the table and rolled it over to Jelena.

"Permission to speak?" Jelena asked through clenched teeth.

"No. You will give me the instruction that you were given in the containment room, or you will enter into an entirely new realm of pain," he quietly said as he bent down to retrieve a bucket from the bottom shelf of the cart.

"Bruce, I swear to you that I was not given any instruction," Jelena pleaded.

"AAAHH!" she screamed as Bruce dumped the bucket of freezing water all over Jelena's mostly naked body. "Please!" she begged.

"Jelena, begging does not become us," he scowled. "This will hurt you more than it will hurt me...a piece of free advice...don't clench your jaw...you don't want to break your teeth."

Jelena had no idea that electrocution was part of this deal. *I don't think that I can survive this,* she thought, trying to brace for whatever was to come. *Please, God! Please, God, help me survive this!* she prayed silently, as tears formed in the corners of her eyes.

Bruce put on thick tan electricity-resistant gloves and attached the battery to the cables with long metal prods on each end. "Now, Jelena, tell me the truth," he said. "What was the instruction you were given?"

"I don't...AAAAAAAHHHHHHHHHHHHHHH!" she screamed as the prods came into contact with her wet flesh, leaving small burn marks after they were removed.

Jelena was now panting and shaking, processing the pain and torture that this sadistic fuck was putting her through.

"Does the cat still have your tongue, girl?" he wickedly asked. "Let's see if we can loosen that up. Just tell me the instruction that you were given, and this can all be over."

"There is nooOOOAAAHHHHHHHHHHHHHHH!" she screamed again as the prods contacted a different part of her body.

This must have continued for a while, with this asshole asking the same question ten or so times over, with Jelena only able to provide the same pain-inducing answer each time. Somewhere in the midst of it all, she remembered spewing chunks of protein bar all over herself and Bruce before her broken body simply gave out, and she was once again surrounded in black-out darkness.

Each time her body gave out, her mind ventured into the past, allowing her the comfort of her memories. This time, she remembered, a short day trip her family took out to the ocean. The sun was bright and high, warming every inch of her. The water was warm and soothing, yet there was something rather refreshing about it.

"JELLY!" her father called out. "Come get in the water. It's great!"

Jelena remembered running down the beach and splashing into the water to join her father for a swim. They played, and he kept throwing her up into the air, and she would come down splashing into the water.

"Oh NO!" her father cried out, "my ring!" he exclaimed.

"What, Papa? What happened?" Jelena asked, quite concerned with the upset look on her father's face.

"My college ring...it fell off into the ocean...DAMN!" he said.

Without any hesitation at all, Jelena dove down and felt around on the ocean floor and, by some miracle, scooped up her father's treasure. She came back up to the surface with a glimmer of gold in her little hand.

"Here, Papa...is this your ring?" Jelena asked as she opened her palm.

"Oh My God! Jelena, you are AMAZING!" he stammered. "My little miracle...you found my ring! Oh, my wild girl...You're my HERO!"

Jelena and her father made their way back to their blanket, where he told her mother and brother just what she had done.

"I swear...this girl is something truly amazing!" he shouted with pride as he pulled her in again for a super huge bear hug. "I Love you soooo much, my little JellyGirl!"

Jelena opened her eyes and found herself back in her little barbed wire cage, lying on her cot but hooked up to an IV. Adam was nowhere to be seen. *I hope he's okay,* she thought before closing her eyes again and drifting back off to sleep.

Jelena was out cold for what must have been hours but seemed like only minutes before a bruised and bloodied Adam was flung back into their cage. He fell to the floor limp. Jelena rolled her aching body off the cot and crawled over to him. "Adam?" she whispered. He didn't respond. She rolled him over to find that, thankfully, he was still breathing. She tried to lift him onto the small cot, but she was too weak from her own trials. Instead, she placed her broken body under his to try to make him as comfortable as she could, but under these circumstances, comfort seemed nearly impossible. She brushed the bloody blond hair out of his swollen, beaten face, closed her eyes, and drifted back to sleep.

The next morning, Jelena woke up and saw that two protein bars and two metal cups of water were on the floor inside their cage. She also noticed that her IV had been removed at some point.

"Jelena?" a weak Adam called out.

"Adam. Thank God you are alive," she said. "I was worried about you."

"Worried about me?" he said with a weird smirk. "I was worried about you. Your screams echoed through this entire place. Are you okay?"

"Yeah, the 'bat man' introduced me to a very unfriendly car battery for some electro-shock therapy," she quipped.

Adam broke out into a chuckle. "Damn...oww...do you always have such a good attitude about such fucked up things?" he asked.

"Well, I know that if me and old 'bat man' in there are ever on the same field and I am not all tied up...I plan on ripping out his lying tongue through his asshole," she bluntly stated.

"Yikes!" Adam said. "Bit of a grudge holder, are we?"

"Hey, these little fantasies are what help get me through, I guess," she replied. "He said that he was going to break me. Yeah, we'll see about that. I am not as breakable as he thinks."

"I got the same talk too...this is the farm...blah blah blah...I'm gonna make you bleed...ya ya ya...I am gonna make you scream..." Adam explained.

"Jesus...what do these guys do, read from a fuckin script? They REALLY need some new material," Jelena responded.

"HEY...LOVEBIRDS! THAT'S ABOUT ENOUGH OF THAT LOVEY DOVEY SHIT...I'M GONNA FUCKIN PUKE!" the guard yelled from his station.

Jelena and Adam looked at each other and quietly scarfed down their protein bars and water, knowing that it may be the only sustenance they get for God knew how long.

"Not like this is going to stay down," Jelena said to Adam in a sarcastic whisper. "But hey, at least I got to puke all over, dmmm dummm dummmm...... 'the bat man.' Who, by the way, WAS the guy at my interview, and now he said that I could call him Bruce, although I highly doubt that is his actual name."

No sooner than the syllables left her lips, Bruce appeared outside their cage. Jelena glared at him with her one good eye and nothing short of murderous contempt. This only spurred Bruce on as he looked at her with a toothpick hanging out of one side of his mouth and his ominous half-grin.

"Well, aren't you two the cute little couple," Bruce snarled at them as they were crouched down in the far back corner of their cage, like trapped animals.

"What now...Bruce?" Jelena snipped as she got onto all fours, slowly advancing in Bruce's direction. "More beatings? More electrocutions? Do I get more *face time* with your *bat*? Well, do I...Bruce?"

"Jelena! NO!" Adam begged. "He will kill you...he can kill you...don't."

"No, Adam. No more...begging!" Jelena hissed at her new friend. "Well, do you...Bruce? Do you want to kill me? Do you want **me** to bleed out at your feet? Do you?" Jelena asked in a sadistic tone of her own.

Jelena had crawled to the front of the cage, within six inches of Bruce and only the razor wire of her cage separating them. She slowly rose to her feet, even allowing the barbed wire cage top to press into her flesh. As each sharp prong punctured her, it released small droplets of blood that started to stream down her skin. While never unlocking her eye with his, she continued, "You see now, I have something to tell you...I don't give a flying...rat...fuck...what you do to me, you fuckin skanky piece of lying shit. None of that matters. Here's what you have to understand." Jelena did not blink once and merely glared at Bruce under her brow through her one good eye. She didn't even seem to mind the little streams of blood trickling down her face from the barbed wire punctures. "Are you paying attention, Brucey?" Jelena mockingly asked. With her tone returning to a low somber level of seriousness, she continued, "You...will...NEVER...break me...EVER."

SMACK! Bruce had shoved the business end of his bat in between the wires of the cage and punched Jelena in the face with it, knocking her out. As she fell backward, Adam jumped to catch her limp body and gently placed her head on the ground.

"And that's about enough togetherness for the two of you," Bruce said as he opened the cage door. "This little bitch has gotten even mouthier bunkin' with you...little beastly bitch."

"You've unleashed the beast alright," Adam said, looking at Jelena's battered face. "If that's what you're trying to do, then you've done it."

"Trust me, she's got a bigger beast inside of her..." Bruce quipped as he bent down to grab Jelena's foot. "And I'm gonna dig it out."

Bruce stood up with Jelena's foot in his hand and dragged her out of the cage, shutting the door and leaving Adam caged alone. Adam's heart sank as he saw the lifeless body of Jelena being dragged down the hall by Bruce. Adam feared that he might not ever see Jelena again, and if he did, she might have no humanity left in her. All he could do for Jelena was to pray for her. He knew she was strong, stronger than anyone else he had ever met, including himself.

In fact, he knew that she would physically survive this place...this pit of pain, torture, and despair. He worried about her softer parts surviving it...her kindness, compassion, and empathy...he felt her brushing the hair out of his face, and he felt her use her own body as a cushion to make him more comfortable that night...Adam was afraid that whatever Bruce would do to Jelena would kill whatever good was in her, leaving only a shell...a hollow killing machine no longer capable of love or joy.

What Adam hadn't gotten the chance to tell Jelena, was that before he went into the Marine Corps and became an intelligence specialist officer, he was a Christian minister. His college degree was in Theological Studies. He never had any plans or intentions to enter the military at all, so it was completely understandable how he had no idea that even the Marine Corps had ministers, called Chaplains. He just took the best job that he could think of that would grant him access to the information that he needed and that was as an intelligence specialist officer.

He was raised on a Minnesota farm in a loving family. Adam had three brothers and two sisters, all younger than himself. They had family meals, birthdays, worked on the farm together, and went to church every

Sunday. His mother was nearly a saint, and his father was a Deacon at their church. They were what some would consider the perfect family.

However, when the youngest of all, Matthew, turned eighteen, he decided to enlist in the Marine Corps. Adam watched as his father beamed with pride at Matthew's boot camp graduation. He held his mother as both tears of pride and worry flowed from her eyes, knowing that this was not the safest path for her youngest child. His father always said that patriotism was a noble trait for any American. Adam was also quite proud of Matthew, but he knew that Matthew had a bit of a temper and didn't always think things through before showing some kind of knee-jerk reaction to damn near any situation...even the pettiest ones. Adam feared that Matthew would do something to get himself killed. Since he was born with a chip on his shoulder, he always felt like he had to prove himself and compete with his older brothers.

Matthew had served five years already and was on his third tour in Iraq. He had collected so many accolades and medals for bravery and always putting his team's welfare first. Adam's opinion of Matthew had changed over the years. He truly thought that enlisting in the Marine Corps was the best decision that Matthew had ever made, until one afternoon, when there was a knock on their family farmhouse door. Adam's mind plays this scene over and over in slow motion trying to find a flaw in it somewhere. Something to make it not real, but it always is.

Adam's mother finished placing flowers she had picked from her garden into a vase. She wiped her hands and went to answer the door, shooting Adam a cross look for not getting up to answer it himself. As she opened the door, Adam could see the two Marines, in their dress blues, with stoic yet somber expressions upon their faces.

"Mrs. Burke, it is with deep regret that we have to inform you…" one of them began.

"No…no, no, no…just no…you…you both go away…get away from here," Adam's mother said to both men.

"…that your son, Staff Sergeant Matthew L. Burke has been killed in the line of duty," he finished.

"NOOOOOOOOOOOOOOOOOOOOOOOOOOOOOOOOOOOOOOO!" Adam's mother screamed as she fell to her knees, sobbing beyond control.

In between her sobs, the man finished by apologizing that he had to bring such news and that she would receive a letter shortly, stating when Matthew's body would be returned for a military burial. As they turned to walk away, Adam, who was now on the floor trying to comfort his distraught mother, yelled out to them, "What happened? How was my brother killed? What happened?"

The Marines turned around, and one said, "I am sorry, truly sorry…but we are not at liberty to say. We don't know. It is classified. Again, we are very sorry for your loss."

They turned around, got into their government vehicle, and drove off the farm property, leaving a trail of dust behind them.

Adam had to deal with that, the not knowing what had happened to his brother. He had to watch as his mother became gravely ill, most likely due to the stress associated with the tragedy of losing her youngest child. He had to watch as his father became silent for the next several years, consumed by his grief and responsibility. Matthew's death took such a toll on his family, and the biggest part of it was the fact that his family had no closure at all. They never got to come to peace with what happened, because they never got to know what really happened on that tragic day.

Adam had a plan, though. He was going to find out what happened to his brother, no matter what he had to do. So, he took his college degree and became a commissioned intelligence officer in the Marine Corps. He did eventually learn what had happened to his brother and was inspired by what he found. His brother had given the greatest sacrifice he had ever known of another person, his life. His brother, Matthew, was indeed a hero.

The letter that Adam found and copied, written by Matthew's commanding officer read as follows:

Staff Sergeant Matthew Burke's team had been pinned down with in-coming fire for over twelve hours. They were running low on ammunition and were told, via radio, that they would have to be at the evac point in exactly thirty-seven minutes. The evac point was easily a mile or so down the road, and his team was trapped from almost all angles. Matthew came up with a plan for his team to take the clothes off of the dead insurgents and put them over top of their USMC fatigues. As his team was covering their uniforms, Matthew was gathering up everyone's remaining ammunition for one final stand against the enemy.

Matthew then jumped out into plain sight and laid down cover fire while taking on-coming fire himself to create a distraction so that his team could escape to the evac point. His team said that Matthew had been shot over twenty times before they lost sight of him but that they could still hear the gunfight continue until they were in the air. Later that night, another special forces unit was sent to retrieve Matthew's body. Staff Sergeant Matthew Lee Burke received the medal of honor for ingenuity, tenacity, and selflessness displayed to save every member of his team that day. That medal of honor and a copy of that classified letter still hang in Adam's family farmhouse to this day.

Adam's mind moved from his brother back to Jelena and then back to his own precarious situation. The hallway filled with cages was eerily quiet. No screams, no voices…just silence.

Damn, Adam thought. *Where is the guy who sprays out our cages every day? I wonder what time it is? I can do anything through Christ who strengthens me. Please, Lord, set us free. Help us in our time of need. Please, Lord, protect Jelena.*

Adam sat back down on his ass, with his knees up and his head down resting on his forearms, trying to pray and keep his mind occupied on anything other than this God-forsaken place. His thoughts continued to bounce from his brother to his parents to Jelena. His mind kept circling the questions, *How much longer will I have to be here? How much more do I have to prove?*

"Hi there, pretty boy…you didn't think that I forgot about you, did you?" the guard snarled as he opened the door to his cage.

"Of course not," Adam began. "Where's Jelena? Is she still…"

Adam's sentence was cut short with a brisk punch to the face. The guard reached into the cage and grabbed Adam, pulling him into a headlock as he began to drag him back down the hall again.

Adam's mind jumped back into the present as he quickly realized his troubles were far from over. He could only hope that Jelena was alive and look forward to the time when they were back in their cage together, after whatever heinous acts they were certain to endure. At this point, all he could do was pray for mercy.

CHAPTER 6: THE DARKNESS

Jelena opened her eyes and found herself lying on a cold, damp floor in complete darkness. At first, she began to wonder if these bastards did something to her eyes to blind her, but after a moment, she reassured herself that a blind asset wouldn't be much of an asset at that point.

She once again stuck to her routine of feeling around in the dark, trying to figure out where she was exactly...a question that she may never answer. As she ran her fingers over the walls, she could feel that they were wet and kind of slimy. She groped around to see what else she could find...if there was a bench or cot, maybe...but there wasn't. Just a drain in the floor and three wet slimy walls and one wall that she was pretty sure was a door, but only because it felt slightly different than the other three.

Jelena focused her attention on the presumed door. She felt around the seam, checking for hinges or the like, and while running her hand along the side, she felt what she was fairly confident was an actual, old-school, skeleton keyhole. She crouched down to try to see anything on the other side, but there must have been a hole flap covering it because all she could see was a dark nothing.

She got down onto her knees and laid on her belly to try to see under the door but again...a dark nothing.

"DAMN!" she hissed. "These fuckers are merciless! I can't even have the goddamned crack under the door??? Like REALLY?!"

Jelena plopped back down onto her behind and remained quiet for a moment, just trying to listen to her surroundings. Nothing. She was once again faced with the combination of solitude and utterly deafening silence.

"So, this must be solitary...Ha...*I* am in solitary confinement? Get a load of that..." She chuckled. "Shit...I must be movin' up in the world...Well, they don't know me very well then...I can do this...Sure beats the shit out of getting face time with Mr. Bat or getting prodded by my least favorite form of electricity. So, I guess I'm sittin' here in the dark then." Jelena tried to find a comfortable position to lay down in and closed her eyes, trying to escape her hellish confines and trick her mind into drifting off to the pleasant peacefulness of dreamland.

She spent days in and out of her dreams. She let them soothe and comfort her most of the time. However, after a while, Jelena had no idea how long she had been in the hole. Hours? Days? Weeks? Months? They must have had some kind of invisible night vision camera in there with her because they seemed to know exactly when she was sleeping and managed to put a protein bar and a cup of water in her cell every so often without even waking her.

Everything was so erratic here, and the Marine in her craved a daily routine. She tried to figure out ways to keep time, but in the dark, time seems irrelevant. She knew that she had had her menstrual cycle at least once while in the hole...or at least she thought that she did. Hygiene was not their focus in this place. She had no idea how long it had been since she last saw or spoke to another human being.

Again, her dreams were so vivid that the lines between reality and fantasy became quite blurred, making the differentiation between what was real and what was in her head nearly impossible. All she knew, in her core, was how absolutely grateful she was that she could stand up and stretch in this cell, so maybe it wasn't all that bad after all. For Jelena, sitting in time-out was a far better option than being beaten to a bloody pulp daily or being raped or electrocuted. It was lonely and dark, and the stench after a while was pretty horrendous if she stopped to think about that for too long. But she always managed to find a silver lining...endless naps...her bones hopefully healing...and best of all, NO BRUCE TIME!

Every now and then, Jelena would hear what she thought were the screams of the other guests here at Chateau d'Shit-Storm. It would never last long, and to be quite honest, she wasn't even certain of what she heard...perhaps, it was the voices now living in her own head that were doing the screaming. Better yet, maybe that was the sound of Bruce getting that bat shoved right up his ass!

Most of the time, Jelena found ways to use the darkness and the silence to make her memories even more vivid and realistic than usual. Most therapists would probably say that isn't the best coping mechanism. However, desperate times call for desperate measures, and dream diving was Jelena's favorite way to pass the time.

During one rather nostalgic dream, she remembered one of her first times learning what it meant to 'fight the good fight.' She was perhaps in the seventh grade and was a bus rider. On this particular day, she walked to the bus stop and got onto the bus, choosing a seat in the middle but toward the front of the bus. She noticed that up front, these two larger older boys were picking on a small, frail boy with pale white-blond hair named Mitchel. He was the standard type that bullies would go after, complete with coke bottle glasses that magnified his big gray eyes. Jelena wasn't always great with names, but she and Mitchel both had the same bus stop, so she at least knew his.

Mitchel was sitting right behind the bus driver, and Jelena knew that the driver could see what was going on less than a foot away from him through the rearview mirror. Jelena watched from a distance as the boys teased Mitchel and pinched and poked him. She watched as they took Mitchel's books out of his backpack. Faster than she could react, one boy swung the book around and hit Mitchel right in the face, breaking one of the lenses of his glasses, which left his upper cheek with a sizable gash.

Jelena jumped up and grabbed the older boy by the arm. "HEY, YOU! KNOCK IT OFF! YOU HURT HIM!" she yelled. "Aren't you going to do anything to stop this?" Jelena asked the bus driver.

"Nope...just driving you little assholes to school, and that...is...it," the bus driver replied.

As Jelena turned around to get her backpack, one of the older boys grabbed her flowy blue skirt and ripped it upward, exposing Jelena's thigh.

"STOP IT!" Jelena screamed.

She retrieved her backpack, returned, and sat next to Mitchel for the remaining ride to school. When Jelena got to school, she went directly to the principal's office and told him what had happened to Mitchel on the bus. Most kids would have probably thought about the ramifications of that and would have just kept their mouths shut, but not Jelena. Her only concern was poor Mitchel.

The principal brought in the school resource officer and asked Jelena to make a statement, which she did. She didn't know the older boys' names, but she had no problem identifying them from the previous year's yearbook. The principal and the school resource officer both assured Jelena that the older boys would be kicked off the bus for the remainder of the school year and that they would have the school nurse attend to Mitchel's injury. They failed to remind Jelena that these boys probably knew where she lived and that she should be careful.

After school, Jelena told her parents what had occurred throughout her day, and no one seemed to pay any attention to it. That didn't shock Jelena too much. After all, she was raised to do the right thing solely because it is the right thing, not for any pat on the back, so she didn't press the issue. She did what she felt was right and was okay with it. However, much later, in the middle of the night, Jelena heard a huge commotion in front of her house, waking both of her parents. Everyone went outside, and Jelena was mortified by what she saw. Someone had vandalized both of her parents' vehicles. Eggs, ketchup, mustard...all over each car. Jelena felt awful seeing just how upset her father was and knowing it was all her fault.

"Papa..." Jelena called to her father. "Papa, I am so very sorry. This is all my fault."

"Jelena, don't be ridiculous!" her father said, irritated at the situation.

"No, Papa, this *really* is all my fault," Jelena said as she told her parents about what had happened earlier that day...again.

Jelena hung her head and began to cry when her father came close to her. He lifted her chin with his finger and said, "JellyGirl, today you fought the good fight. You protected someone else. NEVER be ashamed of fighting the good fight because *that's* the one that's worth fighting. Some of the hardest fights you will face will be the good fights. You can't quit, though. Not even if you're fighting alone, standing there by yourself. Not even if no one believes you. You must never be ashamed to stand up for what is right, and you should never quit protecting others...NEVER. You did a good thing today, Jelly, and this is nothing that cannot be cleaned up. Okay?" Jelena felt better and helped her family clean off the cars before everyone headed back to bed.

She visited this memory quite often, along with others similar in nature. Fighting the 'good fight' had always been inside Jelena. She was simply incapable of standing idly by while someone else was being injured. The strong pull of justice, equality, and kindness were undeniable, almost to the point of compulsion. She just felt that she was responsible to right the world's wrongs and protect those who were not strong enough to protect themselves, no matter the cost.

Jelena's mind was brought back to the present when something unknown in the darkness brushed up against her leg.

"Shit!" she exclaimed as she jumped up to her feet. "What in the flippin' frog nuts was that?"

Being in the dark silence can drive anyone to the brink of insanity...having visual and auditory hallucinations are a common side effect of being locked up in solitary confinement, but tactile hallucinations?

Jelena knew that she had felt something touch her sensitive skin in the darkness. She sat back down and waited for whatever it was to come in for a closer look, and when it did, with the speed of a viper, Jelena snatched it up, showing more evidence that she was becoming more feral by the day. The loud squeaking sound it made when Jelena grabbed it, along with how it felt in her hand, let her know exactly what it was. She was not alone in this cell.

"Rats...Fuck my life!" she whispered.

Jelena had never really been a fan of rats or rodents of any kind, really...not even hamsters. The idea of anything that could shimmy up her pant leg was just an unpleasant image for her. However, it was somewhat comforting to know that even in the darkness, Jelena could have a friend.

"Well, it's you and me, buddy...and that's what I will call you...Buddy. Hi, Buddy, I am Jelena, your cellmate. So here is the deal, I'm not real fond of rodent vermin types...no offense, of course. However, I have to admit that it is nice not to be the only living, breathing thing in here anymore. So, tell ya what...you can have that side of the cell, and I will have this side of the cell. Okay?" she said. "For Christ's sake...I swear if you start fucking talking back to me, I may very well shit a purple twinky," Jelena said to herself and her new furry pet.

Nonetheless, each time Jelena received a protein bar, she chipped off a corner of it and fed it to her newfound pal, and eventually, she was numb to the fact that she cohabitated with a rat...or rats...What would have freaked her out before, she no longer seemed to mind at all. She just knew that no matter the species, no one deserved to die in there...not of starvation at least...and certainly not while she had a say in the matter. As long as she had a protein bar, both she and Buddy would have a little to eat. "I'm friends with a friggin' rat. I think I have actually lost what was left of my mind," she whispered.

As she drifted back to dreamland, Jelena visited yet another memory. She was around fifteen years old, and on this night, her mother had come to pick her up from her aerobics class. Jelena got into the car, and as they drove through the dimly lit parking lot to get to the main highway, she saw something...something that she simply couldn't ignore.

Jelena saw an unknown woman on the side of the highway get struck by a car. Again, without any hesitation, she jumped out of her mother's moving car and ran in that direction. Jelena knew that part of the highway was so poorly lit that another motorist would never see the woman lying in the street, unconscious, and would run her over again, possibly killing her. Jelena ran with everything that she had toward the motionless woman, hearing her mother screaming her name from the car behind her.

"JELENA RADOMIR PRAZICH! WHAT IN THE HELL ARE YOU DOING? COME BACK HERE RIGHT NOW!" her mother screamed.

Jelena just couldn't obey her mother this time. She continued to run to the highway. She looked and saw that more cars were coming in her direction. She approached the lifeless woman's body and called to her. No response. Without any further hesitation, Jelena scooped the woman up, and with every bit of force she could muster, got the woman into a fireman's carry and carried her off the road. A millisecond later, a car zoomed past, traveling over fifty-five miles per hour, not even aware of the life-ending tragedy that could have occurred. Jelena gently laid the woman down on the soft grass when her mother pulled up onto the easement.

"WHAT IN THE HELL WAS THAT, JELENA? YOU COULD HAVE GOTTEN YOURSELF KILLED, YOU FOOLISH GIRL!" her mother reprimanded.

"Mama, she would have died! I had to do it, Mama. I had to save her," Jelena pleaded with her mother, who had by then composed herself.

"JellyGirl, you are truly something rare and amazing with a genuine heart of gold. You nearly gave me a heart attack. I am just so happy that you are okay," her mother said, hugging her. "You can't save everyone, Jelly. You have to remember that, or one day you may not be okay. Sometimes, you must save yourself. I love you so much that I don't know what I would do if anything ever happened to you."

Her mother's words echoed in Jelena's mind, but once again, Jelena was brought back into the present when a small beam of light came piercing through the darkness, landing on her face...

*The keyhole...*she thought.

Jelena sat up and watched as a key was slid into the hole blocking the beam of light. She heard the locking mechanism move, and then the heavy door opened. The light landing on Jelena's body felt like scolding laser beams. She never knew that light, itself, could be so painful. It was only the dim light coming from the few working bulbs they had in the hallway, but any light, after so long in complete darkness, seemed like it was coming from the surface of the sun.

Her eyes squinted shut as she tried to identify the person standing in the doorway, but all she could make out was a shadowy silhouette. Before her eyes had time to adjust, the person charged in at Jelena and grabbed her up by one arm. Still not knowing who this person was, Jelena was dragged into another room and sat in another wooden chair. Her eyes were beginning to adjust to the new levels of light available, and she could begin to identify the person in front of her.

"GODDAMN YOU, JELENA!" a familiar voice yelled out at her.

"Ummm, ehhh?" Jelena said groggily, still allowing her eyes to focus on the man before her.

"Six weeks!" he yelled. "Six fucking weeks!"

Jelena's eyes were now focused enough to tell that it was none other than Bruce yelling at her.

"Not a scream, not a cry, not a GODDAMNED FUCKING PEEP OUT OF YOU!" he said, rather irritated by her lack of reaction to being locked in a hole for what was apparently six weeks.

"Disappointed, Bruce?" she said snidely.

"We broke every single man...EVERY SINGLE MAN...in less than half that time. We figured that we couldn't leave you in there indefinitely, so here you fucking sit," he snarked.

"I told you, Bruce. I am not as 'breakable' as you think," she replied.

"WHAT'S THE FUCKIN INSTRUCTION, YOU CRAZY BITCH!" he

screamed.

"As I have told you from the beginning... YOU FUCKING PSYCHOTIC SADISTIC FUCK...there was NO GODDAMNED INSTRUCTION! Now, if you like, I can happily make one up for you, but I know that both you and I are well aware that NO FUCKING INSTRUCTION was EVER given! So, what will it be? Which instruction shall I make up for you, Bruce? Okay, I got one...GO GET MY FUCKING DRY CLEANING!" she screamed at him.

He charged at her as if to backhand her again, but this time he stopped, his hand millimeters from her pasty dirty face as she braced for impact.

Instead, he grabbed her face with one hand and looked her dead in the eye. "You sit here. DO NOT MOVE a fuckin' muscle!" he ordered as he launched himself out of the room with the door slamming behind him.

Jelena was so tired and hungry and weak that it was simply easier for her to obey his command and just be grateful for the chair she was allowed to sit in, as opposed to the floor with rats, although she did miss Buddy and hoped he and his little rat family would be okay.

In a few minutes, Bruce returned, a lot calmer than he had left. He had another toothpick hanging out the side of his mouth, which made her wonder if he was trying to quit smoking or something.

"So, there really *was* no fuckin' instruction?" he asked briefly, glancing at her and then to the floor.

"Nope," she said. "What? You didn't know?"

"No. The powers that be don't tell us what instruction is given. We are told to basically beat it out of you, no matter what. When a potential gives us what we ask, we go back and verify it. If they give it up, they have scrubbed out and are sent packing...back to wherever the hell they came from...and if they don't give up the instruction, if they can manage to keep their shit together, they move to the next level. We have never had a situation where an instruction just wasn't given," he explained.

"So do I win, or do I lose?" Jelena asked sarcastically.

"Never in my nineteen-year career have I ever seen ANYONE endure what you endured and not break. Fuck girl! You didn't even crack. I do have to say that it was somewhat dissatisfying. I rather enjoy watching them break," he confessed.

"Yeah, you would! You crazy bastard!" she snipped. "I told you once, and I will tell you again fucker...YOU WILL NEVER BREAK ME!"

At that moment, the door flew open, and two more men charged in.

"Get her up. We are moving her," one of them said in an unfamiliar voice.

The two men pushed past Bruce, grabbed Jelena, one by her hand and one by her foot, and dragged her out. Jelena was weak but kept trying to pry her hand free. Before she could even get his grip remotely loosened, she felt them swing her up and drop her in a wooden box that was much smaller than she was. She immediately tried to get up to try to get out of the box, and one of the men punched her in the face, knocking her back down and causing her lip to split back open, releasing a stream of blood from the reopened wound. He then put his boot square in the center of her chest, and with his weight, he pressed her down.

"STAY!" he commanded.

Jelena looked around and saw that they had dragged her into what appeared to be some airplane hangar with a huge open bay door. She could see Bruce running in behind the men.

"WAIT!" Bruce yelled. "WAIT! She wasn't given an instruction! Goddamn it, WAIT!"

The men placed a lid on the top of the box and began to nail the edges into place, sealing Jelena inside. She saw a small two-inch hole on one of the upper sides of the box, near her head, and tried to look out of it. She couldn't hear much with the hammering. It echoed inside the box, making her ears ring. Once the hammering stopped, she could make out a little of what was said between the three men.

"She doesn't have a fuckin' instruction. Hasn't she proven herself enough?" Bruce asked on her behalf.

"She's staying in the box. If she is still alive after this, then you can have her! The powers that be say that she stays in the box," one of the men said sternly.

The other man leaned down to the hole and whispered in, "Welcome to the box, sweetheart. Let's see if this don't kill ya."

They both chuckled as they walked away. Jelena peered out of the hole, trying to see Bruce, but the light was so bright that it was incredibly painful. She felt the box being hoisted up and had no idea what the hell was coming down the pike.

"What the fuck next?" she asked. "Cobras? Crocodiles? A Fiery death? Am I supposed to Houdini my ass out of this getup or what?"

She felt the cables release and heard a huge splash. Slowly she felt the water seep into the small holes in the bottom of the box. The water was rushing in through those holes faster than she had expected. The way they squished her down inside, she couldn't even get any leverage at all to try to push against it, let alone barely breathe.

The water continued to rush in as Jelena tried to think of some idea to fight her way out. This, however, would prove to be futile. The next fifteen minutes of her life would seem like hours. Jelena honestly didn't know if she wanted to beg for her life or if this would be the thing that would make her beg for death more than she had ever before.

Maybe she was being punished for telling the truth the whole time, that she really was **never** given any instruction. Maybe this was just a colossal fuck up from whoever was in charge of this torturous fiasco. Why was Bruce so upset? Did he really not know that they never gave her any instruction? Did he feel bad for all the hell he unleashed onto her? Could he really not make this stop? Question after question kept flooding her mind faster than the water flooded her new, yet unpleasant, accommodations.

"Why in the hell would they actually want me dead? Did I hear something I shouldn't have? Do I know something that I shouldn't know? This shit isn't fucking training...it's attempted murder! Why are they trying so hard to kill me? What did I do?" she said in the dark.

CHAPTER 7: THE BOX

As Jelena thrashed around in her tiny coffin, she could taste the blood from her reopened split lip. The water rushed in so fast that she couldn't help but wonder just how long she would have any air left to breathe. She could feel her panic get a violent shove into high gear as she pressed her face as close to the hole as possible.

"Fuck...this is a realllly bad time to not be able to grow gills!" she said sarcastically.

She scratched and clawed at the wooden walls of her watery tomb, hoping to find some little flaw that she could exploit. Her breathing was rapid and irregular. Jelena had difficulty regaining her composure, not to mention that thinking straight seemed to be impossible now.

Even in the midst of this, Jelena's mind took her back to a memory of her mother.

Jelena was learning how to drive with her mother in the car. It was raining, as it usually did throughout every Floridian summer when she felt the car jolt suddenly. Jelena realized that something was wrong, and she could only barely steer the vehicle in the pouring down rain. She began to panic while telling Charlotte what was going on. With the panic came Jelena's tears, just knowing that she was going to crash the car.

"Jelena," Charlotte said in a very calm and soothing tone. "You have to control yourself and not panic. When you panic, you cannot think straight, which only makes the situation that much worse. Now calm yourself and think. What are you going to do?"

"Okay, Mama," she cried, making every effort to slow her

breathing and force herself to calm way down.

"Talk your way through it, Jelly. You can do it," Charlotte reassured.

"Okay. I am going to take my foot off the gas, and I am going to put my hazard lights on. I am going to gently tap on the brakes and puuuulllll the wheel over to the right...okay...until...I...am...stopped," Jelena said.

"Mama! I DID IT!!! WE DIDN'T CRASH!!" she exclaimed excitedly.

"Good job, JellyGirl! Good job!" Charlotte replied. "Now, let's find a phone and call Papa to get us out of this mess."

This memory allowed Jelena to slow her breathing and regain some composure. "I gotta think straight. Now, what in the hell am I going to do?" she asked. "What are you going to do, Jelena?"

She racked her brain, trying to think of any possible thing that she could do to get herself out of this damn death trap. As the water rose to her chin, Jelena realized that there was no stopping this. She realized that this box would fill up with water, and there wasn't a goddamned thing that she could do to stop it. She could only hope that somehow, she would survive.

This is it, she thought. *This is how I end. They are going to kill me in this box, and there is absolutely nothing I can do to change that.*

Jelena began to pray, "Umm, dear God. So, I am sort of stuck in this box. I definitely got myself into this box, and I am really sorry that I made the crappy choice to come here. I only wanted to help. Please take care of

Papa and Mama and my brother and make my death come quick."

As the water had nearly filled the small tomb, Jelena had to make peace with the fact that she may not make it out of this alive. She had to resign herself to what became her new fate. Jelena took one deep breath and let it out...then another...and another...the time came, and she took her last final deep breath as the water filled the last remaining corners of the box.

She sat there, calmly, surrounded by the cold dark water, just listening to her heartbeat. Slower...slower...slower. She closed her eyes, let only a tiny bit of air out at a time, and relaxed all of her muscles. As she sat there, crammed into this tiny wooden tomb, her mind took control of her again...

Jelena remembered a scuba diving trip that her father had taken her on. It was her very first time out in open water. She grabbed her mask and regulator and took the plunge, immediately surrounded by clear blue emptiness. She looked around and saw her father motioning to her under the water to follow him. She kicked her fins behind her and headed in his direction.

Just beyond a small sand bar, they came to a beautiful ocean reef filled with so many colorful fish. It was like she was swimming inside of a rainbow. Jelena took her time inspecting every nook and cranny of that reef, as her father did the same. She was so excited to see this new fantastic world under the water. She was quite distracted looking at a small Morey Eel hidden in a tiny spot on the reef when she realized that she was having difficulty breathing. She looked at her air gauge, as she had been trained to, and realized that she was running out of air.

Jelena swam to her father to try to show him her gauge, but he, being an ocean lover himself, was also distracted by all of the wonderful creatures to see in the reef. Finally, Jelena grabbed her father's vest and pulled him to her. She pulled up her gauge and showed him that she was now out of air. His warm brown eyes immediately went from relaxed to shocked, once the severity of the situation struck him. Still, his experience and calm prevailed when he looked at her and gave her the signals to let her know that they were going to buddy-breath to the surface.

Radomir took a breath and then took the regulator out of his mouth and put it into Jelena's for her to take a breath. They did this back and forth until they reached the surface of the water. Just as that memory brought them breaking through the surface of the sea, another memory brought her right back down to the bottom again.

She was still scuba diving with her father, but this was a different memory of a trip to the Florida Keys. Again, Jelena felt the rush and excitement of visiting the local sea life. She felt more confident during this trip and managed to spot a stingray gliding along the bottom of the ocean floor. It was the first one she had ever seen that wasn't in a zoo or aquarium. She turned to see her father and waved at him to get his attention and show him the stingray. She didn't realize how big of a gap there was between them. As she turned back in the direction of the ray, something massive hit her in the head and not only knocked off her mask but also knocked the air regulator out of her mouth. What she didn't see, on the other side, was that she was on the edge of a huge school of

Tarpons. Tarpons are large fish that can measure up to eight feet in length and weigh up to two hundred eighty pounds, with a head shaped like a bluntly rounded bullet. A Tarpon swimming on the outer edge of the school had hit her in the side of the head, resulting in her predicament. She knew not to panic, but when you're sinking in the dark with no air, it can be hard to find that silver lining.

The next thing she remembered was feeling someone grab her by the back of her vest and shove a regulator back into her mouth. Followed by someone handing her the mask. She put it on, cleared the water out of it, and to her relief, it was her father who had saved her. Once again, his experience and calm demeanor spared Jelena from what could have been a tragic event. He signaled Jelena to see if she was okay. Although she was a bit shaken and a little more than ready to return to the safety of the boat, she was okay. She looked at him and knew that calm was key, especially when shit gets a bit dicey.

SNAP* CRASH* The waterfilled box containing a barely conscious Jelena had come crashing down onto the hangar floor, smashing open, releasing her limp body. She was so focused on every detail of her memory that she hadn't even realized that the box was being lifted out of the tank.

Jelena choked and gasped for air almost immediately after the box broke.

"NO FUCKIN WAY!" one man yelled. "THAT'S GODDAMNED IMPOSSIBLE! NOBODY CAN HOLD THEIR BREATH THAT LONG!"

Ignoring their comments, but not without a cross look, Bruce quickly scooped Jelena up and carried her to the medic's bay.

"Jelena...Jelena?" the nurse called softly. "Dr. Simms, she is coming around."

"Jelena, my name is Dr. Simms. How are you feeling?" he asked as he shined his penlight into her eyes, checking for a pupillary response.

Jelena slowly opened her eyes and looked around to find herself in a clean white room. She was hooked up to an IV, and there were monitors around her beeping rhythmically in time with her respiration and heartbeat. She was clean and in an extremely comfortable hospital bed that, quite frankly, felt like it belonged in a suite at the Hilton resort...but after God only knows how long she was in that pit, it stands to reason that her standards may have been lowered a tad.

She was in a white hospital gown with small blue diamonds on it, and she even had a few super soft blankets covering her that felt magical to her hands and fingers. She reached up to feel her face, and as she ran her finger over her lip, she discovered that it was now a decently healed scab covered with ointment.

"Jelena, can you hear me? My name is Dr. Simms. How are you feeling today?" he asked again.

"Umm, I don't know...okay, I guess. I have a bit of a headache, but nothing I can't manage," she replied in a raspy, unused voice. "How long have I been here?"

"The farm can be quite rough on even the toughest potentials. You survived the box and were brought here four days ago. Your oxygen levels were so low that we put you in an induced coma and let you rest in a hyperbaric chamber for a bit, just until your levels came back up. I have to say, that was quite impressive. Most potentials don't or can't do that, even those that get as far in the process as the box, require CPR…and some, unfortunately, don't make it beyond that. The fact that you show no brain impairment at all makes you quite the marvel young lady," he explained.

"Marvel, my ass…" she said, trying to clear her throat. "Those bastards tried to kill me."

"I know it's hard. The process is designed to challenge you in every way conceivable. It can seem harsh and unfair, but please believe me…For anyone to succeed, we all must trust the process. Now, it is to be expected that you have a bit of a headache. We will keep you here for another day to let you rest and eat to get your strength back. Then you will go on to the next level. Get some sleep, and I will check on you tomorrow. Okay?" Dr. Simms said as he left the room.

"So, my dear…boy, aren't *you* the talk of the town. My name is Belle, and I will be your nurse for the night. So, tell me, what would you like to eat? Got any cravings? You deserve a five-star meal for sure! Cookies? Jello? What's your pleasure?" Belle said with a smile.

Belle was a small round woman with kind brown eyes and a sweet smile. Her gray hair was pulled back into a low bun just above the nape of her neck. She was soft-spoken, soothing, and warm. She seemed like she could be the grandma you always wanted.

"Uh…Food?" asked Jelena. "Like real food?"

"Yes, deary. Real food," Belle said with a soft giggle. "What can I get you? We should probably keep it light since you haven't had a lot of *real food* in a good long while, I assume."

"Yeah…no…just protein bars and water…the last real food I had was a sandwich I ate right before they got me," Jelena said, "but I ended up puking that up all over the floor, not long after arriving."

"Yes, entering into your line of work is never easy. How about some chicken noodle soup, saltine crackers…and maybe some apple juice? Sound good?" Belle asked.

"That sounds great, actually!" Jelena said with an enthusiastically appreciative tone.

"Okay, dear. I'll be back," Belle said chipperly. "Ooh, and I'll stop by the kitchen to see if I can find you a cookie too."

"Oh, hey, Belle!" Jelena called out.

"Yes, dear?" she responded.

"Did you tend to a man named Adam Burke by any chance? Lieutenant Colonel Adam Burke? White male, six-one-ish, dirty blonde hair, kind deep blue eyes?" Jelena asked.

Belle looked down quickly as if all of the happiness were wiped from her face and then responded, "We aren't supposed to talk about potentials, dear. I'm sorry. I'll be back with that cookie."

Jelena's mind, for some reason, was focused on Adam. She didn't even get to say goodbye. She was so focused on her hatred of Bruce that she didn't realize that would be the last time she saw Adam.

"I hope he made it out alive," she said before closing her eyes and entering into the first dreamless sleep that she'd had in a very long while.

"Jelena? I have your soup," Belle said quietly. "I'm sorry dear...I couldn't get a cookie."

"Ohhh, Belle, thank you...I was just...um...resting my eyes," Jelena said as she pushed herself up in the bed.

Belle placed the food tray on the cart and rolled it over to Jelena's bedside. As Jelena continued to push herself into an upright position, Belle went behind her and fluffed her pillows, grabbing another one from a lower cabinet. "Here you go, deary. You can lean back on this," Belle said, trying to make Jelena as comfortable as possible.

"Well then, I will be back in a little bit to take your dishes to the kitchen. Okay?" Belle asked.

"Okay, Belle. Thank you so very much. I truly appreciate your kindness," Jelena said.

The chicken noodle soup melted in Jelena's mouth and tasted better than she had ever remembered. The crackers seemed a bit salty but were so crunchy and good. Jelena couldn't believe that she had forgotten what a friggin saltine cracker tasted like. What a crazy notion. As she opened her apple juice and began to sip at the tiny straw, she expected a certain taste, but when it hit her taste buds, it seemed so much sweeter than it ever had in the past, almost syrupy. For some reason, Jelena felt like she needed just plain water...and, sickeningly enough, in a metal cup. She felt like she had splurged on all this super-rich food when in reality, it was only her extreme deprivation that made her simple meal seem so extravagant.

"Jelena...Jelena...I found one! I found a cookie!" yelled Belle as she came flying through the door.

Jelena couldn't help but laugh at Belle's excitement over a cookie, although truth be told, she was a bit ecstatic herself.

"Oh boy, deary, I have never gotten quite that excited over a cookie before." Belle chuckled. "So, all done, are we? Let me get these dishes out of your way."

"Belle, can I ask you a question?" asked Jelena as she munched on the best cookie that she had ever had.

"Certainly, dear, but unfortunately, I cannot guarantee that I will be able to answer it," Belle replied.

"Fair enough," Jelena began. "Belle, do you know how much more I have to take? I just don't think I can keep surviving things here if I am not even close to being done. It is definitely NOT what I expected."

"All I can say, deary, is that most of the hardest and riskiest parts are behind you now. You really shocked the hell out of 'em when you held your breath in that box. No one has ever come out of that like you did.

You'll keep those boys talking for a good long while, and I must also say that you have set the bar incredibly high for those who come after you. You're a legend," Belle answered wide-eyed and charismatically.

Jelena smiled. "I am sorry to ask again, but are you sure you can't tell me anything about Adam? Can you at least tell me if he is alive? He took care of me in there, and I took care of him, and then before you know it, I got dragged away and never saw him again...I didn't even get to say goodbye...I just want to know if he made it out alive," she said as she looked away, almost getting choked up just thinking about him.

"I am sorry, dear. We are just not allowed to talk about other potentials. I wish I could, but I can't. I'm sure you understand. Now, now dear...let's get you all tucked into bed...all snug and cozy," Belle said. She approached Jelena and began straightening her sheets and tucking her in tightly. As Belle was tucking her in, she leaned over in a very sly manner and whispered into Jelena's ear, "Adam is alive. He survived the box, too but needed a brief stint on life support until he could breathe on his own again. He came into the hospital three or so weeks before you, but I don't know where he is. His code name is John Jack."

"There you go, deary...all snug as a bug in a rug. Sweet dreams, Jelena. It was nice to have met you. Good luck on all your adventures," Belle said before blowing Jelena a kiss and shutting the door.

The next morning, Jelena woke up with the warmth of the sun on her face. The morning nurse must have come in and opened the drapes. As she opened her eyes, she stretched her arms long and wide. She hadn't felt this good since they trapped her in this pit. She rolled over to get some water and jumped a bit when she saw Bruce.

He was sitting in the chair next to her bed, with his forearms resting on his thighs but his face looking up at her. Seeing him up close in good lighting, he didn't look like she had remembered from her interview. He seemed cleaner back then, in a fancy business suit... clean shaven. Today, he was wearing a black t-shirt and ripped jeans with black boots, almost like he was preparing for some grunge rave. His dark wavy hair, cut short, was complimentary to the angled shape of his scruffy face and high cheekbones. His tan Mediterranean skin tone made his appearance even more appealing. His eyes, in this light, were the perfect combination of green and brown. His lips were full, his teeth were straight and white and hanging out the right side of his mouth was that stupid toothpick.

"Well, hello, Bruce. Where's your bat...or your prods?" Jelena asked snidely.

Bruce may have brought her into the medic's bay, but Jelena was not conscious enough to know that, and as far as she was concerned, she still felt nothing but rage and contempt for him. It would be a long time before she ever got over the sadistic things Bruce did do her...if ever.

"Stop it," Bruce said. "How did you do that?"

"How did I do what, Bruce?" Jelena sighed. "How did I piss you off? Disappoint you? Make you want to kill me? Well, gosh, I don't know."

"Jelena, knock it the fuck off and answer the damn question! How did you do that? How did you hold your breath for over twelve minutes? We have never, and I do mean NEVER, seen anyone do that before. Every single potential that has come through this program has required CPR and a vent for a bit until they can breathe on their own again. Yet you...you came out of the box still breathing...How is that even possible? How in the fuck did you do that?" Bruce demanded.

"Wait...what? Twelve minutes? You left me drowning in that fucking box for twelve minutes! Go back to the part about twelve minutes," Jelena said.

"Somehow, you were able to hold your breath in that submerged box for just over twelve minutes, and I need to know how you did that," Bruce replied.

"Well, I don't know what to tell you, Brucy. Your 'Jelena breaker box' must be on the fritz because here I am...bruised perhaps, but definitely not broken," Jelena said bitterly sarcastic.

"GOD DAMN IT, JELENA! I NEED TO KNOW!!! HOW IN THE FUCK DID YOU DO THAT?" he screamed at her.

"I DON'T FUCKIN' KNOW, YOU PSYCHO BASTARD! I DIDN'T DO IT ON PURPOSE!" she screamed back at him.

Just then, Dr. Simms came through the door looking rather irritated, "**Excuse me,** you two, but people are trying to heal here, and that is the absolute last thing that they need to hear, so if you don't mind, please keep it down," he sneered.

"Sorry, sir," Jelena responded. "It won't happen again." Dr. Simms nodded at her and looked down at Bruce in disapproval before leaving and softly shutting the door behind him.

"Bruce...you could have apologized too, you know!" she scolded, but Bruce, who just couldn't take his eyes off her, appeared to be in some sort of trance or something. "Ummm, Bruce...Helllooooooo..." she sang as she waved in an attempt to get him to even blink before giving up and looking out the window instead.

"Ummm, Jelena..." he said, "what do you mean you didn't do it on purpose?"

"I don't know. I was pretty sure that I would die in that fucking box. I didn't plan out anything...like...ooooohhh I will just hold my breath until they let me out...I didn't hold my breath like that on purpose. Shit...I didn't even know that I *could* hold my breath for that long," Jelena confessed.

"Tell me what you were thinking? What happened in that box, girl? Tell me!" Bruce demanded.

Jelena looked out the window at the green trees that were outside. That was the most color she had seen in months. As she gazed, she took it all in, all of the little things that she had taken for granted. She spotted a red-breasted robin on a branch. It was so beautiful. It was so peaceful. Jelena couldn't wait to be free again...to be outside...to feel the wind and the snow and the rain.

"Please," Bruce said quietly. "Jelena...Please...tell me."

"Wow...so, Mr. Baseball Bat knows the word 'please.' Now THAT is unexpected," Jelena scoffed. "But alright...I will tell you. I really don't know what happened. The box was filling up with water really fast, and I learned a long time ago how to meditate and kinda free my mind...I guess...I don't know...I just let my mind take me to different places and different memories and stuff. I was thinking of my mom and how she taught me to not panic so that I could think clearly...and then I was thinking of a dive trip that I took with my dad, where I ran out of air seventy feet under the ocean...and another where I got smacked by a big fish, and it knocked my mask off and my air regulator out of my mouth...and then I wake up a week later in a hospital room not really knowing what all happened myself," Jelena explained.

"I'm sorry, Bruce...but I can't answer this question any better than I was able to give you an instruction that I was never given. If it's okay, I would like to spend my few remaining hours getting some more shut-eye and real people food before I have to go back and eat whatever other shit sandwich you have planned for me, and I can't do that with you here. I have learned that closing my eyes around you never seems to end well for me. Can you please just go?" she asked.

"Sure. I will be back to escort you to the next phase of your training in about four and a half hours. Be ready," Bruce replied.

"SIX!" she scoffed.

"You don't make the fucking rules, Jelena! Four and a half hours...and be ready," he curtly replied.

Jelena's eyes followed Bruce to the door, and as it shut behind him, she rolled her eyes, shut the drapes, and tried to drift off to another peaceful dreamless sleep. Still, no matter how hard she tried to relax, she couldn't help but feel anxious over something Bruce said... 'the next phase of training.'

*Dear God...what's next? Disembowelment? Cutting off my body parts? Do I even want to know what comes next? Shit...Not fuckin really...*she thought to herself.

For a brief moment, she wondered if she could just make a break for it...just get up and walk out of this sick torture festival...just leave it all behind...she finally accepted that any attempt to leave would be in vain...she knew that she was in far too deep to get out now. She closed her eyes and slowly began to clear the cluttered chaos and anxiety from her mind, which was something she had become quite masterful at.

"God, I hate that man!" she said under her breath.

CHAPTER 8: MRS. APPLEBIE

Jelena woke from her nap and found that the nurse had left a tray of food, consisting of a chicken sandwich, an apple, some orange juice, and what ended up being a cookie wrapped in a napkin with a white ribbon and a sliver of paper that read 'From Belle.'

She looked around her room to find the clock and saw that she still had about two hours until the devil showed up to drag her back to hell. She also noticed that hanging over one of the chairs was what appeared to be clothes on a hanger in a dry-cleaning plastic sleeve.

"What the??" she whispered.

Jelena hopped out of bed and walked over to the chair, expecting to find her own clothes that she was picked up in, but instead, she found a lovely soft ivory peplum blouse carefully matched with sleek, black, slightly pinstriped trousers. Around the neck of the hanger, she found a bag containing a new, nude-colored bra and pantie set. In the seat of the chair, she found a shoebox containing a pair of patent leather heels with a cute MaryJane rounded toe that just happened to be in her size.

This can't be for me? she thought. *Where's the tag? This must be a mistake.*

She fumbled around for a moment, searching for the dry-cleaning tag to find the name of the correct owner. She finally found a tag stapled to the bag which read, *Put this on. - B*

B? she thought, *Uggh BRUCE! God, I hate that man! Well, shit, at least he has good taste.*

Jelena's mood was one of the happiest she had had in months. She jumped into the shower and took her time, washing every part of her body...twice. She washed her dark chocolate brown hair and scrubbed her scalp, trying to remove any evidence of anything that may have decided to take up residence there during her stay at the Roughneck Resort...where the manhandling is guaranteed to knock you out...or your money back. She even found a razor and shaved her legs and pits. Singing in the shower and coming up with all kinds of names to call that hole she just crawled out of.

Club Canker...Asshole Alley...Sadist's Sanctuary...Hell's Haven...I could do this all day! Oh. My. God! I feel amazing! she thought as she got out of the shower and dried off.

Near the sink, she found a cabinet with all kinds of goodies. Deodorant, a hairbrush and hair ties, a toothbrush and toothpaste, a small spray bottle of a fruity kind of perfume, and a little bag of make-up.

"Ooooohhhhh!!!!" she exclaimed excitedly. "I am allowed to be a human again...Let's see what do we have here? Concealer...yes. Powder...yes. Blush...yes. Eyeliner...and mascara. I swear it must be Christmas! Either that or I am about to be pimped out to the nastiest bidder. Please God, just don't let it be friggin Bruce!"

Jelena danced around her room, taking bites of her food here and there while getting dressed. She ran the hairbrush through her hair and pulled it back in a tight clean bun at the back of her head. She finished her food and went into the bathroom to apply her make-up, humming a happy little tune the whole time. After she gave herself a little spritz of the perfume, she stood back and took a look at herself in the mirror.

Jelena was not a petite gal. She wasn't really considered short or tall for that matter. She was really kind of a plain Jane, but she was muscular and quite athletic, although she appeared slender from a distance. She also had some sweeter-looking feminine features, such as fuller lips, rounder eyes, and a heart-shaped face. At certain times she definitely fit the bill of 'the girl next door,' but make no mistake about it, she was all muscle and all heart with an iron will and a questionable disposition. Under the right circumstances, Jelena could be sweet and kind and even loving; but under the wrong circumstances, she could rip out your throat and carry on with her day.

"Damn! I look great for a dead chick!" She chuckled as she gave herself one final up and down in the mirror.

Jelena turned around to leave the bathroom and paused when she saw a man standing in her doorway. The instant she saw him, the smile was erased from her lips. It was Bruce.

"Ahh fuck!" she said quietly, but not at all trying to hide her disdain.

Bruce was nothing if not punctual. There he stood, smiling...at her door. He apparently had showered, shaved and changed into a more casual dark gray suit, sporting a red patterned tie. He extended his hand gesturing that he was ready to escort her to the next phase of her training as promised. Jelena looked up at the clock and saw that she still had four minutes left.

"You're early," she said in a manner that made it quite obvious that she was less than thrilled to see him.

"I have always been told that if you can't be on time, then be early," Bruce replied with a grin. "You look great, by the way."

"Yeah, at least you have decent taste in women's apparel," she said sarcastically. "Thanks, I guess."

"Oh, actually, my assistant picked it out for you," he confessed.

"Well then, once again, I have given you too much credit there, Bruce," Jelena snipped.

"Jelena, we are going to be working together for a while. Can't you just play nicely? I mean, what's it going to take for us to get along and for you to drop the attitude toward me?" he asked.

"Well, how about you get strapped to a table, and I get to shove the electrical prod up your ass this time for funzies...ummm and that's just for starters," she said snidely as she rolled her eyes, grabbed her cookie, and walked out the door in front of him.

"Damn, you are really..." he started.

"What? Feisty?" she asked.

"Ummm, no. I was going to say a bitch, actually," he replied.

"Yep. Bitch works too...So...which way is it to hell, there Satan?" she asked.

Bruce pointed to a sidewalk leading to a large, plain tan-looking multi-story building. Jelena looked around her surroundings as she nibbled on her cookie. It looked like it could have been a college or university campus at some point. Trees, grassy areas, benches, and buildings that looked to have maybe three to four stories. No school insignias were visible, though...anywhere.

"Where are we, Bruce?" Jelena asked.

"I told you...the farm. You only got to see the dark side of the moon so far. Now we are going into one of the main training buildings. You will learn a shit ton of stuff...guns, cultural etiquettes, laws, rules, gadgets, languages...you know...all that squirrelly spy shit," he explained.

"Oh, yippee. I am on the edge of my seat..." she started.

"Stooooop," Bruce emphasized, rolling his eyes at her.

"Okay...alright, so let me get this straight," Jelena began as she stopped dead in her tracks and pulled Bruce to face her. "No more prods? No more bats? No more boxes?" she listed. "No more solitary? No more rats? No more protein bars? No more 'What's the fuckin instruction Jelena?' bullshit? Is that right?"

"Yep. That's right. You have already passed all those tests," Bruce explained.

"And now what? Now that that's all over, you want to be my friend or something???" she said as she began walking again toward the building.

"Well, maybe not your friend...but maybe your mentor. You know, your ally," he replied, retaining a glimmer of hope in his eyes.

Jelena stopped again and faced him. "Bruce, I hate to tell you this but, thoughts of doing you great harm brought me nearly orgasmic joy in that pit. And yes, I am still fantasizing about ripping out your lying tongue with my bare hands, even to this very second. You made a lot of false promises, Bruce! You spewed a lot of bullshit, and you did a lot of things in that pit...things that I cannot yet overlook. I can promise to be civil to you, and that is all," she said, her voice filled with contempt and tempered rage.

"Fair enough," Bruce said, conceding to the terms of her civility.

Jelena and Bruce entered the building through two large glass doors. The ceilings were super high, and everything inside was about as plain and neutral as possible. The floors were a tan-ish, light-colored marble and the click of Jelena's heels made an echo as they walked through the entry hallway. She continued to look around and observe that there were no paintings or pictures of any kind on the walls. They came to a gated security checkpoint.

"Badge, name, and ID?" the security officer ordered firmly.

Without hesitation, Bruce opened his jacket, retrieved a small leather wallet-looking sleeve containing his badge and CIA identification card, and showed it to the guard as he said, "6831 Lima."

"Who's this?" the guard said, eyeing Jelena up and down.

"Potential 518 Papa," Bruce replied. "We are here to get her set up to begin Phase Two."

"Fine. One at a time, please step into the scanner," the guard said as he pointed.

Bruce placed his gun, badge, wallet, and keys into the tray and then stepped into the scanner.

"Clear. Step out, please," the guard said. "Now you."

Jelena raised her hands as if she were surrendering and said, "Umm, I don't have anything."

"Fine. Step in," the guard replied.

Jelena stepped into the scanner as Bruce waited for her on the other side.

"Clear. Step out, please," the guard said.

Bruce gathered up his items and holstered his sidearm, and as he looked at Jelena, he smiled and asked, "Impressed?"

"Not really. This place needs a woman's touch," she quipped.

"Without a doubt." Bruce chuckled. "Let's go."

The two walked down another series of hallways, with Jelena's heels making a clickity-clack sound the entire way. They eventually came to a tall tan door with no window and a small placard that read, 'Rm 106-Admin.' Bruce knocked twice, and his knocks were followed by a loud buzzer and the sound of the door unlocking.

"Geez, you guys have a lot of security deals up in here," she said.

"We can never be too secure...Right?" Bruce said to her while opening the door.

On the other side of the door was a large, cubicle-filled room. Probably around twenty or so, good-sized cubicles, but it looked like only two or three people were there.

"What? Is everybody on vacation or what?" Jelena asked.

"No. Here's a piece of good advice...While you are here, don't talk so much. That can only get you into trouble. Learn what you are here to learn and get out. Sarcasm doesn't really fly too well within these walls," Bruce explained.

Jelena raised her eyebrows for a second and responded, "Okie dokie."

They navigated around the cubicles and came to one occupied by a tiny little woman with almost mouse-like features. She had a frizzy, messy bun of light brown hair perched nearly on top of her head. She wore glasses in front of her crystal blue eyes and had an extremely oversized tan sweater covering her tiny physique.

"Hey Lucy," Bruce began politely, "I got another one for you."

"Sure thing, Lima Bean," Lucy responded quirkily with just a hint of an old-fashioned southern accent.

Jelena raised her eyebrows as she looked at Bruce and mouthed the words, 'Lima Bean,' with a quizzical look on her face. Bruce just rolled his eyes at her and continued, "Lucy, I would like you to meet my newest Potential, 518 Papa. Originally, Jelena Prazich," Bruce said with a friendly and pride-filled tone.

"Ooohhh, so *you're* the one everyone's buzzing about, huh? The famous 518 Papa..." Lucy started, only to be interrupted by Bruce.

"Lucy? We talked about this, right?" he asked with an almost reprimanding but soft tone.

"Oh, yes, sir! Lima Bean...Not another word on that," Lucy said with a smile and a salute that barely showed her fingertips sticking out from beyond the long tan sleeve of her sweater.

"So, 518, let's get you all A'd and J'd and squared awayed. Today you're gonna slap your John Hancock on another insurance document and fill out some basic paperwork. Then I'll take you over to them digital fellers, and we'll get your fingerprints all scanned in and take care of your retinal scan too. Now, every door in this place is locked. Certain ones you'll be able to open with either your fingerprint or your retinal scan. Once you finish all of your trainin' and you get your official credentials, then you'll be able to open more doors, access safe houses, safes, cars, and all them cool little gadgety things them R&D guys come up with," Lucy explained.

"Okay then, I will leave you ladies to it. I have a meeting, and I will be back in about two hours. Good luck. Oh, and Jelena...watch out for this one. Lucy here is a ton tougher than most folks know," Bruce said as he smiled and gave a little salute back to Lucy.

"Pffft, ohhh, he's just joshin' ya," Lucy quipped. "Well...Let's boogie."

Lucy took Jelena around the office and introduced her to the few people there, always introducing her as 'you know...*that* one' with a quick wink in her eye. They got back around to her cubicle and quickly filled out the little bit of paperwork that required Jelena's signature. Most of her personal details were already filled out, just like before.

"Alrighty-dighty," Lucy said. "Let's head on upstairs to them digital guys...but just to let you know, they don't really have any sense of humor up there, so it's probably best to zip the lip, if you catch my drift," Lucy finished as she made a gesture of zipping her lip with an imaginary zipper and throwing the key away.

Jelena smiled and repeated the gesture back to Lucy to show that she understood.

"Here we are...Room three-o-three. Now, remember..." Lucy said, repeating the zipping gesture.

"Got it, Lucy!" Jelena said.

Lucy bent down and opened her left eye as wide as she could in front of the scanner. It made a beep, and a line of green light scanned it up and down and then right to left. It made three more beeps and then the sound of the door unlocking. "Well, howdy, fellas!" Lucy said.

The room was a truly monochrome gray, and two heads popped up from behind the half wall in the middle of the room. "Hello," one of the men said.

"I got, 518 Papa here for her fingerprint and retina scannin'," Lucy explained.

"Fine. 518 Papa, please have a seat at that desk in the corner," the man replied.

Jelena walked over to the desk and sat down as Lucy patiently waited for her by the door. The man quickly placed each of Jelena's fingertips on a small white box with a glass top. Then he took her over to another station, with a device that looked like something the DMV used to check your vision before issuing you a driver's license. "Press your forehead into the top bar and open your eyes as wide as possible. Do not blink," the man said with zero personality in his voice.

"Okay. Please sit back and look straight at this blue dot. No smiling," the man instructed.

Jelena did as she was told and realized that she was probably getting her picture taken for various IDs.

"You're done," the man said.

"Umm, that's it?" Jelena asked.

"Yes," the man responded.

"Welllll, umm okay. Thank you then," she said as she headed to the door to meet back up with Lucy.

"All done?" Lucy asked.

"Yes, ma'am," Jelena replied.

"Well alrighty then…let's boogie right on outta here. Maybe we can stop at the snacky thing to get a treat," Lucy said.

The two walked back to the Admin room, to Lucy's cubicle, and waited for Bruce to come back. Lucy saw Bruce before Jelena did.

"Lima Beeeaaannn. Your girl is all done and just as pretty as a picture too," Lucy exclaimed.

"Thank you, Lucy. You are an absolute gem!" Bruce said.

Bruce guided Jelena out of the Admin suite with his hand on her lower back. "This way," he said softly. "Bye Lucy!" he hollered out as the door shut behind them. They began heading out of the building the same way they came in.

"Where are we going now?" Jelena asked him.

"I am taking you to your accommodations," he replied.

"Oh really?" she quipped. "Can I have a light this time? Maybe a bathroom?"

Bruce shot her a side-eye warning as they walked through the grassy courtyard along the sidewalk, heading toward yet another plain tan building. As they continued to walk in silence, Jelena felt the undeniable need to ask Bruce about Adam.

"Bruce, may I ask you a question?" she asked hesitantly, figuring that this question would probably not yield a pleasant response.

"Go for it," he responded.

"Where is Adam?" she asked.

"Jelena, we do not talk about other potentials...ever," Bruce said.

"Come on, Bruce. Where is he? I never got to say goodbye before you punched me in the kisser with your fuckin bat. Please just tell me where he is?" Jelena pleaded.

Bruce stopped abruptly and turned to Jelena, and said, "EVER. I will not tell you where Adam is. I can't. When assets have too much information about each other, it only puts everyone at risk. So just don't ask. You have to focus on *your* training here, not Adam's. YOUR TRAINING! Got it? DO NOT EVER mention the name Adam Burke ever again!"

"But..." she pressed.

"LEAVE IT, JELENA!" he demanded. "And another piece of free advice is don't get attached to ANYONE! In this line of work, you will have to play your little mind games more than ever, and you will have to develop relationships that are critical to your mission at the time, whatever that may be, but people in this line of work die. A lot. If your focus is fractured thinking about someone you have gotten attached to, then your mission is at risk...you are at risk...and they are at risk, not to mention the whole fucking establishment here. That attachment can be used against you, and that never ends well for anyone."

Jelena understood what Bruce was talking about, but she also knew she needed to find Adam. She felt some kind of forbidden connection to him. She didn't think it was love, per se, but she just felt this need to find him deep in her gut. Regardless of Bruce's warning, she had already decided that she was going to do whatever it took to find Adam as soon as she had the chance.

As they approached the door, Jelena saw a small station attached to the wall. It was a fingerprint station.

"Here, you try," Bruce said to her.

Jelena placed her right index finger on the pad, the scanner made a beep and the same familiar unlocking sound.

"Damn...that was fast," Jelena said, surprised.

"Yes, things happen quickly around here." Bruce chuckled.

The door unlocked, and Jelena opened it and felt the refreshing blast of cold air from the air-conditioned space. They walked to the elevator and got on, and Bruce pressed the button for the seventh floor.

"Seven, huh?" Jelena asked.

"It's your lucky number, isn't it?" Bruce said with one of his sly grins.

DING. The doors opened, and it was more of the same. Tan hotel carpet with no designs, other than the occasional coffee stain here and there. There was nothing on the bland beige walls, and all the doors were equally spaced down the hall.

"Here we are. Room seven-sixty-two," he said as he flipped the plastic guard covering the fingerprint scanner. He pressed his finger down, and the panel displayed a red light with an accompanying buzzer sound. "See? Mine doesn't work," he began, "So, you *do* have some privacy here. Now you try."

"Will any of my fingers work, or just the index fingers?" she asked.

"Any one of your choosing. All ten have been entered into the system," he explained.

With a smartass look on her face, Jelena placed her middle finger on the pad, and the panel then displayed a green light and made a happy little beeping sound, along with the familiar unlocking sound.

"Funny," he said as he opened the door for her, "Welcome to your accommodations. You will be staying here for the next eight weeks of your training." Bruce went through the small living space and turned on all the lights.

The room was simple and undecorated. The walls were the same plain beige color as the hallway walls were, with no pictures or color evident in the room. There was a twin-sized bed, a small dresser, and a locker-like closet, all matching the same beige tones. There was a private bathroom with a stand-up shower, a tan waterproof curtain, a toilet, and a sink/vanity combo.

"This is like my old barracks room...and HOT DAMN Bruce! I even get a bed. I certainly must be movin' on up," she said with a chuckle.

Bruce smiled at her. "The linens for the bed and the towels are in the top of the closet. I will let you get all settled in then. Okay?" he said.

"Can I leave? Like, go to the store or something?" Jelena asked.

"No, you are not permitted to leave the farm until we tell you so. If you need something, tell me, and I will get it for you if I can. There is a small commissary next to the cafeteria here, where you can buy your hygiene and toiletry items. Sometimes, they have other things too that you might like. There is a map on the back of your door so that you can find your way around. A hint... Be where you are supposed to be... exactly when you are supposed to be there. And if you cannot be on time... then be early. Get some sleep. You officially begin your next phase of training tomorrow morning. I'll be here at o-five-hundred hours," he replied.

For the next eight weeks, Jelena trained under Bruce and various other instructors at the farm. She learned just about every conceivable weapon system, how to operate various vehicles from motorcycles to cars to heavy equipment, and even how to fly small planes and helicopters. She didn't quite have enough time to become an expert at all of them, but she certainly learned enough to get the job done.

She learned Spanish, Russian, Italian, and French, and that feat even amazed her. In reality, Spanish, French, and Italian all have the same root language, and her father was Russian and taught her a bit, so it really wasn't as amazing as her peers and instructors felt it was. She learned about computer systems, programming, and various hacking techniques.

She learned how to build things from make-shift shelters to bombs. She learned the various cultural etiquette and manners associated with damn near every country in the world. She learned how to blend herself into any city or survive in the wild with no modern-day conveniences. She mastered psychological warfare and learned how to change her appearance in the blink of an eye.

She was now one of the world's most versatile chameleons, able to be hidden in plain sight. She was a machine, molded, sculpted, and finely honed to give the CIA the sharpest edge they possessed in nearly a century. Jelena was now a fully trained CIA operative, ID 518 Papa.

She graduated from the farm with higher marks than any of her peers, which by certain standards, would place her at the top of the class. Graduation at the farm was slightly different from your average boot camp or college graduation... but then, nothing was ever typical or expected there, and 'traditional' was nothing more than an obsolete term of endearment.

"You did it. I am so proud of you," Bruce said as he came in close to hug Jelena.

Jelena put her hand out in the center of his chest to stop his advance and instead reached her hand out to shake his.

"Man... still holding that grudge, I see," he quipped as he shook her hand.

"Well, you still have your tongue, don't you?" She chuckled and raised her eyebrows, making a funny face.

"Yes...Yes, I do. So, are you ready for Phase Three? The final phase," he said to her.

"WHAT? But I am done. I have done everything you guys have asked of me. I was the best. What else could you possibly want from me, Bruce?" Jelena asked with her voice showing her level of frustration.

"Jelena, I would like you to meet someone," Bruce said, guiding Jelena over in another direction.

As he guided her, she could see that she was heading in the direction of what she would describe as one of the most beautiful women in the entire world. She stood so tall, even taller than Jelena, so she must have been around 6'0 or maybe even 6'2 in those heels. She had waist-length, blonde, flowy hair and bright ocean blue eyes. Her skin was a pristine porcelain ivory with zero defects visible. On each side of her smile, she had just a pinch of rosiness in her cheeks. She was wearing a white pantsuit with a gorgeous blue silk blouse underneath that made her eyes pop. Jelena was stunned by her beauty...but then again, who wasn't.

"Hi, there!" the beautiful woman began, with a southern Texas accent. "I'm 8993 Delta, but you can call me Kate," she said, reaching out her perfectly manicured hand to shake Jelena's. "I'm gonna be your Senior Asset for your first walk," she said as she shook her hand. Kate held onto her hand and pulled Jelena in close for a semi-hug to congratulate the new graduate and whispered in her ear, "Code Name: Mrs. Applebie, I'll be in touch."

CHAPTER 9: THE FIRST WALK

Jelena had just finished cramming the last bit of her stuff that she had accumulated over the past eight weeks into the little suitcase that she bought from the commissary and was waiting for a driver to come get her. She was so excited to finally go home and sleep in her own bed after this whole experience. She went to the bathroom to wash her hands, and before she was done, she heard a knock at her door.

"Just a sec! Be right there!" she yelled out as she shut off the water and dried her hands.

Jelena opened the door to see Mrs. Applebie standing there. Her long and perfect body was covered in a white A-line dress with sunflowers on it, fitted at the waist, and tailored to a snug fit around her shoulders and breasts. She had her hair pulled into a smooth, sleek ponytail that hung down her back. She was wearing large sunglasses that peeked out from underneath a wide-brimmed woven hat with a band around it made of the same material as her dress. She finished the look off with some white strappy high heels. She looked like a drawn model right out of an issue of *Home and Gardens* magazine from the 1950s.

"Well, hello there, darlin'. Surprised to see me?" she asked with a slight southern giggle in her voice.

"Mrs. Applebie... or I mean Kate..." Jelena stammered, rather stunned to see her new mentor so soon. "What *do* I call you? I'm sorry, but they were a little vague on that point."

"You can call me Kate, sweetie," Kate said as she walked past Jelena into her room, pushing the door shut behind her.

"Okay. Kate. I can do that," Jelena replied. "What are you doing here?"

"It's time for your first walk, angel, and I am here to take you. This is Phase Three of your training. The final phase," she said excitedly, waving her hands and squeaking a barely audible 'Yaaayyyy.'

"Okay, well, when do I call you Mrs. Applebie?" Jelena asked with a confused look.

"Well, darlin', you don't. Your code name is only used in a brief and specific manner. Like when I met you at your graduation, for instance. As soon as I whispered my code name in your ear, your little buzzy bee antennas should have perked right up. Sometimes, when we need to leave a coded message for another asset, we will label it with our code name, but it is not unusual at all for assets who haven't worked with each other on a specific mission or 'gone on a walk' together to know each others' code names. Those kinds of cards should be played close to your chest," she explained.

As Jelena stood there, she opened her mouth to ask another question and Kate interrupted, "I am terribly sorry, darlin', but we really don't have time to play twenty questions. We have a walk to go on after all," Kate said as she went back out the door to retrieve a garment bag and satchel that she left in the hallway. "Here, put this on and go get prettied up for me now while I organize some things for you. Hurry, we don't have much time."

Kate seemed friendly and kind to Jelena, but she was definitely a direct-and-to-the-point kind of gal. Jelena went into the bathroom and slid on her own A-line 'costume' with a similar fit. Her's was white as well but instead was covered with vividly colored tropical flowers. She put on some modest make-up slid on her own pair of white strappy heels and her sunglasses before walking back out to Kate, who was now perched on her bed, waiting and fidgeting somewhat impatiently.

When Kate heard the bathroom door, she stood up to look at Jelena. "Ohhh, now don't **you** just look delicious!" Kate said enthusiastically with her hands pressed together, palm to palm, in front of her chest. "Just marvelous! Okay, darlin', so here are your things..." Kate said, returning to Jelena's bed, where she had everything spread out.

"Here is your driver's license, social security card, credit cards, some cash, your passport... oh and some of my favorite shade of coral lipstick. I thought it would look great with that dress," Kate said. "Our walk entails finding out what a player on the other team knows about our operations in Moscow, and then we report back with our findings. We're just there, you know, to see if there's a problem and if so, then we're there to provide a solution. Don't worry, darlin', I'll hold your pretty little hand the whole time, but as I'm certain you already know, our employer is rather...hush-hush on some topics, and there is nothing worse than a nasty rumor."

"Sabrina York?" Jelena asked, confused, looking at her new driver's license with her actual picture on it and everything. "So that's my new name?"

"Yesss, darlin'... you know of the Atlanta Yorks'?" Kate began.

"When you're going on a walk, you must completely embrace your new, albeit temporary self, as well as sear your backstory into your mind so that you will be as convincing as possible and raise no suspicion. And you dear, are now Mrs. Sabrina York, and I am your sister-in-law, Mrs. Elizabeth York, both of the Atlanta York family. We are rich southern aristocrats who are coming through town on our way to see our dear ailing mother on her death bed. Our great cousin has offered us a place to stay for the night there. We just need to find the cousin. But no worries, the florist in town knows the address. Shall we go?" Kate said just as smooth and sickly sweet as possible.

*Damn...*thought Jelena. *She's good!*

Jelena took the small, thin, white pocket-style handbag and put all of the items Kate had given her inside.

"So, wait... Kate, where are our guns or weapons or stuff?" Jelena asked naively.

"Not every walk requires such heavy artillery, darlin'. We have everythin' that we need in hand already. Now chop chop...the clock's a tickin'," Kate said as she opened the door for Jelena.

The two ladies, dressed in their Sunday finest, walked together to the taxi waiting out front of the dormitory building.

"Saddle up," Kate said as she opened the car door for Jelena.

They both got into the car. The driver said nothing as if he already knew the destination. Approximately fifteen minutes later, they pulled into an underground parking lot where Kate and Jelena exited the taxi.

"Thanks a bunch, sweetie!" Kate said to the driver as she shut the taxi door. "Bless his heart."

Jelena followed Kate over to a beautiful pearl-colored Cadillac DeVille, to which, Kate apparently already had the keys. "Come on, get in," Kate said.

Kate drove for about two hours to a tiny little town. As they pulled through the first little stop sign, Jelena spotted the town flower shop. "Kate, right there," she said.

"Good eye, darlin'," Kate replied as she pulled into a parking spot on the side of the street.

"Now remember, we're just trying to find our great cousin. I'll do the talkin' in here, okay?" asked Kate.

"Got it," said Jelena, still feeling a bit unsure about this entire facade.

The bell on the door jingled as they entered the flower shop. "Be right with you!" called out an unfamiliar male voice from the back in a softened New York accent. The ladies waited for the flower shop owner to appear at the front desk. It was easy to tell that he was rather busy that day due to all of the rustling they heard coming from the back of the shop. Before he appeared, a few more ladies came into the shop and began browsing the flowers. Jelena gave Kate a concerned look, not expecting outsiders to come into their little theater. Kate simply looked at her and patted her hand gently with a warm sweet smile on her face.

Perhaps a minute later, the shop owner, a shorter man, maybe 5'8, came bustling around the corner. He was stout but appeared sturdy and strong. He had short, salt and pepper hair, a round face, a long angular nose, and the kindest blue eyes that Jelena had seen in a long time. When he lifted his head to see Kate and Jelena, he had a huge grin on his face, showing the slightest gap in his front two teeth.

"Mr. Titan? Mel Titan?" Kate said quietly and ever so politely. "Is that you, dear?"

The look on the man's face instantly changed as his grin was wiped away in that second and a half. He looked over at the other ladies and then back to Kate. His face showed a slight sign of relief when he realized that they were so busy chatting over the flowers that they didn't hear what she had called him.

"Yeah... that's me?" he said, visibly uncomfortable. "What can I do for you?"

Just as he finished his sentence, he noticed one of the other ladies flagging him down for help. "Hi there, be with you in just a minute, okay," he said to her, trying to paste his smile back on.

Once they went back to their chitter-chattering, Kate looked at him and said, "Hello there, I'm Mrs. Elizabeth York, and this here is my sister-in-law Sabrina. We're just trying to find our dear cousin who lives here in your quaint little town, but unfortunately, we seemed to have misplaced the address. I was so hoping that you could help us."

The man, still rather pale, responded, "Umm Yeah...sure...what's your cousin's name?"

"Mrs. Sally Peters," Kate said as sweetly as possible.

"No, ma'am. I'm afraid that I don't know any Sally Peters. She must not come in here much. But I just got some beautiful purple sage and poppy flower bunches in. Let me just run to the back real quick and wrap 'em up for you...You know, for your trouble. No charge," he said as he ran back around the corner.

"This big show all for nothing..." Jelena sighed under her breath.

"Never for nothing, darlin'. Always accept the beautiful gifts from a stranger," Kate reassured.

The man came back with beautiful flowers wrapped in red and white paper and handed them over the counter to Kate.

"Oh, sir! They *are* absolutely gorgeous! Thank you so much for your time and these beautiful flowers," Kate said as she turned to leave the shop. "Come along, Sabrina. There must be another way."

"Oh and hey...Good luck finding your cousin. Sorry again that I couldn't help," the shop owner said.

"No worries, darlin', we'll manage to find our way just fine. Thank you kindly," Kate responded with a cheery sing-songy tone to her voice.

As the ladies made it back inside the car, Kate began to open the paper containing the flowers.

"What the hell was that, Kate? So, we just took flowers? Like what just happened here?" Jelena spouted off, visibly frustrated at Kate and not quite yet understanding just how this game was played.

"Soooo naïve. Listen here, girly, in this business, everything means something, so you're gonna have to jump on this train and catch on a little quicker if you want to get good at it. First off, Mr. Titan was his code name... you know... he's another asset, dumb-dumb, in case your brand-new little brain didn't get that. Second off, I knew I had the right man solely from his reaction when I called him that. Third, when I gave him the name Sally Peters he responded with Sage and Poppies...'S' and 'P'...come'on girl you gotta get one of these...'S'...and...'P'...Sally Peters...catching on yet?" Kate explained, quite irritated that Jelena was not catching on as fast as she had hoped. "Sweet Baby Jesus. I thought they said you were the best of the best. Christ almighty, Jelena."

Kate continued unwrapping the flowers that the florist had just given them. She held onto the paper and gently laid the flowers on the backseat of the Cadillac. Carefully she inspected the inside of the paper, and neatly written was *Sally Peters, 605 Thornbush Road*. "Got It!" Kate whispered.

"Wow!" Jelena exclaimed. "So, you knew his code name, but why didn't you tell him yours?" she asked.

"Because he didn't need to know mine. I knew his, and that was all that mattered, and since I knew his, he knew that I was there to go on a walk and attend to some company business," Kate explained.

"Okay," Jelena said, "I think I am finally starting to understand. Man! You are one smooth operator!"

"All in good time and with good experience. One day you'll be pretty doggoned smooth too girly," Kate replied. "So now onto the next step, 605 Thornbush Road, to see our long-lost cousin. But before we get too far ahead of ourselves, I gotta give you the next tidbit of info, so you don't fuck it all up. Listen, I did **this** part, but you're up to bat next, so I hope you're good and ready to jump on outta the bullpen."

"I'm ready... well, I think I am ready," Jelena said, thinking immediately of Bruce and his damned bat.

"Mmm-hmmm, we'll see about that," Kate replied. "So here is the situation, Sally Peters is really Svetlana Petrov. She is a known KGB agent, and our intelligence has caught wind of some chatter goin' back and forth from her to her people in Moscow. That's why old Mel Titan has taken over the florist shop... to keep tabs on Svetlana. The agency sent the real owner on an all-expenses-paid six-month vacation around the world, so he's a happy little camper for at least the next two more months...All I know is that they are planning some kind of coups, and rumors are buzzin' that their folks in Moscow are planning an attack on one of our classified Intel sites located in a remote area out there. Svetlana, AKA Sally, has the plans stashed away somewhere with her. Those plans have all the info on who's goin' where, when, how, and do what. We gotta get those plans. I've been told that they're on some sort of thumb drive, so that tiny thing could be damn near anywhere. The only other things that we know about Sally are that she spends most of her days out in her garden or bakin' pies and cakes for the local bake sales," Kate explained.

"So, wait," Jelena said. "We are really just people watching people?"

"Pretty much," Kate began. "We also play a little interference every now and then, too... you know, when it's necessary."

"Like now?" Jelena asked.

"Yes, ma'am. So, we're gonna go out to Thornbush Road and pay Sally a visit. Remember, we're just interested in buying some of her pies and treats for our family back home," Kate replied. "This is your show, kiddo... show me whatcha got."

Jelena felt anxiety and anticipation about this meeting with Sally. She really didn't want to let Kate down and jack up the plan. She felt ready and trained and also, at the very same time, not so ready and incredibly ill-prepared. She went over everything that Kate and Bruce and everybody back on the farm had taught her. Get the drive and get out. Seems simple enough, or was it?

"Here we go, darlin'... six-o-five Thornbush..." Kate said as she pulled the Caddy into the gravel driveway.

At the top of the driveway was a simple farmhouse. Two stories, light blue with white trim, and a white picket fence surrounding the edge of a pretty fantastic garden filled with all kinds of plants and flowers. Jelena had taken some deep breaths, and right as she was about to get out of the car, she had an idea. She grabbed the flowers from the back seat and wrapped the stems with the ribbon that the florist had used.

"Okay," Jelena said to Kate. "When we get in there, you search, and I'll distract. Flowerpots, pie pans wherever you think that little drive could fit. Got it?"

"Aye, aye, Captain," Kate replied.

Jelena pressed the doorbell and gave the screen door a little knock. "Hellooo?" Jelena called out in her best southern accent.

A taller, thicker woman with a bun of messy gray hair and a stern, rather cranky expression came around the hidden corner of the porch from the direction of the back garden. She was wearing a simple farm dress and an apron with little red chickens on it. "Can I help you?" Sally asked, trying to mask her Russian accent.

"Hi there, Sally," Jelena said as she handed Sally the bouquet. "A friend from town sent us. My name is Sabrina York, and this here is my sister Elizabeth, and we were told that you make the absolute best pies and cakes in town, and we just wanted to see if we could buy a few from you to take back home to our family. Would that be possible?"

"Well ya, they are pretty good," Sally agreed. "Sure... okay... come inside, and I show you what I make."

"Ohhh, Sally," said Kate. "Would it be okay if I just looked at your beautiful garden? I have never seen its equal."

"Oh yes, Sally, your garden is truly amazing!" Jelena agreed.

"Okay… suite you self," Sally said. "You come in to see pies, yes?"

"Oh yes… most definitely," Jelena said while giving the go-ahead glance at Kate and following Sally inside the house.

Sally's house was cluttered and filled with endless knick-knacks and tchotchkes and smelled of some kind of smoked meat.

Fuck! Jelena thought. *That goddamned thing could be friggin' anywhere.*

"So, what kind pie you want?" Sally asked.

"Well, what kind do you make?" Jelena asked as she looked at as many little trinkets as she could without becoming too suspicious. "Oh my, these little things are so very cute. Wherever did you get them?"

"My family send to me. I can make cherry, blueberry, apple, rhubarb, strawberry… Here, you taste, I just make this morning," Sally said as she handed Jelena a slice of apple pie on a blue and white paisley patterned plate. Jelena picked up the small fork and cut through the crumbly crust of the apple pie. The small bite melted in her mouth as she could taste the sweetness of the cinnamon and brown sugar, the tartness of the apples and the smooth buttery flavor of the crust. It brought back memories of apple pies that her mother used to make for special occasions. Jelena forced herself to stay present in the moment and refocus her attention on Sally.

"Oh my, that is so tasty, Sally! My friend was right. You DO make the best pies in town, that's for sure," Jelena raved as she looked closely at a little ceramic pie figurine. As she tried to lift it, she discovered that the top lifted up and there it was...

PAY DIRT! Jelena thought.

"Who is this friend? I must thank them," Sally said.

Jelena pretending to not hear her continued, "So do you have another one of these delicious pies ready? My husband and children would go absolutely crazy over it."

"Ya," Sally said. "In oven, hold on."

As Sally went to the kitchen to get the other pie out of the oven, Jelena quickly snatched up the drive from the inside of the pie figurine. At the same time, Kate walked in from searching the garden with a blank and disappointed look on her face shaking her head at Jelena to let her know that she had not found the drive.

"Hi there sister, how was the garden? Did you see all your favorites?" Jelena began, now really hamming up that southern accent. "Elizabeth, you must try this pie. It's simply to die for." As Jelena handed Kate the plate, she whispered into her ear, "I got it."

"Oh, indeed, Sally, this is magnificent pie," Kate exclaimed as Sally came out of the kitchen and handed Jelena the small white baker's box containing the pie she requested.

"Sally... I have a fantastic idea," continued Kate. "Why don't you put on some tea, and we can sit and chat a bit. I would really LOVE to talk to you about how you got your magnolias so thick and full this year. I can't quite get mine to grow so well at all."

"Okay," said Sally in the same monotone voice, "I make some tea."

"Now, don't forget one for you too, Sally!" Kate hollered.

As soon as Sally left the room, Kate whipped around to Jelena and handed her a small plastic baggie containing a white powdery material. "Put this in her tea," Kate ordered under her breath.

Jelena looking confused, asked Kate, "I thought we were only here for the pie?"

"Plans change. No negotiations. Put this in her tea," Kate ordered again under her breath.

Jelena took and palmed the baggie and then headed into the kitchen to help Sally with the tea tray.

"Oh, here, Sally...Let me help you with that," Jelena said sweetly as she picked up the tray with the three cups and the kettle and headed into Sally's sitting room.

Jelena quickly emptied the baggie into the cup closest to her and poured the tea right on top of it. She stirred it and then handed the cup and saucer to Sally as she sat down in one of the upholstered chairs in her sitting room. Jelena then handed a cup to Kate and took one for herself.

"So, Sally," Kate said as Sally was taking her first hearty sip of tea. "Those magnolias are..."

Before Kate could finish the sentence, Sally slumped over sideways in her chair, dropping her teacup and saucer and spilling what was left of her tea onto the floor next to her.

"SALLY?" called Jelena in an alarmed voice, still not really sure what the hell was going on. "SALLY??"

With a sly smile, Kate sat back in her seat, crossed her legs, and sipped her orange blossom tea. From behind those cold and icy blue eyes, Kate said to Jelena, "She's dead, sweetie... And you killed her."

CHAPTER 10: REALITY CHECK

"WHAT THE FUCK, KATE!" Jelena screamed as she felt for a pulse on Sally's neck and struggled to mentally process the situation. "WHAT IN THE PSYCHOTIC FUCK IS THIS?

"Jelena, now darlin', you need to calm yourself right down," Kate said, nonchalantly putting her teacup onto the wicker side table. "This is not really somethin' to get yourself all worked up about."

"NOT WORKED UP??" Jelena screamed as she waved her hands and paced the sitting room floor back and forth in front of a now-dead Svetlana. "HOW CAN YOU POSSIBLY FUCKING SAY THAT! WE JUST FUCKING MURDERED HER!! WE JUST FUCKING MURDERED HER IN COLD BLOOD, KATE! THIS IS DEFINITELY SOMETHING TO GET WORKED UP ABOUT! WE ARE MURDERERS! Oh my God! We are fucking murderers. We are going to jail for fucking murder!" Jelena continued as she sunk into the other wicker chair.

"First off, sweetie," Kate began in her sickly-sweet southern voice, "*you* murdered her. Second, if we do our job right, then ain't nobody going to jail. And third...for the record, the correct term is assassinate, not murder."

"OH, FOR FUCKS SAKE, KATE...IT'S THE SAME GODDAMNED THING!" Jelena continued loudly.

"Listen here lady. You really need to lower your voice before the neighbors hear, start to get suspicious, and then we'll really have a problem on our hands. There should never be any extra wet-works involved on a simple little walk. You need to breathe, calm down, and recognize that you were just doing your job, darlin'. And you did a damn good job too... well, except for the fact that I had to give you an instruction twice. On a walk, there's usually no time to tell ya somethin' twice. So that's somethin' you can work on... you know for in the future," Kate said, still as calm as if she was at a Sunday brunch with the church folk.

"I cannot believe that you are this calm," Jelena said, heeding Kate's warning and lowering her voice. "Especially when there is a dead woman, right here, in the same room, and we killed her."

"Again, darlin'... **you** killed her... And I can't believe that you're over there, losin' your ever-lovin' mind, bein' all dramatic and getting' all crazy over a damn dead spy, who would'a slit your throat just as soon as look at ya. If she would'a known who we were, we wouldn't had made down the damn street, let alone into the livin' room, eatin' **pie** and drinkin' **tea**. For Christ's sake, lady... She wasn't one of the good guys, Jelena... She was a flippin' bad guy, and you need to start wrappin' your brain around that fact. We had a damn job to do, and we got it done. Now, let's go find her computer and see what's on this drive before anybody else comes up for **pie**," Kate responded, defending their actions.

Kate and Jelena ran upstairs and found Sally's computer on a tiny wooden desk in a closet. They turned it on, and like magic, the desktop screen came right up with no password required.

"Oh, honey..." Kate began. "I'm startin' to feel like this is way too easy. Nothin' good happens when things are too easy. That ole' sayin' is right as rain... if it's too good to be true, then it ain't."

"Kate, that's not how that saying goes… but I get your point," Jelena replied.

"Look here, kitten, I don't give a rat's ass about any damned sayin'! Let's get on with it so we can get the hell on outta here!" Kate snapped back.

They plugged the thumb drive that Jelena had found inside the pie figurine into the USB port and tried to pull up its files. Only one file appeared with some kind of 'image-only' icon. Jelena carefully clicked on the icon. One single image came up with the letters, 'ОТВЯЖИСЬ!'

"Ha," Jelena squeaked, finding humor in what she saw.

"Well?" Kate snarked at her. "What the hell does *that* mean?"

Without thinking, Jelena responded with a bit of a chuckle, "It's pronounced, Ot-Vya-Shes… Basically, I'm pretty sure that it means 'Fuck Off' in Russian."

Kate stepped back, looked at Jelena, and exclaimed, "YOU speak Russian?"

Jelena looked right back at her and asked, "YOU don't?"

With a bit of an irritated expression, Kate said, "No, I don't. Well, this is obviously the wrong damn drive. Let's keep lookin'. It's gotta be here somewhere. And we probably won't be able to open it. Some Russians might not be the sharpest tools in the shed, but I do know that the Russians *we're* dealin' with aren't stupid enough to have all their secrets on some non-encrypted drive stashed here in Po-Dunk-Nowhere-Ville with Sally-I'm-So-Dumb-I-Drink-Poison here watchin' it for not-so-safe keepin'. Let's go. Let's look around up here, and then I reckon I'll take the kitchen this time, and you take the garden."

Jelena and Kate searched the upstairs bedroom and bathroom. Every little hidey-hole and nook and cranny was thoroughly scanned.

"I got nothing here in the bedroom," Jelena called out. "How about you? Find anything?"

Kate came around the corner shaking a box of opened condoms that she found under Sally's bathroom sink. "Well, I didn't find any drive... but ole' Sally had herself a little friend to keep her warm on those cold and oh so lonely nights... but that's a rabbit hole we really don't have time for."

"Did we miss something with this drive? I mean, you saw what I saw, right?" Jelena asked Kate, starting to question her own eyes.

"Naw, honey, there wasn't anything else on that drive," Kate reassured.

They headed back downstairs to continue searching feverishly for the missing thumb drive. Jelena grabbed some pink gardening gloves on the porch and headed out into the garden. She planned to turn over and dump out every pot she found. The very first one had a little bit of muddy water residing in the bottom, and when she dumped it, probably about half of the mucky juice jumped back up and onto her white flowery dress.

Shit! Jelena thought. *And THAT. RIGHT. THERE. is why I do NOT wear white anything.*

Jelena saw something shiny in the muddy pile that she had just dumped. It was another thumb drive in a tiny plastic bag. She picked it up, examining it carefully when the notion struck her that this seemed far too easy to be found on the first try. She put the drive back into the pot that she had just emptied and set it aside to keep track of what she had found. She grabbed up the next one to dump. In the bottom of that messy pile of dirt was another baggie with another drive.

Jelena dumped out every single potted flower and plant on Sally's property and found a tiny bag containing a thumb drive in each. By the time she went back inside to find Kate, she had found over twenty-two tiny thumb-drive-filled baggies.

"KATE!" Jelena called out from the garden. "Umm...I think we have a little problem here..." Jelena scooped them all up and brought them into the house. Kate looked right back at her, with her own hands also filled with little thumb drives, and replied, "Boy! You're tellin' me."

Kate and Jelena continued to tear apart Sally's house, finding tiny silver thumb drives all over the place, and continued to pile them up on the kitchen counter for over two hours. After searching just about every nook of that farmhouse, they had found more than seventy little silver thumb drives.

"Hmmm," giggled Jelena. "Perhaps Sally wasn't so dumb after all. What a pain in the ass."

"Well, damn. Let's get on back upstairs and start going through these, I guess. Damn Sally and her wild goose chase," Kate said, quite clearly frustrated by the fact that even in death, Sally was one up.

One by one, they plugged each thumb drive into the USB port on Sally's computer. And one by one, they kept coming up with single image files containing various Russian profanities that they chucked into the crap pile.

"What number are we up to, Kate?" Jelena asked.

"Oh hell... honey, I don't know, maybe fifty-three or fifty-four. Come'on. Plug'er in," Kate sighed.

Jelena plugged the next small silver stick into the port and visibly crossed her fingers as the computer made its little buzzing and whirring sounds.

"REALLY, Jelena?" Kate said, rolling her eyes at the crossed-finger superstition.

"Well, it couldn't hurt..." Jelena defended. "We've been here all damned day... you wanna be here all damned night too?"

The buzzing and whirring sounds stopped as Jelena and Kate fixated on the computer screen. A large red triangle popped up on the screen with 'Зашифрованныл Файл...Требуется Пароль!' typed in large red letters.

"FUCK YEAH!" Jelena exclaimed excitedly.

"Ummm... you wanna shed a little light here, darlin'?" Kate asked.

"Oh… right… I forgot you can't read…" Jelena began.

But Kate, with great annoyance, interrupted with, "RUSSIAN! I can't read Russian. Smartypants. Now, what does that say?"

"It says… that we are done with this bullshit wild goose chase. It says, 'Encrypted File…Password Required," Jelena quipped sarcastically. "We got it, Mama… Time to bounce!"

"AMEN, and thank the Lord!" Kate said as she picked herself up off the floor, straightening her dress.

"Oh, one more thing… I almost forgot," Jelena said as she picked up the chair and raised it with the intention of smashing Sally's computer.

"Oh, HEY… darlin', darlin', darlin'… there's just so much that I have to teach you. Those fellas at the farm are seriously slackin' off," Kate said as she reached into her handbag and pulled out a thin, white envelope and a thumb drive of her own. "Here, use this. Put this little envelope into the disc reader and then plug this drive into the USB port. Now once you have done that, we have about thirty seconds to get the hell on outta here before things get too hot."

Jelena did as Kate instructed and then the both of them high-tailed it right down the stairs with the encrypted drive snuggly tucked into Jelena's bra. Just as they had shut the front door behind them, a little 'BAM-POOF' sound came from the upstairs; and as they got back into the car, they could see a tiny wisp of smoke exiting one of the upstairs windows.

"What was that you handed me for Sally's computer?" Jelena asked from the passenger seat of the Cadillac.

"Oh, that little thing... That was just a little somethin' from the R&D team, designed to specifically destroy a computer. No recorded keystrokes, no fingerprints, not a lick of evidence left to identify us... at least not on that computer. Now the clean-up crew will be along shortly to tidy up whatever we may have missed and to take care of Sally's body," Kate said, with her cheery disposition returning to her normal sickly-sweet manner.

"Hey, Kate... what was the white powder in the baggie that you had me put in Sally's tea?" Jelena asked quietly.

"Oh, that was ricin, sweetie. A deadly poison made from the castor bean plant. It's odorless and flavorless and well... as you've already seen... it's rather fast-acting. Even faster than cyanide if memory serves me," Kate explained in a tone that sounded like she was teaching kindergarten.

"Why didn't you just shoot her?" Jelena asked.

"Ooh... you Marines *do* like to do things the messy way, now don't you?" Kate retorted. "I, myself, prefer to keep things nice and neat. I fancy pretty dresses and nice shoes that I would really prefer no one to bleed on. When I first started, I went through so many shoes. Girl! It was plain crazy. Shame, really to throw 'em out, but those damned blood stains just won't budge. I also do prefer to keep things civil. Once you whip out a gun, then they whip out theirs, and it turns into a damn free-for-all. Just not my style. I do have to admit, though, that for certain walks, you just don't really have much of a choice. Sometimes things get messy. And if they get messy, well then I guess it's just time to buy some new shoes."

Jelena quietly sat and watched the passing trees and scenery as they drove back to the farm. She was thinking about everything that she had just witnessed, as well as everything Kate had explained along the way. She felt like she had learned more on this 'walk' than she did during her entire time at the farm. She especially learned quite a bit about her new mentor, Kate, although she also saw a side of her that she could never have imagined, not even in her wildest dreams.

Jelena really liked Kate, and for most of their brief time together, found her quite relatable. Kate reminded Jelena of her mother, Charlotte. Charlotte was a country girl from Nashville, Tennessee, and retained her southern accent to this day. Even when Charlotte was in an unpleasant situation, she always maintained the grace of a lady, and Jelena saw that exact same trait in Kate.

Still, Jelena not only felt totally off her game, but also, she felt like she was way behind the curve. Kate had all these expectations for her, and Jelena truly felt like she didn't have a friggin' clue about what to do or how to act. She really thought that they were just going there to steal a thumb drive... not to assassinate anyone.

As she repeatedly replayed Sally's death over and over again in her mind, Jelena felt disappointed in herself and, worse yet, she felt that she had let Kate down on their 'walk.' She had never killed anyone up close and personal before. This feeling must be the shell shock of killing someone... She couldn't believe that she actually did it... She can never take it back... She knew that Kate said that Sally was not a good person but, Jelena was used to saving people, not killing them. She just couldn't figure out how she was supposed to feel. Good? Remorseful? Numb? How could she feel like she let Kate down when Svetlana actually lost her life today?

Jelena couldn't help but wonder who her gentleman caller was... would he be sad that she was dead? Does she have any children or grandchildren who would miss her? This was supposed to be the completion of Jelena's third training phase, but if Kate didn't give her a good report, then that probably wouldn't go very well. Jelena couldn't help but question how much more of herself would she have to prove? And did she even want to anymore? Hell, at this point, she wasn't even sure how she could do a job like this and live with herself.

"What's on your mind, sugarplum? You've been awful quiet this whole ride," Kate asked as she pulled in and parked in front of the farm dormitory.

"Hmm, well, I have just been thinking about today. How dumb I was to think that we were just going there to steal a stupid thumb drive... How I actually killed another person... How I reacted and couldn't keep my cool when Sally died... The fact that I was the one who killed her, I am really struggling with that... I didn't get the florist thing... I just... I just feel like I didn't do a single thing right today... so much stuff Kate. I don't even know how to begin to process it all. I just wanted to impress you. To show you how freakin' badass I was, that I was the top of the class... the best of the best... and today... today I feel like an epic failure," Jelena confessed emotionally.

"Well... darlin'... I absolutely could not possibly disagree with you more," Kate said, gently taking Jelena's hand in hers and smiling. "You see, Jelena, I wasn't assigned to you, darlin'... I chose you. That's right! I chose to be your mentor... the mentor of the infamous 518 Papa... the girl who survived the box. Hell, we were all fightin' over you. By definition, you're already pretty badass. Yes, you may have missed the florist's subtleties, but you learned somethin', right? You learned that sometimes the most important things are found in the tiniest, ittiest, bittiest, little details and that nothing should be overlooked... right?"

Jelena looked away and said, "Well yeah... I guess."

Kate continued, "And yes, I did have to tell you twice to put the poison in Sally's cup, but you learned that there isn't always time for two sets of instructions... right? And yes, killin' Sally may have seemed a bit harsh and unnecessary, but you learned that even though we don't get to make up our own orders and we may have an order to do something unpleasant that we can always try our best to be as gentle and graceful as possible about it... right? And yes, you may have been just a tad dramatic when Sally died, but you had to learn, honey, that one of the bigger parts of your job description is killin'. Now it ain't easy, and it ain't fun, but it doesn't always have to be messy. I thought you did a spectacular job Jelena! How you just chimed right in with good ol' Sally, goin' on and on about those damn pies. You kept to the story, and honey, you got the job done. At the end of the day, that's what it's all about, and you did it. Shit! Had I been on my own, I would'a walked right on outta there with the wrong damn drive because I can't read... Russian." Kate giggled before continuing, "You learned four languages in eight weeks... that's insane... Back when I started, honey, they didn't do that. I'm lucky I can speak enough country just to handle business in this part of the world, but after seein' you today... I think I'm gonna go pay a little visit to those farm instructors and get myself some language lessons. Jelena, sweetheart, you ARE one of the best... maybe not the best of the best... yet... but honey, you are definitely at the top. I'd be honored to walk with you anytime."

With tears in her eyes, Jelena whipped around to look at Kate. She just still didn't understand what Kate and Bruce and everyone else saw in her, but to hear Kate's kind and encouraging words brought up emotion in Jelena that she hadn't let herself feel in years.

"Oh, Kate," Jelena said as she reached over to hug her. "I want to learn so much from you. I don't ever want to let you down. Thank you so much for today... and for your help."

Jelena got out of the car and went to shut the door but caught it as she remembered something. "Oooh, Kate, before I forget," she said, reaching down into her bra and pulling out Sally's thumb drive. "Do I... ummm... turn this in somewhere?"

"Oh, hell, honey... It ain't homework. Give it here. I'll give it to Bruce. He'll know what to do with it," Kate replied. "Good night, darlin'."

"Good night Kate... Thanks again," Jelena said as she closed the car door and began to head up the walkway.

Jelena walked up to the dormitory building and pressed her finger on the pad to unlock the heavy metal door. She proceeded up to the seventh floor to her room and repeated the process to unlock her room door. She walked into her room and found it exactly as she had found it the first time she walked in with Bruce. The linens and towels all cleaned and put away in the top of the closet. All of her personal possessions were gone, and the room was back in its original pristine condition, all ready for the next potential.

"Shit!" Jelena whispered. "Moving day…"

CHAPTER 11: TRANSFORMATION COMPLETE

In the midst of all the spy-killing action, she had completely forgotten that she was supposed to move back home today. The driver must have come and taken her stuff back to her own house. Jelena turned off the light, closed the door, and went back downstairs to call a cab to get her and take her home.

When the cab pulled up to Jelena's house, she expected to feel a sense of relief, but she didn't. Instead, she still felt an immense mental clutter and chaos weighing down her mind. Questioning her own choices to become this secret weapon and missing the farm in some sick and twisted way. That was what she had learned... what she had become used to, and now when left to her own devices, she almost didn't know what to do with herself. She had been so incredibly controlled and monitored at the farm that this new freedom was extremely overwhelming and even a little frightening.

Jelena peeked through her living room window from the outside and saw all of her things neatly placed next to the couch. For some reason, she just couldn't bring herself to go inside. She found one of her old lawn chairs and sat down. It was one of those red, plastic ones in a permanent reclined position. She sat there, still dressed like a doll from the '50s, just looking up into the sea of stars above her and allowing her mind to drift.

When she would allow her mind to drift, it was almost supernatural. She would dive into the sea of her memories and find comfort there. Occasionally, at the farm, she would go and sit on top of the dormitory building, just counting the stars and getting happily lost inside old times. Although, she didn't always have the time or energy to tend to her mind once she entered her second phase of training, she managed to stay on point. But, sometimes... when she hadn't done it in a while, things in her head could get a bit cloudy and confusing.

Memory-dreams and dream-diving were Jelena's ways of organizing her thoughts and clearing the gunk out of her mind. Sitting here in this lawn chair, she realized just how much gunk had accumulated and how important it was for her to clear all that shit out and get her head back in the game. She almost had no control over it now. She was tired and brain-fried and shell-shocked, and she had absolutely no desire to move a single muscle. So, she sat... and she allowed herself to dive in.

As she thought about the events of the day, she still had a particularly hard time accepting that 'doing her job' equated to 'killing Sally' or KGB Agent Svetlana Petrov or whatever. She had never thought of herself as a murderer... a killer. She knew that when she enlisted into the Marine Corps and took the job of aerial door-gunner, she would be shooting bad guys... killing them for sure... and like a trooper, she did her job and did it quite well. But until this point, it had never been so up close and personal and even more importantly... without reason... at least not any reason she was allowed to know.

She thought about everything that Kate said. How she learned things today. How she did things today. That everything meant something and that there was always a reason. But Jelena still questioned the morality of killing someone for someone else's reasons. The 'just doin' my job' angle was an extremely bitter pill for her to swallow and one that possibly no amount of Scotch could get down smoothly. She struggled to accept that she was now basically a paid assassin. How could she let herself get this far without any real and actual understanding of what would be expected of her? As a door gunner, she laid down fire to protect her guys on the ground… not specifically to hunt someone, not to see the life drain out of them… just to protect her guys… just to help keep them alive.

Throughout her life, when Jelena's conscience was at odds with itself, and she was conflicted in some manner about some topic, she could usually find resolve in one of her memories… most of the time a previous lesson learned.

Sitting in her front yard, Jelena, once again, allowed her mind to drift. She dove into an early memory of her father, Radomir. He was teaching her marksmanship. How to shoot and maintain various firearms. Jelena, at first, thought that this particular item, a firearm, was no different than a football or a tennis racket, as she only used it at the range to shoot paper targets for points. She never affiliated it with a loss of life, only for fun and competitions.

She remembered coming out of the range and seeing a woman passing by who looked at her father with disgust, and Jelena didn't understand why.

"Papa," Jelena said, as she tugged on her father's hand, "Papa, why did that woman look so mad at you?"

"Aahhh, well, Jelly, she probably thinks that you are too young to come to the range and shoot and that I must be a bad papa for bringing you here," he explained.

"I don't understand, Papa. If my brother can be younger than me and play soccer, then why can't I come shoot my targets?" she continued.

"Ohhh, my innocent JellyGirl. So much you don't understand yet," he sighed as they got into the car.

"Papa, can you help me understand?" Jelena pressed. "I want to understand everything."

"Jelena… you are nothing if not persistent," her father said with a soft chuckle. "You see, Jelly, no one sees harm in soccer because no one has ever died from a soccer ball, silly girl. That is nothing more than a toy. Guns are tools… they are NOT toys. They were designed as tools for war…to deprive men of their lives… to kill them. Now in this country, we have a Constitution that says that we, the people, are allowed to have our own guns… our own tools… to prevent a tyrannical or bad government from hurting us. Guns can also help us hunt animals for food, or we can use them in sport like you do, shooting paper targets for points and fun. Unfortunately, some people choose to only see the death… the harm that can be done… the damage, and the bad things…" he explained.

"Like that lady?" Jelena asked.

"Yes, Jelly, like that lady. But one thing that a lot of people don't understand or don't want to understand is that sometimes the only thing that can stop a bad man with a gun… is a good man with a gun… or in your case, a good girl with one. Guns are powerful and must be treated with respect because they can cause a lot of harm. A bad person with a gun can kill lots of people. Sometimes, the only way to stop that bad person from hurting or killing others is for a good person to shoot and kill them. It is not one of life's happier facts, Jelly. I love you, and I hope and pray that you are never faced with having to kill anyone, but if you must, to stop them, then I want you to win, and I want you to live. So that's why I bring you here and teach you myself. She doesn't have to like me, Jelly, but I have every right to teach you how to stay alive. Do you understand better now, Jelena?" he said to her.

As she refocused her eyes on the stars above, Jelena made the mental connection. *Maybe Svetlana was doing very bad things to hurt and kill other people, and the only way to make her stop was for me to kill her*, Jelena thought, trying to rationalize her actions and her feelings. Her father was right, it was definitely not one of life's happier facts, but Jelena still couldn't help but feel that taking the life of another was the most intimate thing one could do. It was incredibly personal. She still didn't know just how she was going to cope with this job responsibility and still be able to look at herself in the mirror and sleep soundly at night.

Jelena was diving from memory to memory, swimming through the deepest parts of her subconscious, analyzing every detail, every comment and every lesson, searching for the pieces to help her make sense of everything incomprehensible. Bouncing through memories, reviving old emotions, and virtually re-living lessons learned from all parts of her life… learned as a child, as a teen, as a U.S. Marine, and even at the farm, trapped under some of the harshest conditions possible. All she wanted was that one piece of the puzzle that would help her connect the dots to find peace with what she would become. A killing machine.

Jelena found herself in another memory of her mother. Jelena had gotten herself into some trouble at school. She was probably about in the tenth grade and had gotten rather disrespectful with one of the teachers over political and philosophical differences of opinion. The teacher had overstepped his bounds with Jelena to the point where Charlotte became involved. Charlotte had come to Jelena's school to intervene on her behalf. She was a literary professor and could always handle teachers because she too was one. She was a fierce protector of both of her children. There was absolutely nothing that Charlotte wouldn't do for them.

Jelena was sitting in the classroom alone with the teacher in detention when Charlotte briskly entered the room.

"Good afternoon," Charlotte said, in a sickly-sweet southern manner, eerily like Kate. "I'm Mrs. Prazich, Jelena's mother. I think we need to have a conversation."

Feeling like she needed to excuse herself for the 'grown-ups' to talk, Jelena got up to leave when her mother whipped around and calmly said, "SIT," to which Jelena complied immediately.

Re-focusing her attention on the teacher, Charlotte continued, "Now, as I was sayin', I believe that we need to have a conversation about my daughter and perhaps, more appropriate teaching methods. I'm just not sure that bringin' in and teachin' your personal political agenda is classroom appropriate, and I do not condone anyone forcin' anything on my children, to include any self-serving, erroneous ideas. I, myself, have been teaching for thirty-five years, so I'm well aware of what is acceptable and what is not. This, sir, is not. I'm gonna take my daughter home now, and I do hope that we don't have any further complication regarding this issue. Thank you so very much for your time, and I do hope you have a wonderful rest of your day. Jelena, come along, dear."

The teacher did not get a chance to utter one single word and probably wouldn't have anyways, as he seemed to be under her spell. As soon as Charlotte would open her mouth to speak, her words became like music to a cobra, enchanting her listener and, for the briefest moment, removing any power or momentum from their lips. Jelena was stunned at how smooth and cunning her mother truly was. She was dumbstruck as to how someone could be so tough and sound so sweet simultaneously. It was like watching a lumberjack with a smile hack down a redwood without so much as a hair out of place.

On their way home, Jelena asked her mother, "How do you do that?"

"Do what, darlin'?" her mother replied.

"Be so mean and so nice at the same time..." Jelena elaborated.

"Well, darlin', sometimes you have to be a bit tough to get your point across. However, no matter how unpleasant a deed you must do, you should *always* be a lady about it. You should conduct yourself with grace and elegance, no matter the circumstances. Instead of raising your voice, you should consider raising the quality of your vocabulary. Educated speakers catch more ears."

Maybe this is exactly what Kate was talking about, not being messy, being graceful instead... 'No matter how unpleasant a deed I must do, I should always be a lady about it.' Hmmm, this is exactly what Kate was talking about, Jelena thought, as her mind allowed her to just focus on her mother's words and repeated them, nearly in sync with the memory of what Kate was telling her earlier in the day.

Her mind was busy tracing the delicate features of her mother's face within this memory when reality once again made itself known and pulled Jelena back into the present. She had sat outside her house, in the front yard, all night long and was so deep inside of her memories that she didn't even realize that the sun had come up. When she opened her eyes, she flinched a bit when she saw Bruce standing there in front of her with the sun to his back.

"Heyyyy… you're not dead yet," he said jokingly.

"Good observation. No, I'm not. What do you want?" Jelena asked pointedly.

"I just wanted to see how my newest asset was doing after her first walk. Kate said you did great. So how ya doin'?" Bruce asked, in a chipper, new dad kind of way.

"Well… umm, I have been sitting outside, all night long in this chair, so that should tell you something," Jelena replied in a much less enthusiastic manner.

"Do you want to talk about it? Sort it out?" Bruce asked, flipping his tone to serious.

"Bruce… why did you join the agency?" Jelena asked.

"Man! You jump straight to the double jeopardy questions, don't you?" he quipped.

She shot him a crass look through her squinted eyes.

He grabbed the other lawn chair, sat down next to Jelena, and continued, "Okay. Okay. I joined because it was there, and it was an opportunity presented to me. At that time in my life, I didn't care about much. My mother had just been murdered on the subway…"

"Oh my God, Bruce! I am so sorry!" Jelena interrupted.

"Meh… it was a senseless act, really… she was just in the wrong place at the wrong time. My father, though, well, he had to be committed because when my mother died, he basically lost his mind and stopped taking care of himself. He just sits there day after day. He doesn't talk, doesn't do things… just sits there in his chair… It's just like when she died, so did he. Really a part of me died too. They trained me, just like I trained you. Hard and merciless but incredibly effective. I remember my first walk. I think it wasn't even fifteen minutes before I had slit the throat of some international arms dealer. My mentor noted that I was 'blood thirsty' in my review. I wasn't, really. But when I saw that guy… it was like I saw the man that murdered my mother. I saw red and killed him. No muss… no fuss. And here I sit… 6831 Lima… Code Name: Cainen Abel. I became one of the agency's top assets within the first six months, and then five years later, they asked me to train other potentials, so I agreed," he explained.

"Damn, Bruce! Again, I am so sorry to hear that about your family. I can't even begin to imagine. I still have both of my parents, and I can't bear to think about something happening to them. So, Cainen Abel, huh?" She asked. "Why did they choose that for you?"

"My trainer said that I was like the two brothers... inside... ya know? He said that throughout my training, it was evident that I had some internal struggle going on inside my head, like the two brothers duking it out all the time. Part of me wanted to handle things peacefully, and then the other part of me was sheer blinding rage, willing and able to kill at a moment's notice. Although I denied it back then, he was right. I still struggle with it sometimes, so it's more than appropriate," he replied.

"Huh... I haven't gotten my code name yet. I wonder what it will be," Jelena confessed.

"No?" Bruce replied, his tone sounding a bit surprised. "It's already been issued. You mean, no one has told you what your code name is yet?"

"No... what is it?" she said as she pushed herself up to the edge of her seat?

"Jelena, your code name is Jane Doe," he said.

"What???? Why did they give me Jane Doe? That's a nobody name... like literally," she asked, looking slightly disappointed. "I mean, Kate got Mrs. Applebie, and then there is Mel Titan... even you got Cainen Abel... I don't get it. Why weren't they more creative with my code name? Like, Lethal Lady or Deadly Damsel... something cool."

"Jelena, you're not a superhero. You're a spy. You need blend in, not stick out. Anyways, are you sure that you want to know the answer?

It's pretty intense," he warned.

"Yeah… I want to know. Why is my stupid code name Jane Doe?" Jelena asked again.

"Usually, the immediate first-hand trainer has a lot to contribute to the assigning of code names. They usually know more about the potential than anyone. The trainers must get into the heads of their potentials to really be able to see both, their strengths and weaknesses…. the light and dark side of each potential. But your code name is actually not my doing… other than agreeing to it," he started.

"Okay. So why then?" she pressed.

"Because you don't exist on paper. Only a few folks at the very top of the food chain here know about you… and of you… and of what you are capable of. Sure, there are folks still talking about the 'girl who survived the box,' but they don't exactly know who 'that girl' is. They don't need to know to keep the legend alive and give new potentials something to aim for. Jelena, you are not one of the best… you ARE the best. We have NEVER seen anyone do what you have done. We have never seen anyone maintain their sanity for six fucking weeks in the hole. Six fucking weeks Jelena… Damn! We have never seen anyone memorize four fucking languages in eight weeks… most potentials get through one if they are lucky. Kate only speaks hillbilly, for Christ's sake! We have never seen anyone memorize how to build eighteen different types of bombs. Damn, most of these potentials can barely tie their shoes, let alone *not* blow themselves up. AND, No one has EVER survived the box. Jelena… YOU are the fucking unicorn. The mythical creature that doesn't exist. However, unicorns draw too much attention, so the powers that be went in the opposite direction. Jane Doe is everyone, and she is no one. She is everywhere and nowhere at the same time. You're like a fucking vapor. We gave you the code name Jane Doe because you are now the most lethal phantom that the world will never know. You are the CIA's newest and deadliest secret weapon, and they want to keep it that way. This agency will never allow your identity to be compromised, no matter who they have to silence to protect it. You are the fuckin unicorn, girl. The infamous 518 Papa, Code Name: Jane Doe."

"Wow," Jelena said as she took a deep breath and exhaled loudly. "Yeah, you were right. That *is* pretty intense. I guess I just don't see what you guys see in me. I mean, the language thing really isn't *that* amazing. I already knew a little bit of each, so it was really more like completing it. That was no magical unicorn miracle. And like yesterday, I think that I fucked up left and right, but Kate said all these nice things. I didn't think that I would be some deadly killer. I don't want to let anybody down, but I am struggling to justify some things in my own head right now. I honestly thought that it would be some one-time deal, where I meet some guy, pretend to be his girlfriend, steal some thumb drive, give it to you and then get on with my happy little day. I had no idea that things would go this way."

"Well, that makes two of us, lady!" Bruce started. "That *was* our original intent with you... however, in Phase One, we started to see how you were so very different. From the moment we picked you up in the van, we knew that you were different... as your training progressed, we realized that you were not just different... we realized that you were exceptional, and that's when the powers that be, began carving a brand-new path for you. The downside is that I don't think that they would ever let you go. I don't think there is an 'out' on this one kid. I think you are in it for the long haul now... whether you want to be or not. I'm afraid the choice is no longer yours to make. You are just too damn good. You impressed the hell out of Kate, and I am here to tell you that she does not impress so easily. She is not a smoke blower... so if she says that you're a Rockstar, then we know that you are, indeed, a fucking Rockstar."

"Yeah... Rockstar..." Jelena sighed. "Bruce, does it ever get easier? Like do you get used to... you know... doing the stuff we have to do?"

"Not really. I mean, you do get better at it. You get smoother at the lies; you create better personas, and you begin to be able to see opportunities and options where you couldn't before," he explained.

"Options? What do you mean options?" she asked.

"Look, sometimes we are given orders with specific objectives that need to be fulfilled to the letter of the law... it's very black and white... no room for negotiation. But there are other times when we have a little more gray area to work with... a little more leash to make a few calls on our own. Not every mission will be a kill mission. I guess that I mean that you start to learn where your boundaries are. What rules are black and white and cannot be bent, and then where exactly the gray area starts. It's hard to know what you can and cannot get away with when you are so new. Sorry, I guess I didn't explain it all that great," he said, looking down at his feet. "But as you develop, you will begin to see opportunities where you can get the objectives fulfilled without taking anyone's life."

"Well, there's that. Thank you. That's actually quite helpful," she said as she genuinely smiled at him for the first time.

"Oh, hey... you're actually smiling at me. You have a beautiful smile, Jelena. I am glad that I didn't mess that up too bad. Ohh, that reminds me, I have something for you. Here," Bruce said, handing Jelena a flip phone.

"A little outdated don't you think?" she said sarcastically. "I was hoping for... you know... more like an iPhone10 maybe."

"Shut up... It's a burner," Bruce began as Jelena examined the phone. "A burner phone. It's unregistered and untraceable. This is how we'll stay in touch. You need to memorize my number, though, in case you..." he was saying when he was interrupted by the ringing phone in his pocket... "haven't," he finished.

"Nope... I got it. Thanks, though." She giggled.

"You know... that memory shit is really a neat trick. You should teach me sometime." Bruce chuckled.

"As soon as you master those shoelaces, you're on." She laughed.

"OUCH! Alright, well, I am gonna head out... you know... so many people to electrocute and so little time," he joked as he turned to walk back to his car.

"Yeah! NOT FUNNY!" Jelena yelled. "I STILL OWE YOU SOME ELECTROSHOCK THERAPY TREATMENTS THERE, BUDDY!"

As she turned around to go into her house, the little flip phone began to ring. Bruce was not yet out of earshot and whipped back around, staring at the ringing phone in Jelena's hand.

"Are you doing this?" she asked him.

"Nope," he replied. "Answer it... like right now!"

"Umm hello," Jelena said.

"Darlin', it's me, Mrs. Applebie. Mel Titan has disappeared. Be ready in fifteen." click*

CHAPTER 12: THE SEARCH

Jelena looked at Bruce with a stunned look of confusion on her face as she closed the flip phone.

"What? Who was it?" Bruce asked impatiently.

"It was Mrs. Applebie, Bruce. Mr. Titan is missing," she responded.

"What the hell does that mean? Mr. Titan is missing?" he snipped.

"Beats the shit out of me. We met a man she called Mr. Titan when we went on our walk. She said yesterday that that was his code name. Now he's missing, and she said to 'be ready in fifteen.' That is all she said before she hung up," Jelena snipped back.

"Hmm, well, she does keep things nice and tidy... you know, short, sweet, and to the point. That must have been what my call was for too. I was told to get back to the farm ASAP, then they hung up. Phone lines are not the most secure means of communication, so no one really dishes out too much information over an open line," he said.

"Well, what am *I* supposed to do?" she asked.

"I would say, being ready in fifteen minutes for whatever she has up her sleeve would probably be a good place to start," he joked.

Jelena looked at him and rolled her eyes. She was at least starting to find his little quips entertaining, but she still wasn't sure that she wanted to be any closer to him than six feet for any specific length of time. She still enjoyed fantasizing about how much effort it would take to physically rip his tongue out of his head. *Meh... Why ruin the dream?* she thought.

"Okay. Well, you know what to do, and you'll have her there to help you if you don't. So, 518 Papa... go do what you do. I'll go find out what I can about our missing link, and I'll be in touch," Bruce said as he continued to walk to his car, transitioning more to a jog.

Jelena went inside her house, and what was once so familiar and comforting now felt so foreign and strange. She barely recognized the house she had lived in for over a year. She walked around, looking at all of her old pictures and treasures, and for the first time ever, she felt like she was looking at somebody else's life... somebody else's family. She wanted so badly to feel 'at home,' but she just didn't. Her time at the farm had changed her in so many ways. She hoped that maybe it might just take a little bit for her to come back around to a somewhat normal life. Like it or not, this was her world now... her 'new' normal, and she would have to put in the extra effort to make the strange and unfamiliar, familiar once again, but for now, she knew that she only had fifteen minutes to pull her shit together and be ready for Kate.

Mr. Titan seemed so unassuming and unthreatening, but Jelena really didn't know enough about him or this new career field to be able to come up with any ideas of why or how an operative could go missing. *I guess I do understand why someone would want to just disappear and get out of this lifestyle. God knows that I had no idea what I was walking into when I agreed to help the CIA. I had no idea that I would have to kill in cold blood. Maybe Mel Titan just had enough, too, after he caught wind of Sally's demise. Maybe he felt responsible for her death, knowing that he gave us her address. Living this life of lies and deceit and death...I don't even know what to make of all this shit yet. Maybe he just quit?* she thought as she meandered around her kitchen.

Jelena put on a pot of her favorite raspberry chocolate-flavored coffee. She walked into her clean white bathroom to splash some cold water onto her face and give it a good wash. She changed out of her mud-stained, white floral A-line dress and slapped on some jeans and a plain gray T-shirt, her favorite go-to in terms of fashion. She pulled her chocolate brown hair into a messy ponytail and rubbed on a bit of concealer to hide the last little bit of bruising that she had around her right eye.

"That oughta do. Good enough for government purposes at least," she said to herself.

She poured herself a cup of coffee, added her cream and sugar, the way that she used to do, and took that first sip. She couldn't believe how flavorful and insanely sweet it was. She honestly didn't ever remember when a cup of coffee tasted so very good, but at the same time, she couldn't help but wince at how sugary it was. She was no longer used to all the sweetness. She took that cup and dumped it right down the sink as she ran the water to rinse the cup out and wash it down the drain. She poured another cup, this time, just with the coffee and no added sweeteners. The deep rich flavors struck some happier memories in her, making her taste buds do their little happy dance. THIS she remembered. As she drank her coffee, she shook her head at herself, wondering how she could have stayed up all night long after being so damn tired. The sleep deprivation caused her to be slightly startled by the loud knock on her door.

"Damn...that was like the fastest fifteen minutes EVER," Jelena quipped as she opened the door. "Good morning, Kate."

Kate stood there in the doorway and, once again, looked like she was performing some scene in a 1950s musical. She was wearing a pair of baby-blue Capri slacks and a white, button-up tank top with little blue anchors on it. On her perfectly pedicured feet were a pair of white cloth and cork wedge heels and, of course, her signature wide-brim woven hat with a fabric band, matching her shirt. Her smooth flowing blonde hair was delicately pulled to the side of her head in a low gentle pony, draping over her ivory shoulder.

"Don't you ever wear normal-people clothes?" Jelena scoffed.

"Well, hello to you too, there, darlin'." Kate chuckled. "We can't stand out too much in that tiny little town... and what's wrong with looking nice anyways? A coral snake is beautiful... but it can still kill you in a split second, sweetie... Why don't you ever wear nice lady-like outfits?" she asked, mocking Jelena's tone. "Here, I figured you'd be dressed like that, so I brought you another gift," Kate continued as she handed Jelena yet another garment bag containing an outfit for her.

Jelena opened the garment bag and found peach-colored Capri pants and a light blue, button-up tank top patterned with large pastel fruits. At the bottom of the bag were a pair of cork wedge heels with light blue fabric instead of white. "Hey... I do so wear nice lady-like outfits sometimes... just so you know..." Jelena replied as she took the ensemble to the bathroom and quickly changed. She also took a second to tidy up her messy ponytail, resulting in one with a much sleeker design.

"See now... There ya go! You look great, darlin'!" Kate exclaimed as Jelena came back out into the living room.

"Yeah, thanks. So, what's the deal with Mel?" she asked.

"Oh… Mel… I don't know. The intel team just called me up early this mornin' and said that he didn't check in like he usually does. They insisted that we go make sure that it's not a problem or nothin'. We just gotta go find him, I reckon'," Kate responded.

"Don't they think maybe he just slept in? I mean, why send us to a town two hours away for something so simple?" she asked.

"Now honey, we've gone over this already… haven't we?" Kate replied, with a motherly 'I already told you once' tone.

"Yeah, yeah… I remember everything means something. Yeah, I remember," she said, almost mocking Kate.

"Okay, so grab your Joe, we gotta go," Kate continued in a chipper, sing-songy tone.

Jelena grabbed her coffee and locked the door behind her. As she followed Kate, she noticed that she was now driving an entirely different vehicle. It was an older style, silver, Buick LeSabre with the stale grandma smell still emitting from the seats, and as she was buckling her seat belt, she asked, "What? Where's the Caddy?"

"Well… darlin'… It's never a good plan to go back to the wet-works scene, but if you absolutely must, then it's better if you don't use the same horse. Catch my drift? We don't wanna go back and raise any eyebrows, ya know?" Kate explained as she pulled the Buick out of Jelena's driveway and began the long drive back to Po-Dunk-Nowhere-Ville. "

"Okay, then. So, what else do you know about our missing Mel? What's the plan?" Jelena asked.

"Well, like I said, darlin', I only know what I know. I got word early this morning that he done disappeared. Just vanished into thin air," Kate began. "I can tell you one thing, Mr. Titan don't just disappear. Messy ain't my style and disappearin' ain't his. Before I called you, I looked at his asset file. He's about as regular and consistent as a damned prune farmer."

Kate continued, "The only other thing I know is that intel wouldn't just send us somewhere without havin' a damned good reason. So, I think findin' good ole' Mel may end up bein' harder than we think. Now we don't know who has him or where he is, but the only hornet's nest that we done poked lately has been the KGB. Good 'ole Sally must'a been more important that we know. She was clever enough to hide that drive in a pile of look-alikes... like findin' a damned needle in a haystack. Good Lord Almighty. Well, we need to get back to town to look around that flower shop and Mel's house. Maybe we can get lucky and find ourselves another needle."

"Okay, sounds good. So, are we still in town, 'lookin' for pie' there, Elizabeth?" Jelena asked Kate. "I just want to make sure that I have the right story in my head."

"Oh no, dear. Well, I mean, our names and general backstories are the same. We're Elizabeth and Sabrina York, from the York family in Atlanta, but this time we're in town looking for little antiquities and treasures for our cousin's vintage country weddin', and we heard that the florist here in town was the best for miles. Got it?" Kate asked.

"In the vault!" Jelena responded. "So, to the flower shop then."

During the drive out, Jelena looked at Kate and asked her the same question she had asked Bruce earlier. "Hey, Kate, why did you join the agency?"

Kate sighed heavily, and her facial expression made it more clear than ever that that was a topic she really didn't want to discuss as she replied, "Listen, sweetie, I'm gonna need you to stay focused here. Just focus on what we're gonna go do. Think about your story and how in the hell we are gonna find Mel Titan. He's our priority here, not ancient history. We can talk about ancient history some other time. Okay?"

Not long after Kate shut down Jelena's inquiries as to her own personal motivation to serve the agency, Kate and Jelena both found themselves again at the door of the town flower shop, only this time, the lights were all off, and there was a "CLOSED" sign hanging inside of the locked door.

"Damn!" Kate started. "I kinda hoped that someone would'a opened this up so that we could look around a bit, but since that's a no-go, let's go into some of these little shops and see what the locals know."

The first little shop the girls went into was 'Martha's Antiques,' a tiny shop barely big enough for three or four people to fit inside. The outside, along the street, was adorned with little raised flowerbeds filled with various colorful flowers. Stacked along the outside wall was a menagerie of lawn decorations, from flamingos to giant ugly ceramic frogs. The entry to the shop was a glass door propped open with an old telephone book. As they walked inside, they realized that it was quite a tiny space. The shop was crammed full of mismatched shelving that housed tons of weird and obnoxious little trinkets. The shop was so full that it was blatantly obvious that fire codes were not a concern here in Tiny-Town.

Behind the counter sat a little old lady sporting a curly gray hairdo, perched on an old seventies vintage barstool. "Well, helloooo there," Kate sang as they entered the little shop. "Do you mind if we browse your wares for a bit, ma'am? We're tryin' to find the perfect little trinkets for our cousin's weddin'." The old lady smiled and nodded, acknowledging Kate's request.

After perusing the tight isles for a few moments, Kate approached the counter and continued the conversation. "Say, you wouldn't happen to know what time the florist opens up would you?" Kate asked sweetly. "We heard that your little florist is the best for miles around, and we would love to see what he could do for the venue."

As Kate continued that conversation about pies and flowers and such, Jelena decided on her own plan. After browsing the isles herself, she palmed an antique hairpin made of a long strand of brass and had a large tacky butterfly on the end. She silently slipped it into her handbag and began working her way back to the front end of the cluttered tiny space. Without Kate even noticing, she was able to sneak right back out of the front door without the slightest sound.

Jelena headed straight back to the flower shop, cutting one street down and one street over to not be too conspicuous. She enjoyed the fresh air and sunlight, not to mention the adrenaline rush associated with doing something questionable and not being caught. To her surprise, this 'down one-over-one' strategy also conveniently placed her on the back side of the shop. As she pretended to look in her handbag, all the while retrieving the hairpin, she took a moment to scout out the area. She looked around to find a suitable entry point and ensure that no one was watching her. When she spotted the back door, she made a B-line straight for it.

"Perfect!" she whispered. The back door was down about five or six steps and was nicely hidden by an awning and some brick walls. They must have designed it this way because the neighbors probably didn't want to see some alley eyesore from their balcony. Knowing the type that resided in tiny towns like this, the future neighbors probably complained about it at the Town Hall meeting long before it was even built. Nonetheless, the layout couldn't have been any better for an afternoon of breaking and entering.

She pulled out the hairpin from her pocket and began to pick the lock on the back door.

Let's see if any of this crap they taught me even works... she thought.

It didn't take long for the lock to pop. *Shit!* she thought. *It actually worked.* Jelena was stunned that not only did it work, but she was even more astounded that she remembered the correct steps on how to do it.

As she carefully opened the door, she looked for the alarm panel. She entered the code that she had memorized back at the farm for a class called 'Security Measures.' In order to defeat alarms and various security systems, she was taught the codes that were used by most first responders, such as police and firemen. These codes were hard programmed into the system to disable the alarm while the authorities contacted the owners. She quietly slipped inside the shop and shut the door behind her to not raise any concerns for any folks passing by.

Jelena found the area that Mel had been using as the basic office area, complete with a little desk and a phone. The desktop was littered with all kinds of paper, a few old coffee cups, and a calculator, but no computer. It was quite evident that Mel Titan was not much for modern technology and was definitely not one for organizing things, and if his mind was as messy as his desk, then maybe it wasn't so shocking that he got snatched up after all. Jelena could never figure out how certain people could think clearly in such chaos. Quickly, she searched through old receipts from flower deliveries and bills from the electric and utility companies, using only the light coming from the one back window. She continued to search through all of Mel's desk drawers for any false bottoms that may contain any hidden signs or clues as to his whereabouts. When that yielded squat, she began to feel rather frustrated.

"What the hell, Mel?" she whispered.

Giving up, though, was not in Jelena's nature. She stood there for a second and remembered what Kate said, "...disappearin' ain't his style. He is as regular and consistent as a damned prune farmer." Maybe the mess was just another cover... maybe that wasn't the real Mel or whatever his real name was. If Mel was as dependable as Kate said he was... as consistent as the intel guys said he was... then he wouldn't have just left.

There has got to be a clue somewhere in this place. Jelena had an idea and dropped to her knees onto the floor. She crawled under the desk and felt around for any hidden compartments.

As she craned to inspect the underside of the desk, she noticed something odd. Under the center drawer, she saw that it looked like someone had covered the bottom of the drawer with tan, brown butcher block paper, but it was stuck on, sort of like contact paper with wrinkles. She reached up and felt something rigid underneath the paper. She pulled out her pen light and searched the edges to see if she could cut or peel the paper off. She found one of the corners was folded over onto itself, like a dog-eared book page. She slowly peeled back the tan sticky paper and looked up to see what was there. It was a small black square that looked like a small book. Jelena ripped it out of its hidden spot and saw that it was indeed a book, with a leather cover tied in a knot along the side.

As she remained sitting, tucked under the desk with nothing but her purse and penlight, she stuck the penlight in her mouth and began digging through her purse, trying to find that hatpin she had swiped earlier. "Shit, I must have left it in the damn lock. Fuck, that was dumb," she whispered to herself.

Realizing that she had probably been in there for a bit too long anyways, Jelena decided to shove the book into her purse, along with her penlight, and began to crawl out from under the desk. As she backed out, ass first, she got to her knees and slowly stood up, trying to brush the dirt off the light peach-colored Capri pants that Kate had loaned her. "Shit, again... this is exactly why I do denim and wear shit that doesn't stain. That is two for two on trashing Kate's shit. Dammit, she is gonna be pissed," Jelena huffed to herself as she finished standing. Not even a second after she finished standing up, she felt something hard pressing against the back of her head. She was not alone. Regrettably, she was so hyper-focused on the book she had found that she failed to scan her environment before crawling out and, worse yet, failed to notice the other set of feet that had walked in behind her.

She was trying so hard to think of what she had been taught to do in this situation that her mind went completely blank. In that split second, she decided to improvise. She dropped her purse, cocked her fist back as far as she could, and as she whipped around, she prepared for the fight of her life.

CHAPTER 13: DISAPPEARING INK

"Bang!" Kate whispered as she pulled the trigger of her pretend finger gun that she had pressed against Jelena's head. "You're dead!"

"FUCK Kate! You scared the shit outta me!" Jelena whispered.

"You and I are gonna have a conversation about this later... but right now, we don't have time. What did you find?" Kate reprimanded in a whisper.

Jelena bent down to pick up her purse and dig out the small, black, leather leger that she had found taped to the underside of Mel's desk. The cover said something that Jelena hadn't noticed earlier. On the cover, it read, 'Emergency Instructions.'

"Kate, it's tied in a knot. I can't get it open, and I really think that we should get outta here like pronto!" Jelena explained.

"I'm right behind ya, lady! Let's get!" Kate replied in a hushed tone.

Jelena stuffed the little book into her handbag and began reorganizing the mess on the desk, trying to get it back to the way she found it. They both hurried to put the other things back as orderly as possible and briefly looked around for any security cameras. Kate stood by the door while Jelena reset the alarm and locked the door behind them.

As Jelena came up the steps from the back door, she and Kate linked arm-in-arm and walked over to a nearby park they had seen coming into town the day prior, as if nothing at all had happened. Most folks who just committed a little Breaking and Entering along with a little Larceny might appear a bit nervous and twitchy. However, these two truly looked as if they had just come from Sunday Bible school and were still flying high on the delicious crumble cake and coffee served up. As they walked, they chatted and giggled about everything and nothing at all.

They came to the park and found a nice bench under a willow tree next to the little pond occupied by the resident mallards. They sat, and Jelena began digging through her purse to find the book and the hatpin that she had reclaimed from the florist's lock. She sat and picked at the leather knot to loosen it up.

"Emergency Instructions?" Kate began. "What the hell does that mean? I hope we just didn't break in to get some dumb-ass book about what to do if the power goes out. Mel, we really need a few clues here, man!"

"I got it!" Jelena exclaimed. "I got it... I got it... Totally got it! But I don't think you're gonna be happy, Kate. I think it really is about like the power and stuff. Look here... In Case of Fire... In Case of Break-In... In Case of Robbery... Who to call... Insurance documents... In case of Disappearing Ink..."

"Wait, Disappearing Ink?? What the hell does that mean?" Kate whispered with a puzzled look on her face.

Jelena flipped to the 'Disappearing Ink' section of Mel's little emergency book, and there in block print handwriting read, '**IN CASE OF DISAPPEARING INK, GO HOME AND DRINK THE GOOD WHISKEY**.'

Jelena and Kate just sat there for a moment and looked at each other... "Why are some men so stupid?" Kate asked, shaking her head.

"Ha... I cannot... at all... answer that question, but you know that our next stop has to be Mel's house. We gotta go find his 'good whiskey,' I guess," Jelena replied

"Alright," whispered Kate, "this has been fun, but we gotta get the hell outta here before anyone starts asking too many questions. We gotta get to Mel's."

Walking to the car, Kate pulled her company phone out of her purse and called Bruce. "Hey," she said. "We need to know where Titan got his apples? Uh-huh. Okay. Thanks."

"3710 Charter Drive, Unit A," Kate said. "Oh, and don't think for a second that I done forgot about that little stunt you pulled back there, we're still gonna chat about that. Oh, yes, ma'am!"

Kate continued to fuss at Jelena under her breath, "Just leavin' like that. Must be outta her damn mind. Are you outta your damn mind? Go slip off and pick a damn lock... Could'a ended up damn dead. God blessed newbies. Sweet baby Jesus! What in the damn hell would I tell the boss if you went off and done got your stupid ass killed on day two? What then, smartypants? Outta her damn mind!"

Jelena, feeling like she was about to go to time-out for her little transgression, quietly got in the car without a peep. When they pulled into the driveway of Mel's place, she was far less than impressed, but at least by this point, Kate was a lot quieter and less aggravated with her.

Mel Titan lived in a tiny, dilapidated apartment. It looked like possibly four units were all attached to the same building, but the building itself only stood one story tall. The roof had been repeatedly patched and still had shingles that looked like they could blow away if the neighbor had a decent sneeze. The white exterior paint was discolored and peeling off the walls in places. The grassy areas were not so grassy, and on one side, there were endless amounts of piled-up dog shit.

"If this is what I have to look forward to… umm… then maybe I'll pass," Jelena said to Kate with a look of disgust plastered all over her face.

"Now remember my darlin' Sabrina, we just need to water his plants and go," Kate said, clearly back into character and definitely not in the mood for any comic relief coming from Jelena's direction.

They followed the cracked and beaten walkway around the building to Unit A, and as they approached Mel's porch, they noticed his elderly neighbor watching them as they walked up. She was sitting in a rocking chair on her adjacent porch, with a pile of yarn in her lap. Between knits and pearls, she eyed the girls in the perfect 'nosey neighbor' manner.

"Helloooo there," Kate sang to the neighbor and then, under her breath, whispered to Jelena, "You pick the lock, and I'll be a distraction."

Jelena nodded and pulled the hairpin back out of her handbag as if she was getting the keys.

"Hello there dear, we're just here to water our friend's plants while he's outta town. We won't be long at all," Kate said to the neighbor while Jelena was popping the lock on Mel's door.

They entered Mel's apartment, which to Jelena's surprise, didn't look at all like what she had envisioned it to. It was meek and simple but clean, with barely any decorations and only small quaint pieces of furniture. The girls searched the apartment for what Mel would call the 'good whiskey.' Mel had made one of the kitchen cabinets into a make-shift liquor cabinet. Jelena scanned each label. She found one with a name that she didn't recognize and picked it up, and when she did, she could hear something rattling around in the bottom of the bottle.

"Kate, I think I got it," Jelena said as she got two glasses from the neighboring cabinet.

"Now, what in the sam hell do you think you're doin'?" Kate snarked.

"Hey, he said it was good whiskey. It's almost a full bottle. We can't just dump it down the drain. It's a Marine Corps law or something," Jelena said with a giggle as she took her first shot and handed the other glass to Kate.

Jelena poured the last bit of whiskey into the two glasses and shook the bottle out over the sink to knock out the little tube inside. She picked it up and looked at it closely. It was a small white tube that almost looked like a chapstick container. She unscrewed the end cap, and low and behold, there was a thumb drive inside. "Whew!" Jelena said as she started to feel the warmth of the whiskey hitting her system, "This *is* good whiskey!"

"Damn… you people and your thumb drives. This shit is madness," Jelena said sarcastically, "Hey, we got what we came for, now let's get outta here before anyone notices that we are taking a super long time to water the plants."

"Right behind ya," Kate squeaked as she choked down her last little bit of whiskey.

They left Mel's and waived politely at the neighbor as they locked the door and headed back along the sidewalk to the street.

"We gotta see what's on this drive," Jelena said, walking briskly to the car. "Hurry up, Kate!"

"Will you hold your ever-lovin' horses for a hot dang second!" Kate scoffed, obviously a bit tipsy from the 'good whiskey.'

"You don't drink much, do you?" Jelena asked softly.

"Well, not when I'm tryin' to walk, I don't," Kate retorted, her speech quite slurred at this point.

The two of them got back into the car, and this time, Jelena grabbed the keys from Kate and said, "I think I'll drive this time if you don't mind."

"Surley durley, little peach plum sugar pit," Kate said as the slur of her words worsened.

"Alright," Jelena began, "you gotta snap out of it. We have to find a computer where we can open these files and quick. Now, where can we find a computer? I hate to drive back to the farm if Mel is stuck in the other direction. Come on, Kate, think."

"Well, sweety peety, we don't have to go nowhere," Kate mumbled as she opened the glove box and a small screen and keyboard appeared. "Hey, how many pigeons do YOU see sittin' on that there bench? God… There must be fifty or so… I ain't never seen so many pigeons in all my days."

Jesus! Talk about a fuckin lightweight! Jelena thought and then said to Kate, "Okay, pigeon whisperer, you gotta move into the backseat, babe. I got shit to do."

Jelena helped a very uncoordinated Kate flop into the back seat like a dead fish with a bad case of the giggles. She slid over to the passenger front seat and plugged the little silver drive into the USB port located inside the glove box.

"Ha! I had no idea that Buicks had this feature. Sna-zzy. I might have to re-think my vehicle selection," she said while waiting for the drive to load.

The files came up, and one was labeled, 'In the event of my disappearance.' Several others appeared to be organized by dates, along with three others labeled 'People,' 'Places,' and 'Things.' Jelena touched the screen on the icon for the disappearance file, and inside was one Word document.

To whom it may concern; If you are reading this letter, then that means that I am either missing or dead already. I have several files on this drive to help you with additional intel on certain persons of interest.

As for what I have been up to, I have been watching Svetlana Petrov *for the past three months. (*See dated files for specifics). Here, she goes by the name Sally Peters. Throughout several nights of surveillance, I have discovered that she is not always alone but frequently has one male visitor. He appears to be perhaps in his sixties with a thick frame, no neck, a very round face with blue eyes, and straight gray hair. He wears a tiny golden rose ring on his left pinky finger. Every time I have seen him, he wears either a gray or black silk suit with a white shirt and a narrow matching tie. I have learned that her male companion is Vladomir Khishchnik, but the name on the credit card he uses to buy her weekly flowers is Oscar Crunch.*

Vladomir doesn't seem to talk much when he comes into the shop, but he always asks me if I think she'll love the flowers. I believe that their relationship is more than professional, but I currently have no way to prove it. Should something happen to Svetlana, I think that this man may turn to become quite dangerous. I can't prove that yet either, but I have a feeling in my gut, so extreme caution should be considered. I think it's in the agency's best interest to keep Svetlana alive and continue monitoring her and her male companion to learn as much as possible about the KGB's future plans.

If you are reading this, and something has already happened to Svetlana, then most likely, Vladomir is behind my disappearance. I don't know how and I'm not positive, but I think I may have been compromised. Since I wasn't sure, I didn't report it to my handler as policy dictates, so this may have been a fatal mistake on my part. In the past three months, I have found a few places that may be of interest in terms of some place to maybe take someone for questioning and interrogation. I had hoped that it wouldn't be me, but I did know that the possibility was there. If this is the case, I hope you get to me in time. The addresses are listed below:

-Red barn on the old McFarland Ranch. The property is abandoned. 52 McFarland Drive

- Large warehouse behind the paper mill. Also abandoned. 16000 1ˢᵗ Avenue

- Abandoned mine on the outskirts of town off of Hwy 19

Thank you for looking for me. Again, I will hold out as long as I can. Please hurry.

Sincerely, 2112 Tango- Code Name: Mel Titan

Jelena closed the file and closed the glove box before turning around in her seat to face Kate, who was now officially sleeping on the job. She grabbed her handbag and pulled out her company phone to call Bruce. "Hey... It's Jane," she said. "We found Mr. Titan's apples, but... ummm, he wasn't home to return them. We need some help. He may have gone on a walk, but he shouldn't be alone right now. Can you please go see if he's at 16000 First Avenue, and maybe send someone to see if he walked down to that old abandoned mine off of Highway 19, too? Thanks." *click

Jelena hung up the phone and turned back around to Kate. She began to gently tap her face and said, "Hey! Hey! Drunky McDrunkerson! It's time to wake up. I know where Mel might be."

Jelena let Kate continue to sober up in the backseat while she drove to the abandoned barn on the old McFarland Ranch in hopes of finding Mel. As she pulled into the overgrown drive, she could feel that the suspension on that old Buick was being tested by all of the sizable, but hidden bumps. She drove past the deteriorating farmhouse and onto the large red wooden barn. Although she could see that the hatch to the loft was open, the large doors on the front were not only shut but also chained up.

"Well, whatever's in that barn," she said, "somebody wants to keep it hidden."

Jelena parked the car in front of the main chained door and hopped out. She walked around to the trunk and popped it open.

"Hmmm. This ain't your mama's Buick... Let's see what other goodies they have stashed up Grandma's bum here," she said as she felt around the trunk compartment. She found a flap near where the spare tire should have gone and lifted it. The entire trunk was a false bottom. When she lifted that flap, the whole upper board came up, revealing all kinds of tools and gadgets. "Well, hot damn!" she exclaimed. "Maybe I am getting the hang of this spy shit."

She sifted through the tools, and sure enough, there, sitting in its little slot, was a brand-new looking pair of bolt cutters. She grabbed them up and went around to the backseat door to get Kate, who was now at least conscious.

"Hey!" Jelena said firmly. "You sobered up yet? We're at the barn. I think we may have found Mel. The doors are shut and chained too. I need you to get in the game, boss."

"Owwie..." Kate moaned, grabbing her head. "Yeah, I'm ready... ohhh, no more whiskey for lunch, okay?"

"Alright, alright... Let's get you out of the car and on your feet," Jelena said, helping Kate to her feet. "Are you sure that your code name isn't 'Mrs. Lightweight?'"

"Hush your mouth!" Kate quipped back at her after catching her balance.

Jelena led the way with the bolt cutters and snipped the padlock off the thick chain securing the large red wooden barn doors. She chucked the cutters over into the grass, and she and Kate each took a door and pulled them open, over the rocky gravel. What they would see inside would not only jar Kate back into complete sobriety but would rock Jelena to her very core.

When they finished pulling the doors open, they saw a man hanging from the wrists, attached to a thick chain, similar to what was securing the door. He was motionless, and his head was hanging low in between his shoulders. Jelena bolted into action as she ran to him, screaming, "MEL? MR. TITAN?"

As she came around to the front of him, her mind played a very cruel trick on her. For a brief moment, she thought that she was looking at Adam's beaten and swollen face.

"ADAM?? OH NO!! ADAM!! KATE... QUICK! WE GOTTA GET HIM

DOWN… COME ON… HELP ME GET HIM DOWN… WE CAN SAVE HIM. I KNOW CPR. I CAN SAVE HIM. I KNOW I CAN! GODDAMN IT, KATE! WE GOTTA GET HIM DOWN RIGHT NOW! KATE!!! ADAM!!! PLEASE GOD NOOOO!!!" Jelena continued to scream.

Kate, now in a complete state of sobriety, grabbed Jelena by the arms and said, "Jelena… Jelena, honey, look at me… JELENA!"

Jelena looked at Kate with nothing less than panic and confusion in her eyes. Kate continued, "Jelena, honey… he's dead. There *is* no savin' him, sweetheart. He's gone. It's okay. You're okay." Kate pulled her in for a hug until she had managed to calm herself down.

"You alright now?" Kate asked gently.

Jelena pulled herself away and half nodded that she was ok, but in reality, she was anything but. "Okay," Kate continued, "I'll be right back. I have to make a call."

Kate walked back to the car to get her phone and called Bruce to tell him their most recent discovery. It was indeed Mel Titan who was hanging from those chains. Jelena's reaction, though, forced Kate to ask one very important question.

"Jelena, honey, who's Adam?" asked Kate.

"He's no one," Jelena replied in nearly a whisper with her eyes locked onto the ground. She couldn't even bear to look at the tortured carcass of Mr. Titan. Deep inside, Jelena knew that was something else that she would have to sort out, but not here and not now.

"Yeah… no one," muttered Kate under her breath. Then with a new notion, she grabbed Jelena's hand and brought her back in front of the hanging man and said, "Look, honey… this here is Mel Titan. Look at his nose and his face and his shape. It *is* Mel Titan. The man we've been lookin' for all day. Honey, you gotta look at his face… Now Jelena. NOW damn it, I said LOOK!" Kate hollered.

Jelena reluctantly looked up at poor Mel Titan's bruised, battered, and bloodied face, and slowly, the transposed image of Adam disappeared, and the face of Mel Titan reappeared.

"Mel Titan," Jelena said quietly as she looked around, stunned by the cruel trick that her mind had played on her.

"Yes, honey… Mel Titan," Kate confirmed. "And from the looks of it, he took one hell of a beatin'. Now we have no idea how much they know. This is not good. We gotta go, girl. I called Bruce, and he's sending a clean-up crew out, and we can't be here when they arrive. Come'on honey, Let's go."

Jelena picked up the bolt cutters and got back into the passenger side of the car with a whole new sense of heaviness weighing down on her.

Jelena was stone silent for the first forty-five minutes of the drive back. Kate was a bit too unnerved herself to push her new comrade for a deeper explanation, especially after such a confusing and traumatizing experience. Kate still didn't understand who Adam was, and Jelena just wasn't talking.

"Hey Kate," Jelena asked, "can you please stop the car? I need to clear my head, and I really just want to walk for a bit."

Kate pulled the car over, stopping on the side of the road, and replied, "Well darlin', Bruce said that we need to be back at the farm at 6:00 PM for a debriefing in conference room A. I don't know if walkin's such a good idea."

Jelena looked at her watch and saw that it was only 4:13 PM, so that gave her about one hour and forty-seven minutes until she had to be 'ass-in-seat' for the debriefing.

"I got time. Kate, please. I really have to sort this out on my own. I promise I **will** be there. I'll see you at six," Jelena said as she grabbed her handbag and got out of the car. "I promise. I'll be okay," she reassured.

Kate continued driving back to the farm, leaving Jelena to walk. As Jelena got smaller and smaller in Kate's rear-view mirror, Kate's anxiety grew. She kept feeling like she should go back and get Jelena, but she ignored this gut feeling and continued back to the farm.

Sitting in the conference room, Kate looked at her watch, 5:54 PM, and more than ever, her 'bad feeling' had grown bigger and bigger. Jelena was not back at the farm yet. The members of the review and debriefing panel were already there and in their seats. Bruce walked in with a stern and annoyed look on his face.

"Damn it!" he said. "She knows that if she cannot be on time, then she needs to be fucking early!" he scowled.

"Relax, Bruce. She still has time. I'm sure that we're just gettin' all worked up over nothin'," Kate reassured. "I mean, after all, *she's* the damned best. If anyone can handle herself, it's Jelena… right?"

"How the fuck could you let her walk, Kate? You KNEW that she was to be monitored until *I* decided to cut her loose. Now, who the fuck knows? Maybe all this shit spooked her, and she bolted… WITH all the shit we taught her. If she disappears and we don't find her, it's your ass on the line, Kate! I am holding you ultimately responsible!" Bruce snapped at her.

"Well now… hold on right there, Bruce. We don't *let* Jelena do anything. If she wanted to disappear, she would'a gone on and done it already. I think you need to calm yourself right down. She just wanted to walk so that she could clear her head. Today was a tryin' day. She did everything better than you and me would'a done. She thought outside the box Bruce… better than assets with twenty years under their belts, and this is only her first walk for Christ's sake… and she is out there like a boss… kickin' ass and takin' names. But she processes these things differently. She *has got* to get into her head, so her head don't get into her. I trust Jelena, and I just don't think she would'a just not come back," Kate replied.

"Call her!" Bruce demanded. "Call her right now and tell her to stop fuckin around and get her ass in here!"

"Alright… alright… I'm doin' it…" Kate said as she pulled out her phone to call Jelena.

Bruce repeatedly looked at his watch while pacing back and forth. This was supposed to be the machine… the perfect machine… 518 Papa… The longer she didn't show, the more aggravated Bruce became.

"Damn! I can't reach her," Kate said to Bruce as she snapped shut her little black flip phone. Kate grabbed her purse, pulled out her keys, and said, "I'm gonna go out and look for her. I'll bring her back."

Before she could leave the room, Bruce's phone rang. Kate stopped and turned around, waiting to see if Jelena was on the other end.

"YEAH!" he answered, completely expecting it to be Jelena on the other end with a full explanation of where the hell she was at.

Quite suddenly, Bruce's expression changed. The anger on his face was wiped away and was replaced by a stoic seriousness.

"Why not today?" Bruce calmly asked the caller. "Yeah, I got it," he finished as he closed his phone and slid it back in his pocket.

"Bruce?" Kate asked softly. "Bruce, what happened? What's wrong?"

Bruce kept staring blankly in the same direction until he let out a very loud, "FUCK!" which echoed through the conference room and attracted the attention of the seated panel members.

"I can't believe it!" he continued as he ran his hand through his hair. "They have Jane."

CHAPTER 14: BACK IN THE BOX

"What do you mean, Bruce? What do you mean, they have Jane? Who has Jane?" Kate asked, now becoming upset herself.

Bruce explained that he heard an unknown Russian male's voice on the other end of the line when he answered his phone, speaking very broken English. As he explained the contents of the call, he replayed the conversation over in his mind...

(Playback)

"YEAH!" he answered, completely expecting it to be Jelena on the other end, with a full explanation of where the hell she was at.

"Listen carefully," the man said in a thick Russian accent. "I have girl... and you have drive. If you want girl alive, then you bring drive, and we trade. I call you tomorrow with time and place."

"Why not today?" Bruce calmly asked the caller.

"Well... we want to be... thorough. See exactly what she knows before we give her back. The man, he not know so much. Maybe she knows more. We will see. So, tomorrow, I call back to tell you when and where. You come alone. We watch. Understand?" the man asked.

"Yeah, I got it," he said as he closed his phone and slid it back in his pocket.

He stood there for a minute, shaking his head, clearly racking his mind for how to best handle this situation. For some reason, he felt particularly emotionally charged, and he couldn't quite figure out why. All he could do was wait for the phone call.

"WELL??" Kate snapped at him. "What in the damn hell is going on? Where is she?"

Bruce could barely form a reply. His emotions had balled up in his throat, nearly choking him to death, a sensation he hadn't felt in forever, at least not since his mother's murder.

"BRUCE!" snapped Kate.

"We gotta get her back, Kate," he replied. "Why didn't I tell him that she was new and didn't know anything? That she was just a temporary asset, and he could have me instead? Fuck!"

"Bruce... honey, now ain't the time to woulda' coulda' shoulda'. Right now, we gotta figure out where she is and how in the hell we're gonna get her back. We both saw what they did to poor Mel Titan," Kate replied, trying to calm Bruce. "But first, you should probably make the powers that be aware that she's been snagged up by the KGB."

"Yeahhh Kate... that sounds like a fucking GREAT idea! I'll just march my ass right on in there and tell them that the greatest asset that the CIA has discovered in twenty years has just been captured by the fucking KGB! Yep... Let me jump right on that... and then we can both go and dig our own graves... because THAT'S where we'll end up, Kate, and you know it!" Bruce stammered, irritated, and frustrated.

"Well, damn Bruce... when you put it like that... maybe it's not such a great idea. How in the world are we supposed to keep a lid on this? We are ALL supposed to be at a debriefing RIGHT NOW!" Kate said, making every effort to keep her voice down.

Bruce paced the floor just outside the conference room door and thought about how he would initiate a rescue mission and keep it secret at the same time. "I gotta tell them something. Not showing up for a debriefing is not the impression she wants to make around here, especially being so new. Kate, help me out here. What can I tell them about where she is that will buy us some time to get her back? You know when they find out that we lied to them... you know that is not going to go well... you know we'll probably both end up in the goddamned pit!" he said to her in the quietest tone possible.

"Okay, Bruce, just calm down. Nobody's going to the pit... at least not yet... now let's look at this... for Christ's sake we lie for a livin'... certainly we can come up with somethin'..." Kate began to brainstorm out loud, "Ummm... you could tell them that there was a glitch in communication and that you thought that since she was so junior that the debriefing was for just the senior assets, you and I... right? And so, you put her on surveillance detail, watching the area to see if Mel Titan's killer comes back? Right? Then I can come to you and let you know, you know in front of them, that there were some spots out there where the cell service was just God-awful and that we really need the satellite guys to get that better... What if someone were to get stuck without any comms? Right? How does that sound?"

"Well, it's better than the bullshit crap I had floating around my head. I still think I should try to reschedule the debriefing... If we both get sucked into a debriefing right now, then we will lose hours that Jane might not have to spare… so, partly your story and part rescheduling should buy us enough time to get her back without any of us hanging for it," Bruce said, heading back for the conference room door. "So that is what we'll do, sound okay?"

"Works for me," Kate agreed and continued, "I'm gonna go make a call to see if I can get any more information from the fellas that we sent to the other two locations when we were looking for Mel. Maybe they saw something that might be important? It's worth a shot."

While Bruce and Kate were moving heaven and earth to buy some time for Jelena back at the farm, they also didn't like just sitting there helplessly waiting for the phone call. Instead, Kate and Bruce began devising a plan and calling in favors to find out just where she was. Unfortunately, in the meantime, Jelena's world was once again trapped in darkness at the merciless hands of her captors.

SMACK

Jelena felt the percussion of the fisted-up knuckles forcefully bounding off her skull as her head snapped to one side.

"Just tell me why? Tell me why you kill her?" he said.

It was Vladomir Khishchnik, not only a notorious, upper-level KGB agent, known for his incredible, albeit brutal, interrogation skills, but also the man who had frequently been visiting Svetlana Petrov.

Jelena could barely bring her head up high enough to spit out a mouth full of blood onto the ground at Vladomir's feet. She looked around, trying to figure out just where she was. She knew it wasn't the barn where they found Mel Titan, but having never been to the other two suggested locations, she wasn't really sure. The large room was dark, but she could hear the echo from each blow she received. Either the acoustics in this room were great, or her brain had officially started moving around in her head like a marble in a jar.

She was tied to an office chair, her wrists, zip-tied to the arms of the chair, and her feet, crossed at the ankles and tied together. Even in this seated position, she felt incredibly off balance. Before her stood a shorter, older man in a black suit. She figured that this man must be Svetlana's lover. Although she had only seen his picture once in one of her briefing classes, she recognized the man as Vladomir Khishchnik. Mel Titan had described him perfectly in the letter on his Emergency Whiskey drive, but it wasn't until this moment that Jelena put the pieces together.

It was a bit warm in that room, and Vladomir's straight gray hair had become frazzled, making him look extraordinarily psychotic. His blue eyes were dark, and the whites of his eyes were red and continued to fill with tears throughout the beating he was dishing out onto Jelena's delicate flesh.

"I ASK YOU WHY, YOU FUCKING CUNT!" he screamed at her, as his hand came around again, so hard that his golden rose pinkie ring had caught a piece of Jelena's skin, leaving her with a small gash under her already swollen right eye.

Jelena remained silent, and while allowing the ringing in her head to subside, she also noticed three more men in the room watching her and speaking to each other in Russian. Even though she spoke nearly perfect Russian, with the loud monotone ringing in her head, she couldn't discern what they were saying. The windows were blacked out, and the only light in the room was a small desk lamp on a coffee table over in the corner.

She could smell the combinations of cigarette and cigar smoke, along with the body odor of her four captors. Vladomir, at this point, was sweating profusely, and with each strike that he lashed out, Jelena could feel droplets of his sweat splash onto her.

"FUCKING BITCH! SPEAK!" Vladomir screamed. "WHY SVETLANA?! WHYYYY?"

Vladomir was now insanely frustrated with Jelena's silence. He turned away from her and went to one of the other men in the room, where he retrieved something shiny. He approached Jelena again and pressed this item up against the side of her beaten face, on her right temple. She could feel the cold metal, almost soothing her madman-induced injuries. Her right eye was swollen shut, and she still couldn't see exactly what this 'item' was, but she was certain that it would only cause her more pain.

"FINE! You no speak... then I WILL BREAK YOU!" he yelled as he slipped on the set of brass knuckles. "You WILL speak!"

Jelena watched closely, with her left eye, as Vladomir flexed his hand into a fist, adjusting the brass knuckles, but a familiar fierceness came up within her as she thought to herself, *Yeah, I remember what happened the last time some dumb-ass man said that he would break me. We'll see Grandpa...we'll see.*

CRACK

With one blow, Jelena was back in the comfort of her own darkness and found herself in another memory of her father, Radomir, teaching her how to fight when she was about eight years old.

"Jelena... Get up!" he said firmly.

"Papa... I can't," Jelena moaned, beginning to cry. "I can't get up. It hurts."

Radomir stooped down next to his daughter and sat down on the mat with her, as he began to explain, "JellyGirl, winning a fight is not just about how many punches you can throw or how hard you can hit. If you cannot take a hit and recover, then you're all but dead, and you will certainly lose the fight. Winning is about how many times you continue to get up. Winning is about not giving up... not giving in... not quitting, even when every thread inside you wants to. Winning is not a thing, Jelena... it is an attitude... a mentality. Once you've decided, in your mind, to win... then there is no stopping you... but you have to first get up."

Pulling her back into her crappy reality, Jelena found herself dripping wet. The shitbag Russian had doused her with freezing water from a bucket. She couldn't help but make the association of that, with her last electrocution at the hands of Bruce, but she was quite relieved when she opened her eye and saw that, fortunately, there was no car battery around.

Jesus, Jelena, she thought. *Let's not give these fuckers any ideas!*

As she looked around again, she saw Vladomir now on his knees in front of her. His eyes filled with pain and sadness that tugged at her heartstrings.

"Please…" he begged, this time trying a new interrogation tactic. "Please tell me… why did you kill my Svetlana?"

It dawned on Jelena, at this very moment, that Mel Titan was right all along. The pair were not just co-workers but were truly in love.

"You loved her," Jelena said quietly in response to Vladomir's plea.

"Да… Yes… I did…" he said as he looked down, "but you took her away. Why?"

"How do you know that it was me?" she asked.

"Because… I saw you… I saw you put poison into her cup," he said, still trying to hold back the tears.

"Fuck, did you have cameras in there? How do you even know? If you had cameras, why didn't you come to save her??" Jelena asked, now getting a bit worked up herself.

"They weren't our fucking cameras, you idiot," he began. "They were yours! We hacked into them once man told us they were there. That was only useful information we got from him before he died. Pathetic and weak! You need tougher spies," he snipped.

Jelena sat there for a moment, processing what she had just learned, already knowing that there was not a good answer for what Vladomir wanted to know. The one thing that she did know, was that she saw poor Mel and knew exactly what kind of beating he must have taken. She knew he was anything but pathetic and weak. Again, getting upset over the image of Mel's body hanging in the barn, she quipped back with the very poorly timed sarcastic retort, "Be careful what you wish for, big boy."

"AAAAAHHHHHHH!" Vladomir screamed in frustration. He walked over to one of the other men and took his lit cigar from him, carefully blowing on the embers, causing them to glow brightly.

As he walked back over to Jelena's chair with the cigar in hand, he said, "Soon, girl…you will be begging to tell me everything."

He grabbed her hair and thrust her head forward, pressing her chin to her chest. Although she tried to brace herself for the next bout, she screamed in agony as he pressed the embers into the flesh at the nape of her neck. The last thing she remembered before her mind took over was the smell of her own burning flesh.

Her mind took Jelena to another memory of her mother, Charlotte, encouraging her.

"Aww, Jelly. I am so sorry that this didn't work out for you this time," Charlotte comforted as she held Jelena in a warm hug. Jelena had applied to enter a contest for a project that she had been working on for a very long time and had just received the news that she had not qualified to enter. At ten years of age, this was a travesty in her little world, and Jelena felt destroyed.

"JellyGirl, don't cry. You've been down before, and like always, you figure out a way to succeed. I know this was important to you, and I hate to see you this upset, sweetheart. I wish I could take away all the pain and frustration, but if we don't have these downs, then honey, we'll never learn how to get up. I love you, and your journey is gonna have a ton of ups and downs. This is not the end, Jelena. You write your own story, so if you don't like the way it's going... then write a new story."

Jelena's pain threshold had yet again been pushed beyond her consciousness, and she vaguely remembered someone moving her... lifting her like a sack of potatoes into a fireman's carry before being dropped into another dark hole.

SLAM

She remembered her time in solitary and a conversation with her new rat friend, Buddy. "I wonder if they'll ever let me out of this pit Buddy," she said quietly as she stroked his whiskery fur. "Maybe I'll just live here forever. Living on protein bars and water. Yum yum. I wonder if my parents miss me. I wonder if they have any idea, that I am stuck in this pit. Ohhh boy... my dad would be pissed. He was always a hard man to anger, Buddy, but once you did, you quickly remembered why that was never a good idea. They want to break me... ehh... maybe if that's what it takes to get out of here, then maybe I should just break... Naaa... my dad would be mad over that too. I can hear him, Buddy. I can hear his voice ringing in my ears... 'Jelena... Quitters never win, and winners never quit.' Do you have a family, Buddy? A little rat wife and little rat babies? Or are you Mr. Fly-Solo... Mr.

Heartbreaker? Fuck… Listen to me… I *am* losin' my shit in here. I am talking to a rat, and what's worse… I could swear that you understand."

Jelena was brought back to the present when she was jarred with a large familiar bump. She opened her eye and tried to futilely look around in the dark, at the very least, realizing that her wrists were tied in front of her, allowing her to feel around instead.

"Crappy rough carpet… plastic… metal… wires…" she whispered, just as she felt the impact of another bump and saw the lights come on. "Brake lights. I got it… You gotta be fucking kidding me! I am in a goddamned trunk. Can this fucking day possibly get any better? Hello… God… a little help here, please."

Jelena began to wrestle with the wires on the back of the brake light. She was hoping that she would have time to perhaps knock the light out and wave her hands, like she had seen in the movies, in hopes of getting the attention of another driver. Regrettably, just as soon as that thought came, it was squashed when the vehicle came to a stop.

"Shit!" she whispered. "A day late and a dollar short, I guess," she said as she heard the key go into the trunk lock. *Probably best to play a good old game of Possum,* she thought as she forced herself to go limp and closed her one good eye.

She felt the sunlight hit her body as the trunk lid opened. Now that the ringing in her head was gone, she could clearly hear the men speaking to each other in Russian, arguing over who would carry her the rest of the way and asking each other why they couldn't just beat her awake so that she could walk to her own damn grave.

As the man hoisted her up onto his shoulder, he exclaimed in Russian, "Damn, this bitch is heavy!"

Then the other one responded with something to the effect of, "Yeah, this one's not made of sugar and spice." They both chuckled at that notion. Jelena, on the other hand, took exceptional offense to that but reminded herself that her best plan right now was to keep her mouth shut.

She could feel them walking for what seemed to be forever, and every now and then, she managed to catch a glimpse of her surroundings. She saw their black sedan... and a man, who she presumed to be Vladomir, putting out a cigarette as he began following them. Jelena would sneak a peek every five or six steps, trying not to be obvious about it. She saw the grassy ground below and a building that looked familiar.

The farmhouse? she thought, as her carrier stopped to shift her weight.

She snuck another look, and besides noticing that Vladomir was catching up quickly, she also noticed the large red barn, not too far away, where they found Mel Titan hanging just hours earlier.

The old, abandoned McFarland Ranch. That's where I'm at, she thought, actually a bit proud that she had figured it out, especially while hanging upside down with only one working eye.

Seeing the red barn, Jelena's thoughts went directly to Adam. Where was he? What bullshit was he into? Is he still alive? Why didn't Bruce want her to know what had happened to him? Belle told her that he was still alive, and she even told her Adam's code name, but Jelena still didn't understand why she wasn't allowed to talk about these things. Shouldn't they all be on the same team? Don't they want as many allies as possible? So many questions ran through her mind that it almost made her forget how uncomfortable she felt while being slung over some asshole's shoulder, like her stomach was being pressed through her spine.

They finally came to a stop, and Jelena closed her eye as her carrier turned around to see Vladomir for further instruction.

"Put her in!" Vladomir ordered.

Jelena felt the man underneath her shift so that he could throw her down. What she didn't know, at least not until it was too late, was that he threw her right into a coffin-sized wooden box.

As she landed hard into the box, she hit her elbow on one of the edges, with a good enough force to cause her to howl in pain. "Aahhh!" she exclaimed. *Fuck! Guess the jig's up,* she thought as the men looked at her, seeing that she was now wide awake.

"You see this, girl?" Vladomir asked.

Jelena looked around to see herself in another wooden box but quickly noticed that this one had no holes. She sighed and rolled her one good eye in response to this shittier turn of events. As she refocused on Vladomir, she decided it was still a better idea to maintain her silence. She sat there in her box, on her ass, looking up at him, as he was looking down on her. She could see the pain in his face, and perhaps she felt a tiny bit like she deserved her fate for killing Svetlana.

"This, girl, is your grave. I am not going to kill you… but you are going to die. You are going to pay for what you did to my Svetlana. You are going to die slow… and alone," he said with a sadistically calm voice, appearing totally unbothered by the notion of burying Jelena alive.

Jelena suppressed every urge she had to fight back. Every urge to not be in another fucking wooden box, but again, she knew she was outnumbered and that there was no conceivable way to get herself out of this at this point. She knew she was going into the box. She could only hope that Bruce and Kate would find her before it was too late. Mel Titan wasn't so lucky. All Jelena could do was pray, remain calm, and hope that she had better luck than good ole' Mel.

"Okay," Jelena said as she laid down into the box without protest.

Vladomir was stunned and shocked by her submission. "Seal it up and bury her," he ordered his men.

As the men began to hammer on the lid to the coffin, the only thing that Jelena could think to do was squeeze the locking mechanism of the zip tie holding her wrists together under the lip of the coffin. Hopefully, it would hold the tie tightly so that she could break it and at least free her hands once they were gone.

The hammering stopped, and she could hear the men grunt as they lifted the box and put it down in the hole that they had dug in the pasture. She could feel her heartbeat quicken as she heard the sound of the dirt falling into the cracks as they buried her alive.

Knowing that her air was in short supply, she did everything possible to keep herself calm and focused her mind on altering her breathing to a slow, shallow rate. As she did this, she began memory diving, swimming through another memory of her mother and father. This was a memory that she wasn't even aware that she remembered and was truly surprised to find herself there.

She was maybe around two years old, in the hospital. She remembered her mother's panicked and teary face looking down on her as her little body struggled to breathe. Jelena had been diagnosed with a rare condition called Epiglottitis. It was caused by a virus and made the flap in the back of her throat swell up, closing off her trachea.

"JellyGirl! Please!" her mother pleaded. "Fight! You have to fight this! Please! Don't give up!"

She remembered her mother sobbing into her hands while her father tried to comfort her. Radomir said, "Charlotte, my love, she is like you... she is a fighter! If we don't give up, then she won't give up either."

Jelena chimed back into reality and realized just how little air she had. She could feel herself struggle for each shallow breath, becoming more and more concerned that she actually *may* end up no better off than Mel Titan.

CHAPTER 15: FINDERS KEEPERS

Once the shoveling sounds stopped, all Jelena could hear was the tiny pieces of dirt and rock shifting down on top of her. The plan to pinch the zip-tie in the coffin's lid worked, and in one thrusting motion down, Jelena freed her hands. It didn't really help her bigger problem of 'being stuck in a dark coffin buried alive,' but it did give her just a little comfort. At least the illusion was present that freeing her hands gave her more options for a potential escape... even if it wasn't entirely true.

Jelena slipped in and out of consciousness. Every time she passed out, she would dive into more dreams and memories. She found herself inside a memory that had almost nothing to do with her family... she was at boot camp at the Marine Corps Recruit Depot in Parris Island, South Carolina. They were all running an obstacle course. Jelena came to one obstacle that sort of looked like a ⊥-bar. One bar went across horizontally, and then another joined vertically, like the bottom leg of an upside down T. Only, in this challenge, the leg wasn't straight. It was at a very steep incline. As tall as Jelena was, it was much harder to get her legs to swing up over her head to cross over that inclined bar. She tried and failed, and then tried and failed again, but she refused to give up.

"Move along, recruit!" the drill instructor yelled.

"No, ma'am," Jelena said. "This recruit can do this!"

Again and again, Jelena jumped onto the horizontal bar and swung and fell. Over and over.

"I SAID... MOVE ALONG RECRUIT!" the drill instructor yelled louder at Jelena.

"NO, ma'am," Jelena said, defending her refusal to not quit. "This recruit will NOT quit or move along until this recruit successfully completes this obstacle, ma'am!"

At this point, Jelena had rubbed most of the skin off of her palms, and her fingers had become pretty bloody, but Jelena refused to quit. She waited for the next line of recruits to complete the task and move on. She watched intently how they worked the mechanics of their bodies to successfully get over it. She stood to the side, and once the last recruit passed, she went up to do it again.

"You got one more fucking chance, recruit, before I kick your ass out of here myself!" the drill instructor said.

"Aye, aye, ma'am!" Jelena responded. "This recruit just needs one more chance!"

Jelena stood there and looked up at the bar. She took a deep breath and a huge leap. Her sore and bloody hands grasped the bar, and with all her might, she swung her body as hard as she could. This time, her legs hooked around the inclined part of the bar, and she successfully made it past that challenge. As she jumped down, she looked down at her hands. They were raw and bloody. She looked up at the obstacle she had just passed and saw the bloody handprints she had left behind. She turned around, and right there in her face was her drill instructor, looking more irritated and cranky than normal. Jelena, expecting to be the receiver of the wrathful raging screams, was bracing for impact, but then the drill instructor's facial expression softened as she cracked a smile.

"Way to go, recruit! That took heart! Go see the medic about those hands!" the drill instructor ordered.

"Aye, aye, Drill Instructor!" Jelena responded. Bearing was important, but Jelena couldn't help but smile and walk away feeling so proud that she didn't quit, even when ordered to.

As Jelena came out of her memory, she found herself still facing what seemed like another impossible obstacle. How in the hell is she going to get out of this stupid box this time? She felt around the inside of the box, again searching for nooks and crannies to exploit. She remembered that she was not trapped in water this time but dirt. Even if she did get through the box, how would she move so many pounds of dirt on top of her? She couldn't let this prevent her from trying to execute any manner of escape. She punched, clawed, and tried to move in any way she could, but that box just wasn't budging.

"Damn! Did those assholes glue this shit shut?" she whispered in the dark. The longer she was in there, the more difficult breathing was becoming. Between bouts of consciousness, Jelena contemplated two things... praying for life... or praying for death.

Back at the old paper mill, the two men that had buried Jelena got out of their car, and they walked right into a sticky situation of their own.

As they entered the large room, where Jelena had been held, they saw Bruce and Kate, who decided that doing a little research of their own, was better than waiting on a phone call that may or may not ever happen. Earlier, when Bruce talked to the two agents that were sent to this papermill, to look for Mel Titan, the men reported that they saw other signs of recent activity. They found Russian notes left on the table by the lamp, an ashtray full of cigarette and cigar ashes, and footprints in the layer of dust on the floor. Even though no one was there when they showed up, all these things indicated that someone had been hanging out there quite recently. This was enough of a tip off to point both, Bruce and Kate, in the right direction.

When Bruce and Kate arrived, they confronted the one man who stayed behind to guard the mill and waited for Vladomir and the other two men to show up. As soon as the two men came through the door, Bruce waved at them and shouted a loud and sarcastic, "Hey how's it goin'?" while keeping his gun pointed at the third man. When the two realized what was going on, they immediately drew their weapons.

"Who fuck are you?" asked the larger Russian man.

"WE'RE THE FUCKING NEIGHBORS!" Bruce yelled. "Now, where the fuck is she?"

"She?" he replied, with a Russian accent so thick that it made his words hard to understand. He shrugged his shoulders, lit a cigarette, and said, "I not know she." He cocked a mocking half-smile back at his comrades as he took a long drag and slowly exhaled.

"Okay, boys. Let's try something a little different. So, which one of you fuckers is Vladomir Khishchnik?" Bruce continued. "We have a meeting."

"I am Vladomir," one man said, raising his hand smoothly.

"No, No... I am Vladomir," said the second, as he lit his own cigarette.

"No, *I* am the real Vladomir Khishchnik," said the third, as he smiled back at the other two.

"Well, Kate... all these Vladomirs and so little time," Bruce quipped as he looked back at her.

Bruce swiftly swung his gun in the direction of the two men as Kate made a move for the third, who was much closer to her. The shooting began, and Bruce dove down on the ground, pushing the coffee table onto its side to use it more as concealment rather than cover, as he continued to fire in their direction. Kate grabbed the man closest to her and, with all her body weight, used him as a human shield. As he fell, she grabbed his gun, flung herself down onto the ground, and focused her attention on the other men across the room, now crouched down near the exit.

Once the men realized they had shot and killed their friend, the firing stopped momentarily.

Bruce seized the opportunity to challenge the larger, chattier of the two remaining men.

"Hey, we aren't monsters. We aren't cowards either... How about we handle this knuckle to knuckle... like men?" he yelled as he threw his gun on the floor.

"BRUCE!" Kate squawked. "Now ain't exactly the best damned time for a pissin' contest, son."

"Like men?" the man responded.

"Yes... like men," Bruce confirmed.

The man thought about it for a second and threw down his weapon as well, causing his comrade to look at him with the same level of disgust and confusion, matching Kate's.

"Sweet fuckin Jesus!" scoffed Kate under her breath.

Bruce charged at the man, clotheslining him in the first run. Both men scrambled and rolled around, wrestling on the floor until they broke free from each other's grasp. Bruce backed up and, with a great force, whipped around and made facial contact with a spinning roundhouse kick, knocking the man back, a good two or three feet. Bruce kicked him repeatedly until the man fell onto the floor. He climbed on top of the man, straddled him, and began punching him in the face.

With each blow that Bruce released, he emphasized one word at a time, "NOW... (WHACK)... WHERE... (WHACK)... IS... (WHACK)... SHE... (WHACK)?

The man raised his hands in a manner of surrender, as he suspected that Bruce was only getting warmed up. When he did this, Bruce stopped hitting him long enough for him to say, "Мертвый... dead."

Bruce grabbed him up by the collar around his neck, and as he shook him, he also slammed his head down hard onto the floor. Bruce screamed, "WHAT THE FUCK DO YOU MEAN SHE IS DEAD? WHERE IS SHE, YOU FUCKING LYING PIECE OF SHIT!"

This entire time, Kate kept her gun pointed at the one man who was still crouching down, pointing his gun at her. He was visibly dazed and confused at the situation and obviously quite intimidated by Bruce's inner demons. It was rather apparent that he was seriously considering making a run for it to save his own life.

"I don't have time for this bullshit!" Bruce exclaimed as he snatched up the half-conscious man and dragged him to the door. "Let's go, Kate!"

Kate got up from her position and walked over toward the door, where the other man was still crouching.

"Sorry, darlin', nothin' personal," she said softly with a sweet smile as she pulled the trigger, putting a single round right between his eyes.

"DAMN IT, KATE!" Bruce started, looking back at the man she had just shot. "You are one icy bitch!"

"You watch your mouth, mister. I ain't in the mood today," she scoffed back.

Bruce continued to drag the man to the car, showing no more effort than a child carrying a rag doll. He opened the back seat and shoved the man in first, following in close behind him.

"Here," he said, chucking Kate the keys. "You drive. My little Russian helper here is gonna help us find her."

Kate started the car, turned around in her seat, and while looking the man dead in the eyes, she said, "Now mister, I already done put a bullet in your friend's head, and I got plenty more bullets left in this here gun. You got about two shakes to tell me exactly where I'm drivin' this car to."

Just as she finished her sentence, she raised her eyebrows, expecting a response, but the man remained silent. Bruce grabbed him around the throat and gave him another little shake to loosen his tongue. "She asked you for some fucking directions, asshole! Don't be rude!" Bruce demanded.

"Farm... at the farm... with cows," he replied.

"I know where I'm goin'... I think," Kate said. "I was a little groggy earlier thanks to Mel's whiskey, but I think I got it."

"Whiskey? What the fuck did you two get into?" Bruce asked.

"Bruce, honey, now ain't the time for nitpickin'," Kate pressed. "We need to find Jelena!"

Kate drove the three of them back out to the old, abandoned McFarland Ranch. When they pulled up, both of them looked at the Russian, expecting him to point or indicate where Jelena was being held. Then man merely looked back at them with the dumbest expression possible and shrugged his shoulders.

"WHERE?!" Bruce demanded. "Where in the fucking hell is she? I swear to God I will beat the ever-loving shit out of your fucking carcass! NOW! Where is she!?!?"

The man pointed to the pasture and repeated, "With cows! I swear... with cows!"

Kate drove over the grassy land like she was driving a Hum-Vee on a safari while both her and Bruce were looking for fresh patches of turned-up ground. As soon as Kate found the spot, she slammed on the brakes, causing the car to slide on the grass until it came to a complete stop.

Kate jumped out of the car, followed by Bruce dragging the Russian. On the ground was a perfect eight-foot by four-foot patch of bright black soil, the only sign for miles that indicated Jelena's location and possible demise.

Bruce's heart sank as he had no idea how long she had been buried and was truly not expecting to find her alive. He kept telling himself, "She is the girl who survived the box... the girl who survived the box... she's alive... I *know* that she is alive... She *has* to be..."

He dragged the Russian to the trunk and popped it open. He grabbed the shovel, and without a second of hesitation, he struck the Russian in the head with the metal tip, knocking him out. He ran to the patch of ground and began digging as if his own life depended on it.

Kate ran to a nearby stack of hay, where she remembered seeing some farming tool earlier. It was a hoe, not much for digging, but Kate snatched it up anyways and ran to join Bruce. She and Bruce feverishly dug and moved the black soil as fast as possible.

The shovel finally made a thudding sound as it struck the wood of Jelena's coffin.

"FUCK! We got it!" Bruce exclaimed as the two of them continued to dig.

Bruce jumped down into the hole and tried to free the lid with his shovel and bare hands.

"I CAN'T GET IT, KATE! FUUUUCKKKK!" he screamed, as he used every bit of force he could muster.

"Hold on there, Bruce, I think I got an idea," Kate said as she ran back to the car, hopping over the unconscious Russian.

Kate dug through the trunk and found a good-sized length of thick rope. She backed the car up to the hole and threw Bruce the rope to tie around Jelena's tomb.

"HOLLER WHEN YOU GET 'ER TIED TIGHT!" Kate yelled out.

Bruce fought and struggled to get the rope around the center of the wooden box. As he worked the rope into position, his hands were shaking so badly that he could barely tie the knots to secure it.

"ALRIGHT, KATE! I GOT IT! GO!" Bruce yelled back.

Kate stepped on the gas gently and began to pull the wooden box out of the hole. As soon as it was on level ground, Bruce flipped it on its side and began hammering at the side of the box as hard as he could with his shovel.

"COME ON FUCKER! BREAK, YOU SON OF A BITCH!" he yelled as he continued to strike the container.

Fatigued, he paused for a moment to wipe the sweat out of his eyes. During that moment, he felt a sting in his hands and realized that his efforts had rubbed the skin off parts of his palms.

"Here, let me try for a bit," Kate said, taking the shovel and beginning to pound on the box herself with everything she had.

"NOOOO, GOD DAMN IT!" Bruce yelled in frustration as he took the shovel back from Kate and continued to drive the shovel down onto the box like a sledgehammer. Come hell or high water. He was going to bust this thing open. He only hoped that he had made it in time.

CRACK

SNAP

The wooden lid finally gave way and broke, allowing a battered, bloody, limp Jelena to roll out, unconscious. She had managed to free her hands, and based on the ripped fingernails and bloody knuckles, she appeared to have tried to claw and punch her way out as she realized that she was out of air.

Bruce hurriedly knelt beside her and pressed his ear against her chest.

"Fuck, Kate! I don't think she's breathing... I don't hear anything," he said softly.

"MOVE!" Kate yelled as she assumed a similar position to try to listen for a heartbeat or any kind of breathing sounds.

"Well??" Bruce asked impatiently.

"SHUT UP! I CAN'T HEAR!" Kate snipped back at him.

That minute seemed to be the longest minute that Bruce had experienced in a good long while.

"Holy, shit…" Kate said. "It's faint… real faint… but I am choosin' to believe that she's still alive… barely. Bruce let's go. We gotta get her back to the farm… She ain't dead yet!" Kate insisted. "You hear that, Jelena? You ain't dead yet, girl!

Kate sat in the backseat as Bruce gently laid Jelena on her lap. He then dragged the Russian to the hole, dumped him in it, drew his sidearm, and fired a single shot into his head before running back to the car. He Jumped in the car, peeled out and made a phone call.

"Hey, it's me… 6831 Lima. Yeah, we found 518 Papa. It's critical. We're comin' in hot and we need a trauma team in position. Also, we need the clean up crew back out at McFarland's Ranch, in the back forty. Yeah, they need to bring towels back out. Thanks man."

It was a long, racing drive back to the farm, filled with nothing but silent dread.

"Bruce, honey," Kate said as she gently brushed the hair out of Jelena's facial wounds. "This ain't lookin' so good. Can't you please go any faster? Jelena girl, You gotta fight! Don't you go quittin' on me now!"

Bruce floored it and kept it pegged at well over one hundred miles per hour back to the farm hospital. When they pulled in, a team was already waiting to put Jelena on a gurney and take her inside for treatment. Bruce and Kate stood by the car, and once again, all they could do was stand there helplessly and watch as Jelena was wheeled into the hospital.

The hospital waiting area was composed of the same tan walls and floors as the main buildings and had several beige plastic chairs spaced out in the small waiting area. Kate was quietly sitting, with her elbows on her knees and her face in her palms. On the other hand, Bruce was pacing back and forth, like a wild agitated animal, just waiting for someone to come and give him an update. Periodically he would peek through the small windows of the large metal doors.

Dr. Simms came in, and Bruce raced straight for him as Kate stood up from her chair.

"Doc, what's up? Is she okay?" Bruce asked him, still in his frenzied state.

"I'm sorry. We are doing everything that we can for her right now. Her oxygen levels are critically low at seventy-four percent. That's the lowest we have *ever* seen. The lowest, non-fatal percent has been recorded at eighty. This isn't looking good. The last time that she came here, she was at eighty-one percent, and that was hard enough to bring her back," Dr. Simms explained.

"Doc, come on... you gotta be able to do something. You gotta bring her back," Bruce pleaded.

Dr. Simms continued, "Go home... Get some sleep... You both need to prepare yourselves for the worst. She may just not come around this time. She came in here, technically dead. Right now, she's on all kinds of life support, IV fluids, a breathing vent, and we're putting her back into the hyperbaric chamber soon. Unfortunately, right now, she is not showing any good neurological response. Her brain may have just been deprived of oxygen for too long this time. We're trying every trick in the book that we can think of to bring her back. That's all we can do. The rest, I'm afraid, is up to her; but statistically speaking, I wouldn't get your hopes up. I'm sorry, guys... but you may have to make the hard decision to put this one down."

Bruce and Kate just looked at each other. As hard and icy as Kate had become over the years, the idea of having to 'put Jelena down' brought tears to her eyes. "I know that I am not supposed to get attached to anyone, Bruce, but I really thought that Jelena was different... I never thought... you know..."

"I know Kate... I know..." Bruce said as he pulled Kate in for a hug. "You should go home and get some rest... we both should.

CHAPTER 16: BRUCE AND THE MONSTER

Hours later, Dr. Simms passed through the waiting area with a cup of coffee and saw Bruce still sitting in one of the tan plastic chairs.

"Not going home, huh?" he asked.

"No... I can't," he replied.

"Well, come on then, there is a doctors' lounge with a couch around the corner. It doesn't look like much, but it sleeps good," Dr. Simms said empathetically.

"Thanks, man," Bruce replied as he got up from his seat and followed Dr. Simms to the lounge.

As they walked through the hospital hallways, Dr. Simms continued the conversation and said, "You know her coming back is a long shot... right? I mean, even if she comes back, the chances of her not having lasting brain impairment this time are slim to none."

"I know," Bruce started. "But I can't think like that. I *have* to believe that she can pull through this. None of us thought she would make it out of the first box... but she did. It was amazing, and somehow, she did. She is special, and I **have** to believe that she'll be okay."

"Damn, son, with all the potentials that you have put in this hospital yourself, I have never seen you get so worked up over one. What is it with her? You guys got something going on?" Dr. Simms said. "Wait! You aren't involved with her personally, are you?"

Bruce shot him a stern look as he let out a resounding, "No, not even close. Our relationship is nothing more than professional. I... I, uhh... I just know how much our team needs her. She can do things that no one else can do. She thinks differently. This agency **needs** Jelena Prazich to pull through."

"Uh-huh, okay," he said as he entered the door code and opened the door to the lounge for Bruce.

Bruce entered the shabby doctors' lounge. Simms was right. It certainly didn't look like much. There were plain tan cabinets, a counter with a sink, and at the end of the counter was a coffee machine with an 'Out of Order' sign stuck to it with some scotch tape. There was a circular cafeteria table in the center of the room with a few chairs sporadically placed around it. On the other side of the room were tall, tan wall lockers with different initials on each one, and in the corner, next to a potted palm, was a brown leather, beat-up couch.

Bruce sat down on the couch. He ran his hands through his hair and then looked at his fingertips, the nails still filled with dirt from digging Jelena out of her premature grave. His palms were still missing skin, showing bright pink, inflamed patches. From his seat on the couch, he could see his reflection in the long mirror by the door. He looked tired and old. His face hadn't seen a razor in over twenty-four hours, giving him a dirty and disheveled appearance. He noticed the small blood stains on his shirt and wondered which ones were from Jelena and which ones were from the Russians that he had tangled with.

As he laid back onto the soft leather, he could feel himself sink into it. His mind ran wild with the recent events, and he kept asking himself the same type of questions that Dr. Simms had asked him only minutes ago. Why her? Why did he care so much? Why was he there and not cleaned up and at the office? Why did he feel so attached to Jelena when she was supposed to be nothing more than just another asset?

No sooner than he was able to quiet his mind and fall asleep, the lounge door opened. It was Dr. Simms. Bruce sat up, not looking or smelling a whole lot better than he did before, but at least he was able to get a little sleep.

"Hey, we are moving her out of the hyperbaric chamber into a private room," he said.

Bruce got up and headed over to follow him, as Dr. Simms backed up a bit and said, "How about this? There's a shower in the bathroom and some clean scrubs in the cabinet. How about you clean up a bit... and I'll come back in about twenty minutes and get you once we get her settled in. Okay?"

"Alright," Bruce said, sniffing himself and realizing that was probably a good idea.

Punctuality was a must around there, and twenty minutes later, as promised, Dr. Simms appeared in the lounge doorway. "Ready?" he asked Bruce.

"Yes, sir. Much better," Bruce replied as he followed him out the door and down the hall.

"Now, you need to brace yourself. She's in an induced coma. She's still on a breathing vent and hooked up to stuff. She took a beating worse than you, so she's looking pretty rough... Remember... she was technically dead. We treated a severe burn to the back of her neck. She'll have a scar but nothing extreme. There were also some cuts and burns on her wrists and ankles and some large wood splinters in her hands that we removed. Surprisingly enough, she didn't have any fractures in her face other than a broken nose. She has some outline of something on her right temple... I would guess brass knuckles based on the shape. We put some stitches in to close a small facial lac, and we also reset the nose already, so if she comes around, she should heal up nicely. Okay, so she is in room one-o-one, down this hall, and on the right," he explained.

"Thanks, Doc," Bruce said, heading in that direction.

Dr. Simms was not wrong about anything. Jelena didn't even look alive. Her skin was whiter and pastier than Bruce had ever seen it and was covered with so much damage. Her right eye was still much more swollen than her left, although her left also showed evidence of a horrific beating. As he brushed the hair to the side of her face, he saw the outline that Dr. Simms was talking about. It clearly outlined a set of brass knuckles. He gently ran his finger across the small line of stitches under her right eye and saw that her lip was again showing a split in the same spot as before. He sat down in a chair next to her and took her bandaged hand in his own. Her fingertips were cool to the touch, and he felt no tension in her arm whatsoever. His heart sank as he pressed her hand against his cheek, suddenly realizing that he was doing something he didn't even know he could do... he was crying.

Bruce did not attempt to fight his emotions, which was another new experience. He was a 'tough guy,' and stoicism, like Jelena, was his most powerful tool. But not with her... not here... so, he sat there and let himself cry, for the first time in his life, after the murder of his mother, he felt something.

Bruce did not leave Jelena's room for days. He paced, he sat, he yelled, he begged, he asked himself the questions that he couldn't make sense of, over and over again. The staff was nice and brought him a cot to sleep next to her. It was really the only thing to do since he was refusing to leave, and when a 6'6 burly man who can kill you in eighteen ways in three seconds refuses to do something, there is really nothing anyone can do to make him.

Every morning he would wake up, hoping to find her alert and looking at him with the same level of disdain that she normally did... and every morning, there she would be... still on a vent... unchanged... lifeless.

After all this time, he still couldn't explain the strong connection that he felt to her.

"Why? Why her? This is fucking ridiculous!" he said to himself as he continued to pace in her room, looking out the window and listening to the rhythmic pumping sound of the breathing machine.

"Jelena... You salty fuckin' bitch... what the fuck is this hold you have on me? Why in the fuck do I care? You hate me. You should hate me. Why can't I walk away from you? God DAMN, this is frustrating? That's it... I'm out... I'll uhhh see you later... if you can wake your bitchy ass up...

whatever…" Bruce ranted as he walked to the door to leave.

Just as he grabbed the handle, he stopped. He turned to face her as he screamed, "AAAAaaHHHHhhHH!" knowing that he couldn't leave her for a reason that he was not ready to admit to himself… yet.

He walked over to Jelena, and in the heat of his madness, he grabbed her by the shoulders and shook her. "GODDAMN IT, YOU SALTY FUCKING BITCH! WAKE THE FUCK UP! WAKE UP, JELENA! FIGHT! YOU GOTTA FIGHT THIS! YOU LIAR! YOU SAID NO MAN COULD BREAK YOU!" he screamed.

The door flew open, and it was Dr. Simms, who rushed over and put his hands on each of Bruce's shoulders to stop him from shaking her. "Hey… Hey hey… That's not gonna work man. I know you want her back. Come on, let's go get a cup of coffee and take a walk. You need to get some air."

As Bruce and Dr. Simms walked out of Jelena's room, Kate walked up to them and asked, "Any change, Doc?"

"No. I'm sorry, Kate, but feel free to sit with her for a bit. I gotta take this one out for some air," Dr. Simms replied with Bruce by his side.

Kate walked into Jelena's room with a bouquet of bright yellow and white daisies.

"Here, darlin'. I brought these for ya. They're from Svetlana's garden. I thought you'd get a hoot outta that," Kate said, half expecting a response from Jelena, even though she still had a breathing tube.

Kate sat down next to her and continued, "Well, Jelena, I feel like I owe ya an apology there, sweetheart. I feel like I done gone and let ya down. I shouldn't have let ya walk that day. I... I kinda feel like if I hadn't... well... that you'd be okay. You wouldn't be here... like this. So, honey... I'm so sorry. I'm sorry that I didn't look out for ya better. I'm sorry that I let you walk. It's just that... I forget sometimes. You're s'damn good at this that I forget that you're a brand-spankin' new asset... that's no excuse. Darlin', I really hope that you can find it in your heart to forgive me. I promise that I'll do better next time."

Kate picked up Jelena's hand and just held it. She looked around the room, sadly trying to accept the fact that she may be saying goodbye to Jelena sooner than she'd like.

"You know there, darlin'. We still have to have that conversation about you slippin' off to do a little ole' B&E back at that there flower shop... not to mention the whiskey. I can't believe that ya got me all tipsy... while we're tryin' to take a walk," Kate said to her lifeless prodigy.

Not wanting to give up and deciding to change tactics a bit, Kate continued to hold her hand and said, "Alright. Now that's about enough of that shit. Honey... you're gonna **have** to fight this... You're gonna **HAVE** to fight this harder than you've done fought anything in your entire damned life. You've just GOT to come back to us, honey! We need ya! I didn't tell Bruce this but, I think we done killed the wrong Russians. I heard that Vladomir is still alive. We thought that he was one of the three we found at the paper mill, but I just got word this mornin' that he wasn't one of 'em, and he's been spotted back in Moscow somehow. Bruce hasn't left your side for the past seven days since you got in here, so he's kinda in the dark, but honey... Vladomir is **alive**... we need your help more than ever. Damn it to hell, Jelena..."

"Come on, honey..." Kate sighed. "If you're hearin' any of this... anythin' at all... just squeeze my fingers... okay? That's all ya gotta do... just squeeze my fingers."

Nothing... Kate had never felt so defeated in her life. She let out a big sigh, and just as she was about to completely give up, she felt something else. A twitch. She shot her attention right back to Jelena's bandaged hand and watched with extreme anticipation. It happened again, it was faint, but Jelena had tried to squeeze Kate's hand.

Kate shot straight up out of her chair and bolted right out of the room, screaming for Dr. Simms and Bruce as she flew through the hospital hallways. She busted around the corner and ran right into them.

"Dr. Bruce! Simms!" she exclaimed. "I mean, Dr. Simms... Bruce... whatever... she did it! Jelena squeezed my finger... she's there! Come'on! Right now!" Kate hollered as all three of them took off and ran down the corridor and through Jelena's door.

"Okay... wait... watch this," Kate said excitedly.

"I'm back, darlin'. It's me, Kate. Everybody's here now. Bruce... and Dr. Simms... So, I'm gonna need you to do that thing again, okay? Here's my hand. I just need you to squeeze my fingers. Okay, sweetheart. Just show everybody that you're still in there and that you're fightin'... come'on, girl. Squeeze 'em," Kate pleaded.

All three watched Jelena's hand and waited for the slightest movement indicating her mental presence.

She did it again.

"Shit!" Kate shrieked. "She did it! Did you see? She did it! Come on, darlin', one more time! JELENA! SQUEEZE 'EM!"

This time Jelena squeezed and held it for a few moments longer, proving that she was inside her shell and that she could hear what they were asking.

"Oh my God!" Dr. Simms exclaimed as he pressed the large red button next to the door. "Step aside, please… step aside."

Five more medical staff members bustled into the room as Bruce and Kate stayed tucked into the corner, watching them do all kinds of little tests on Jelena.

"She's got a solid Babinski reflex," one of the men said as they scraped the sole of her foot.

"Good pupillary response," said another as he looked into her eyes with a small pen flashlight.

"One-seventeen over seventy-nine, a resting heart rate of sixty-nine strong," began the nurse, "and her oxygen reading is up to ninety-seven percent, Doctor."

"Okay, everyone, let's take the tube out and see if she can go on her own, shall we?" Dr. Simms said as he began to take the tube out of

Jelena's airway. They removed the tube and waited in painful silence to see if Jelena could start breathing independently.

The nurse kept her stethoscope pressed to Jelena's chest and watched her stats on the monitor. "Respiratory rate is dropping, doctor," she said. "Nineteen… seventeen… fourteen… twelve… Doctor, I think we need to re-intabate," she said, beginning to sound concerned.

"WAIT!" said Dr. Simms. "Give her body a minute to respond and remember."

"Ten… DOCTOR! She's going down…" the nurse insisted.

"I SAID WAIT!" he yelled.

"Nine…" the nurse said, shaking her head.

Finally, to break the silence was the beautiful sound of Jelena taking a huge deep breath.

"HAAAA! HOLY SHIT!" Dr. Simms exclaimed excitedly.

"Levels are going back up, Doctor," the nurse said smiling. "Thirteen… fifteen… eighteen… respiratory rate stabilizing… she's breathing on her own, doctor.

"HOT DAMN!" exclaimed Kate. "I KNEW SHE WOULD!"

Kate turned to Bruce and hugged him tight, and all he could do was hug her right back.

"I knew too, Kate," Bruce began. "I knew she was still in there… the infamous 518 Papa… the girl who survived the box… TWICE now."

"Hold on, you two. Let's not get ahead of ourselves. She's not out of the woods yet. She may not even know who you are or be able to come around fully. She needs more time," Dr. Simms said sternly.

"How much more time?" Bruce asked eagerly.

"Listen, like I told you from the beginning," he began, "however long it takes, is however long it takes. It's not up to you… or me. It is up to Jelena and how her body heals. She's made progress that, so far, has me stumped. I am absolutely amazed that she is even breathing on her own and is showing a good neurological response. Things are better than expected. Still… you have to be patient. I know that patience is not a virtue of the good old CIA, but there is no way to rush this. Someone will be in about every hour to check her stats and monitor any improvements. Stay with her as long as you both want. Maybe that was the thing that brought her back. Who knows? I'll be back later."

Dr. Simms left the room as Bruce and Kate sat on both sides of Jelena, just quietly watching as her chest rose and fell on her own accord.

"Atta girl, darlin'," Kate whispered as she stroked the bruised side of Jelena's face. "I knew you could do it. We just need you to keep pushing through it… come on back to us, girl."

Bruce picked up Jelena's hand and held it. "Hey, it's me… Satan… you know you wanna be my friend," he said sarcastically, taunting her to try to get a response. "HEY THERE!" he exclaimed as she squeezed his hand in protest. "I knew you were still in there. Damn it, I KNEW it! We got 'em,

Jelena. We killed every single one of them. Kate shot one right between the eyes. I threw one in the hole they buried you in, and I shot him. I gotcha, girl. We're here... Kate and I... we're both here."

Jelena mustered every bit of strength and squeezed both of their hands, showing them that she was not done with her fight.

Throughout this trauma, Jelena's mind had not left her, but instead continued to swim through her subconsciousness, keeping her alive. She found herself remembering a combination of things... one recent combined with one from her childhood. She replayed her interactions with Svetlana... how she tricked her into believing that she was only there to buy pies for her family. How she had looked at Kate with confusion as she slipped the poison into Svetlana's teacup and how she calmly handed it to Svetlana, knowing down deep that it couldn't be a good thing, but not having the time to truly process the end result.

She remembered as a child when she was crying because she was afraid of the 'monsters' under her bed. Her mother, Charlotte, had come to comfort her, telling her that 'monsters' were not real. They were just figments of our imaginations that we didn't understand, and it was that lack of understanding that caused the fear inside.

Jelena remembered her mother getting frustrated with her as she continued to cry and how her mother asked her father, Radomir, to come in and try to soothe her.

Radomir came into her room and sat down next to her. "Come here, JellyGirl," Radomir said, pulling Jelena onto his lap and holding her tightly. "Your mother says that you are afraid of monsters. Is that true?" he asked.

"Yes, Papa. They live under my bed and in my closet, and they look scary and mean," she said through the sobs.

"Jelena, I have something to tell you. I need you to listen carefully, okay?" he said, looking down into her teary eyes. "Monsters *are* real. But they don't live under beds or in closets. The worst monsters on Earth look just like you and me. They blend in with all the other people here. They are not nice and they hurt people, but the scariest thing about them, JellyGirl, is that they don't carry signs saying that they are a monster. They trick people into believing that they are just like them and don't have any bad intentions. A real monster is a trickster that will make you believe that you are safe with them, and then when your guard is down, they try to hurt or kill you. That is a monster. Now… do you think I could fit under your bed? or in your closet?" he asked in a soft and soothing tone.

"No, Papa. You're too big to fit," she replied, now much calmer than before.

"Okay then, so no monsters can fit under your bed or in your closet. Just remember that. I love you, Jelly. Your mother and I love you with Agape… God's unconditional love… and that love will protect you like a shield… no matter what. Now… you need to go to sleep and dream of beautiful things," he said, as he pulled her in for one final tight hug before tucking her back into her bed.

Jelena couldn't help but make the association between how her father had described monsters and her act of killing Svetlana. Even though she wasn't a big fan of Vladomir, she couldn't help but feel heartache over how much pain she had caused him by killing her. She didn't think about these things when she agreed to work for the CIA. Her mind continued to circle one particular question... that question was the epiphany that brought Jelena back into real-time, 'Was she, herself, one of the monsters that her father had described?'

CHAPTER 17: THE FORBIDDEN FRUIT

For days Bruce stayed in Jelena's room, by her side, watching as the medical staff did their daily ballet around her. Noting down the numbers on her monitors and changing sheets, etc. Kate would also come by every day or two with flowers and to just sit. Kate knew that this was not good for Bruce, but all she could do was sit by and watch as he sucked himself in deeper.

Bruce would not leave Jelena for any reason, not even to go get something to eat. The nurses saw this and began bringing him a food tray at the appropriate mealtimes. He just stayed in that room... sitting, pacing, or just staring out the window, talking to himself or Jelena.

"Why aren't you awake yet?" he asked her. "You're able to breathe on your own now. Why can't you just wake up?"

Bruce was only nineteen when his mother was murdered in the subway near where they lived. She was a waitress at a local coffee shop and was on her way home from work one night. She was just in the wrong place at the wrong time when a man armed with a knife was running from the police. As the police got closer, the man grabbed up Bruce's mother and spun her around, holding the knife to her throat. The police killed him that night, but not before he ran the knife across her delicate neck, killing her within seconds.

He remembered seeing her quietly lying in her coffin. It looked as if she was sleeping. Her delicate youthful features, frozen in time, with the evidence of what took her life so soon, barely visible. He wanted her to wake up... to hold him... to hug him... to tell him how proud she was of him and that she loved him just one more time. He knew logically that none of that was ever going to happen again, but he still wished for it with every thread of his being.

Bruce was enlisted in the Marine Corps and was serving his first tour when all this happened, but was granted Extended Hardship Leave to take care of his father after the fact. Once his father mentally gave up and had to be committed full-time, Bruce found himself in the darkest and loneliest place that he had ever been, emotionally and psychologically. He went back to his enlistment and was transferred to a different ground unit to avoid the pitiful stares of the unit members who were aware of his situation.

He completed three bloody tours in the heart of Afghanistan, earning himself a reputation of 'someone with an impulse control problem.' He would act without hesitation, and in one tour alone, he had more listed confirmed kills than any other Marine in the Battalion. That's when the CIA heard of him. They found Bruce and offered him a deal similar to Jelena's.

He found himself doing the CIA's dirtiest work and actually enjoying it. He could kill without delay and seemed to suffer no ill effects... at least not on the outside. When his mother died, and his father became only a shell of his former self, Bruce sealed his heart off and no longer allowed himself to feel anything at all. It was easier that way... a permanent state of numbness... and maybe a shot of whiskey every now and again.

While sitting there with Jelena, Bruce remembered those times... his mother... his father... how he 'used' to be a good guy. He still couldn't figure out what this hold was that Jelena, a woman who clearly hated his mere existence, had over him. He couldn't believe that he had cried over her. He remembered that he didn't hesitate one bit, when it came down to beating Jelena in the pit... He wasn't the slightest bit reluctant to beat on her or even to electrocute her. In fact, he coldly admitted to himself that he rather enjoyed it. It was his mission... his goal... and he was determined to break her while savoring the steps it took to do that.

What he wasn't counting on was that Jelena was unforeseeably going to give him a run for his money. He had never met anyone whom he couldn't break before, but no matter what he did, Jelena's fire and iron will proved to be unbreakable. Perhaps this is why he felt so connected to her. Could it be her flat-out refusal to give in and break down that he found so intriguing? Was it her internal strength that he identified so strongly with? What the fuck was it about this girl?

He looked at her face and ran his fingers along her newly formed scars, some given to her by his own hand. He picked up and held her cool hand in his. He pressed her hand up against his rugged cheek and just smelled her skin.

Bruce was totally conflicted with himself. He knew that his developing feelings for Jelena was not only a very bad idea, but also against just about every rule in the book.

"Knock it off, man! She's just another asset!" he would tell himself frequently. "You gotta stop thinking about her like that."

He could never seem to get a peaceful night's sleep. Every time he would drift off to sleep, he would find himself dreaming of her. He could feel her on him. He could feel the heat contained in their naked passionate embrace. He could feel the soft silkiness of her skin and how it smelled of sweet honeysuckle. He could feel her deep, slow kisses melting him down to his very core. Especially in his dreams, she had him completely under her spell, and just about the time he would dream of himself telling her that he loved her, he would violently wake up to realize that his mind was doing him no favors at all. He would wake up and remember that she hated every last bit of him through and through. He would remember that he did things to her... things that this woman may never forgive him for.

He woke up from one of his more passionate dreams about her and sat next to her. He held her hand, and he softly whispered to her, "I don't know what this is, but I don't want you to die. I wish you would wake up."

He laid back down on the cot next to her and tried to go back to sleep. The next time he opened his eyes, there she was, sitting up, staring at him with an amused look in her eyes, just sipping the orange juice that the nurse had brought in with her breakfast.

"Hi!" she chirped. "Well, somebody was having a naughty dream." She giggled.

"Ummm... what?" Bruce said, still groggy and not quite fully awake.

"It sounded like you were having a sex dream... so, who's the lucky girl?" she asked.

"How long have you been awake?" he asked her, totally ignoring the 'sex dream' question.

"I dunno… an hour or so, I guess. The nurse got really excited and raced off to get me breakfast, and she even brought you one too," she said, peeling back the yellow skin of her banana.

"You did it again…" he began. "You came back."

"Back from where?" she asked. "You make it sound like I was gone for days… I'm glad you guys found me yesterday. For a second there, I didn't know if you'd make it to me in time."

"Yesterday?" he asked as he sat up and began running his hands through his hair.

She giggled. "You know you have a tell, right?"

"What?" he asked, still processing.

"You know… a tell… like in poker. When you're thinking really hard about something or something is buggin' you, you run your hands through your hair. It's like tick or something," she replied.

Immediately, Bruce caught himself doing exactly that and abruptly stopped.

"So, you think we found you yesterday?" he asked.

"Well yeah. Khishchnik's goons snatched me up. I tried to run in those stupid wedge heels, but they hit me with the car. Next thing I know, I'm getting' my ass handed to me by Vladomir himself, and before I knew it, I was back in a box being planted in the McFarland flower garden. I guess I just needed to catch some zzzs, and well, here you are," she said happily.

"I must say…" she began as she took a bite off of her banana. "I had some really weird dreams, and by the way… you really need to find a razor there, Grizzly Adams. What is this? The CIA's new grunge look?"

Bruce stared at her for a good minute, in disbelief that she was now completely alert and chatting with him like nothing had happened. He had no idea how he would tell her how long she had been down, not to mention that she was technically dead.

He started to run his hands through his hair again as he said, "Uhhh… I don't know how to tell you this, but you have been down… unconscious… for fourteen days. When we brought you in here, you were technically dead, and the doctors didn't know if you were going to make it back this time."

"FOURTEEN DAYS?!" she exclaimed. "I have been down for fourteen days? How is that even possible?" she said, nearly choking on her last bite of banana.

"We don't know how," he stated. "It's like you just came back from the dead."

"Holy shit! I can't believe that I lost fourteen days," she said, looking down at herself. "You're doing it again, the hair thing."

Bruce caught himself running his hand through his hair again, and again he abruptly stopped the motion before saying, "We're just glad that you're back."

"So, wait…" Jelena said as she realized that perhaps her dreams weren't dreams at all. "You were here? You were here the whole time with me?"

"Yes," Bruce confessed.

"Why?" she asked with a quizzical expression.

"I don't know. I just felt that I couldn't leave you in that condition. I wanted to be here when you woke up. I don't know why," he explained.

Jelena thought for a moment, trying to understand how, and more to the point why, the man who beat and electrocuted her would be sitting with her for fourteen days and nights. Why would a man that had such hate and discontent in his eyes sit with her at all?

"Hey... where are my clothes?" she asked. "Do you know?"

"Yeah, they put all your stuff in a bag and stuffed it up in one of these cabinets," he replied as he got up and began to search. "Here you go."

Bruce handed Jelena a white plastic bag filled with her personal effects. She began to rifle through the bag to see her dirty, smelly, blood-soaked clothes all staring back at her. She grabbed her bra and began to tug at the seam.

"I can go get you some clothes. I'm sure that you don't want to wear those. Maybe it's best to just throw them out," Bruce said empathetically.

"I gotta get something out..." she said, struggling to squeeze something out of the bra lining. "Here... A gift..."

Jelena produced a small black stick-looking device and handed it to Bruce.

"What is **this**?" he asked, gently taking it from her.

"Oh just a lil' somethin' that the R&D guys were workin' on and gave me," she replied, with an accent mocking Kate's. "It's a recorder. I put it in my bra that morning just to see if it would work. I completely forgot that it was even in there until I saw you just now. When Vladomir was knocking my brain around like a marble in a jar, my ears were ringing so bad that I couldn't hear exactly what the guys were saying, but I knew that it was something to do with some kinda plan. Everything that they said is recorded onto that little piece of heaven. So here ya go... just like Christmas. Ho, ho, ho, Brucey."

"Holy shit. This is insane," he quipped.

"Naw, dumb luck really," she said.

"Well, shit! I gotta get this over to the linguistics guys for them to transcribe. They can lay it all out for us," Bruce said excitedly. "Even on the brink of death, and you are still thinking outside the box for Christ's sake. Unbelievable!"

"Oh, hey... hang on... do you have your phone? I would use mine, but Vladomir trashed it. Sorry about that... I'm gonna be needing another one. Anyways, I just need an aux cable and your phone, and I can listen and tell you exactly what they were saying, now that the bells in my head are gone. I got this, Bruce," she said, eagerly wanting to help and pushing her blankets off of her bruised legs.

"Listen here… you were dead… D. E. A. D. Fourteen days ago… How about you just take it easy, eat your breakfast and I will run this over and give those guys something to do. So, you stay. Okay?" he insisted as he finished putting on his shoes.

Jelena crossed her arms in protest, let out a huge sigh, and said, "Fine…"

Bruce hopped up, tapped the foot of her bed, and said, "Good. I'll be back in a bit."

As the door closed behind him, Jelena said under her breath, "…Satan."

Jelena got up and looked around the room. She had forgotten to remind Bruce to bring her some clean clothes, and she knew that he was so geared up about the recorder that he probably wouldn't remember.

Desperate times call for desperate measures, she thought, as she slipped on a set of scrubs that Bruce had been wearing at some point.

"Ugg… they even smell like him," she whispered, trying to deny the fact that instinctually, she was more than a bit enticed by his musky scent.

She opened the window and climbed out into the courtyard. Quickly she made her way to the little commissary next to the cafeteria. She used her training account to buy a sports bra, some briefs, a T-shirt, shorts, a pair of socks, and the cheapest pair of running shoes that they had before sneaking back to her hospital room. She chucked the bag in through the open window and slipped back inside, just as the nurse was coming to take her dishes.

Before the nurse could see her, she kicked the bag under the bed and jumped in, quickly pulling the blankets back over her.

"Hi… Yeah… I'm not quite done with that yet if it's okay," she said to the nurse, as smooth as ever.

"Sure, dear. Take your time. I'll be back in a little bit," the nurse replied.

Once the nurse left, Jelena let out a huge giggle, just incredibly entertained that she did something naughty and didn't get caught. She got back up and went to the bathroom to take a shower and scrubbed everything twice. She even used the bar of soap to wash the remaining bits of blood and mud out of her hair.

"No goodie bag this time. Bruce is totally slackin'," she mumbled as she put on the clothes she had just bought from the commissary.

"Ahhh… there we go… all fresh as a daisy," she chirped.

She went back to the white plastic bag containing her crappy stained clothes. She dug out one of the wedge heels that Kate had given her, tore off the cloth strap, and used it as a hair tie. As she scooped up the back portion of her hair, she ran her finger over the spot where Vladomir pressed the lit cigar into her flesh. Other than the horrible memory, all that remained of the event was a large round scab.

Jelena took a minute to closely examine her face in the mirror. She could see that her right eye was still just ever-so-slightly bruised and puffier than the left. She saw where the stitches had been removed from her upper cheek and felt the line in her lip where it had tended to split open. She also noticed another little new scar. It began to dawn on her that she had been unconscious for fourteen long days. As she peered into the mirror at her reflection, flashes of the experience popped into her mind.

Before she dove too deep down that rabbit hole, Kate walked in, wearing one of her signature ensembles and carrying another bouquet of beautiful flowers. "SHIT!" Kate exclaimed, at the sight of Jelena's empty bed.

"Behind you," Jelena called out.

"AHHHHHH!" Kate screamed. "DAMN, GIRL! You scared the shit right outta me. When I saw your bed empty and Bruce gone, I thought... well, I thought..."

"You thought I was dead?" Jelena asked, raising an eyebrow.

"Well yeah... Ooooh, girl, let me get a hug! You're like damned Houdini... dead one minute and lookin' great the next. I swear!"

Jelena grabbed Kate up in the biggest hug possible.

Kate stopped, pushed her back a little bit, and as she looked at Jelena's new clothes that she recognized from the commissary, she asked,

"Hang on... just a hot second there... Was that you? Was that you sneakin' around in the commissary bushes?? What are you? Spiderman? You oughta use the dadgummed sidewalk like ever'body else... you're gonna kill those hydrangeas."

Jelena rolled her eyes at Kate as she plopped back down on her bed.

"So, how' ya feelin' there, darlin'?" Kate asked as she removed the lid and straw from the water container and put the flowers in.

"You were here too..." Jelena said.

"Yes, ma'am... every other day or so at least. But honey... Bruce... we gotta talk about Bruce!" Kate replied.

"What about Bruce?" she asked.

"Well, honey... I have two rather unpleasant news flashes for you, so you may wanna... you know, brace for impact. First off—" Kate started.

Jelena interrupted, "Vladomir got away..."

"So, you *did* hear me?" Kate asked, looking somewhat astounded.

"Yes... bits and pieces at least. Four men held me. One of them was Vladomir. Mel Titan was right. Vladomir and Svetlana's relationship was way more than professional. Vladomir was insanely P.O'd at me for killing her," Jelena explained.

"Yeah, I bet... and girl, we done only killed three, and Vladomir wasn't one of 'em. Intel spotted Vlad back in Moscow a few days ago, but Bruce doesn't know that. He thinks that we got him, and we didn't. I just didn't know how to tell him. But honey… we got bigger fish to fry," Kate said.

"Bigger?" Jelena asked.

"I don't know how to tell you this, darlin', but it's Bruce. He hasn't left this room since they brought you in here. He hasn't eaten much, showered much, slept much, and he hasn't been the office this whole time," Kate explained in a concerned tone.

"Yeah, we talked about that… kind of… it's just so weird. I wonder why he did that?" she responded.

"Honey… I hate to say it… but, darlin', I think Bruce has a thing for ya. You know… I think he's developing feelin's for you," Kate said hesitantly. "Y'all aren't ***involved,*** or anything, are ya?"

"OH MY GOD, KATE! YUCK! I can't believe that you would utter such a thing. I absolutely hate that man! He fucking beat me, Kate! He fucking electrocuted me and got a Goddamned woody from it. The only thing that I want to do to that man is rip his tongue out the hard way!" Jelena scoffed.

"Well, SweetPea, you can say what ya want, but I know. Trust me. You need to keep an eye on that shit. Gettin' all attached is never a good thing in our line of work. That is just how we all end up dead. You may not have feelin's for him, but darlin', if I was a gamblin' woman, I'd bet every last penny that he does for you," Kate warned.

"FUCK HIM, KATE! HE NEEDS TO CHECK THAT SHIT! Have you talked to him?" Jelena asked, quite irate over the mere notion of Bruce having 'feelings' for her.

"No... but honey, I don't need to... He's got that plastered all over his face," she responded, and as she was going to continue, Bruce came flying through the door.

"I know what was on the recorder!" he yelled, louder than intended.

"What recorder?" Kate asked.

"Oh, the one that the R&D team gave me. I shoved it into the lining of my bra and forgot all about it," Jelena explained.

"Yeah... Yeah... So, I know what the deal was. That drive that you guys stole from Sally was a plant. It was a fake. The whole plan that was stored on that thing was nothing but a wild goose chase," Bruce said excitedly.

"Damn Sally and her damned geese," Kate scoffed.

Bruce looked at her for a second, confused as Jelena said, "Yeah, Kate is not a big fan of geese... anyways, go on."

"Well, I just can't figure out why Vladomir would even offer to trade if he knew it was a fake, and he's definitely high-up enough to know that. Why would he even want it back knowing that it was useless?" Bruce asked as he paced back and forth.

"He didn't," Jelena said bluntly.

"What? What do you mean he didn't?" he replied.

"He just wanted to hurt me... and kill me," she said

"You?? Why hurt you?? I don't get it," he asked, still not wrapping his brain around the bigger picture.

"He loved her, Bruce... He was in love with her... Vladomir was in love with Svetlana... and when I killed her, he was going to kill me, and he wanted **you** to know that it was an eye for an eye," Jelena explained.

"Well, none of that matters anyways. He's dead, and the rest is for the bureaucrats to figure out," he quipped, shrugging his shoulders.

"Yeah, Bruce honey... about that..." Kate began in a sweeter than normal tone.

"Ohhh nooo... I know what that 'Bruce honey' shit means... what did you do?" Bruce scolded.

"Well, it's about Vladomir..." Kate began again.

"What about Vladomir?" Bruce asked impatiently.

"Well... ummm..." Kate hesitated.

"Vladomir Khishchnik is still alive," Jelena blurted out.

"WHAT??? WHAT DO YOU MEAN HE'S STILL ALIVE?" Bruce yelled. "KATE!!! How long did you know about this?"

"Well…" she started.

Jelena blurted out, "A few days."

"Stop that!" Kate fussed back at her.

"A FEW DAYS, KATE!!! A FEW FUCKING DAYS!!!" he yelled. "I AM GOING TO KILL THAT SON OF A BITCH!"

"You will absolutely NOT!" protested Jelena. "Vladomir is MINE! He made this personal."

"Knock it off the both of ya!" Kate began. "Well, Bruce, you were here and a… we didn't know if Jelena was gonna live or die… and you just seemed like you already had so much on your plate… I didn't want to add to that. I'm sorry, Bruce, I just didn't know how to tell you," Kate explained.

"SOOO, anyways, guys… come on, let's go get Vladomir!" Jelena insisted.

"Umm, NO WAY, JOSE! You are NOT going anywhere except back to bed until the doc says you are one hundred percent tip top! PERIOD!" Bruce demanded.

"But—" Jelena began but was interrupted by Kate.

"Jelena… honey… you *were* technically dead… just days ago… maybe Bruce is right," Kate interjected softly.

"I was dead…" she said.

"Yes, darlin' you were… so maybe takin' it easy for a few more days isn't a bad idea," Kate continued.

"Well, I think… that I have already had enough 'rest'… fourteen days worth! I am ready to get the hell out of here," Jelena said, hopping off the bed.

"I SAID YOU ARE NOT GOING ANYWHERE! NOW GET YOUR ASS BACK IN BED," Bruce demanded.

"YOU DON'T FUCKING OWN ME, BRUCE! YOU CAN'T TELL ME WHERE I CAN AND CAN'T GO! JUST WHO THE FUCK DO YOU THINK YOU ARE? DO YOU THINK…" Jelena yelled as Kate interrupted.

"Bruce… a word outside, please…" Kate began. "NOW!" she hollered.

Bruce sighed and threw up his hands as he barged past Kate and held the door open for her. They both walked into the hallway, and as soon as Bruce shut the door and turned to Kate, she laid into him as quietly as possible.

"Now you listen here, and you listen good. Whatever **this** is between you and her has got to stop. She is an ASSET, Bruce. You ain't been eatin'… you ain't been sleepin'… you ain't been to work… and hell… your face ain't seen a razor for weeks now. You've been on this girl like flies on shit. Now I know what I think is goin' on, and I'm gonna need you to prove me wrong. YA GOT THAT? PROVE ME WRONG!" Kate scolded in a hushed tone.

"What, Kate? WHAT do you think is going on?" Bruce barked back at her, looking around to make sure their conversation wasn't drawing too much attention.

"I think... I think..." Kate began, knowing that there would be no going back once she finished that sentence.

"YOU THINK WHAT, KATE? SPIT IT OUT!" he yelled a bit louder than intended.

"I think that you're in love with her! I think that you've done gone and let yourself fall in love with that girl... and ever'thing you say and how you're actin' is just proof to the puddin'. Now you **know,** that is not only against the rules, but that shit can get us all killed, Bruce. You can't just keep her in a damn bubble. Come on, honey, it's not worth your career... or your life... or her life, Bruce. You know as well as I do, honey, that love is a luxury that we just don't get. We don't get to have those little 'happily ever afters,' Bruce. You know that I'm tellin' you the truth. You lovin' her... may be just enough to get her killed next time. Do you really want that on your conscience? Her blood on your hands? This has got to stop... and I mean now! You just think about that!" Kate said with a matter-of-fact tone in her hushed voice.

Bruce stood there for a moment, just looking at Kate, wondering if she was right. He had to ask himself, was he in love with Jelena?

CHAPTER 18: THE PLAN

Bruce let out a big sigh. He didn't confirm nor deny Kate's accusations. He stood there, looking at Kate, and ran his hand through his hair before catching himself. Bruce knew that Kate was right and that letting himself feel these things for Jelena was a dangerous gamble. He still couldn't quite say to himself that he was 'in love' with her, but something was definitely there. There was some kind of hold... some kind of connection that he could no longer deny. He knew that he had to suppress these feelings... somewhere way down deep, and he also knew that the best way to keep Jelena safe... was to not love her at all. He just wasn't sure that was something he could do. Worse yet, he wasn't sure if that was something that he even wanted to do. All he knew was that Kate was right, and he was willing to die for Jelena and that alone could be just enough to get her killed next time.

Silently, he walked back to Jelena's door. As he walked back into the room, he was filled with the all too familiar sense of frustration. Kate wasn't too far behind him, and as he just stood there, Kate came into the room and said, "Okay now... What's the plan, y'all?"

Bruce looked at her with an expression of complete exasperation and sighed, "Find the spy, I guess."

"What? She done took off again? Damn it, Jelena!" Kate hollered as she looked out the open window.

Kate and Bruce pulled up into Jelena's driveway and saw her sitting in her red relaxed lawn chair, with her long legs casually crossed, sipping on a wine cooler. As soon as she saw them, she raised the bottle to acknowledge their presence.

Jelena wasn't much of a beer or wine drinker, but she certainly did enjoy some particular liquors and wine coolers. She also wouldn't consider herself a heavy drinker but, in celebration of her recent escapes of both the brink of death and the hospital, she sat there happily sipping with a sly smug smile wrapped around her heart-shaped face.

"Are you fucking kidding me right now?" Bruce scolded her.

"Well, since you two were outside having a bit of a lover's quarrel… I figured that I would take the opportunity to excuse myself while the 'grown-ups' were having their chat," Jelena explained.

"Damn, girl!" Kate howled. "You're hell and far from the hospital… how in the hell d'you get here so fast? Any other super-human skills that you ain't tellin' us about?"

"Mmmmmm nope. I Ubered," Jelena said with a smile. "I mean… I jogged about a mile or so, and then they picked me up. You know, Kate, you really shouldn't leave your phone just lying around. I owe you about twenty bucks, by the way… for the ride."

"WOMAN!! You're just infuriatin'!" Kate snipped. "Don't you ever just do what you're told?"

"Hmm sometimes," Jelena chirped with a smile. "Now that you guys are done with your little drama, how about we come up with a plan to find Khishchnik?"

"And how about we take your ass right back to the hospital?" Bruce insisted. "You were dead less than two weeks ago and in a coma twenty-four hours ago, and now here you are… running and what the fuck… Ubering?"

"How about not," Jelena quipped. "You know as well as I do there, Bruce, after that coming back to life shit, that I wouldn't be leaving that hospital for another month… hell, maybe not another year… just so that they can stick me and run more tests on me just to prove that I'm an alien or something. I **don't know** how I came back. I just do what I do, and I happen to stay alive. Maybe I'm a fuckin' cat?" She giggled. "So, I'm down to what? seven lives now?"

"NOT funny, Jelena! You're GOING BACK!" he yelled.

"Okay, you two… Bruce, now maybe let's just let her get some air, and we'll come up with a plan here and once we've come up with somethin', then maybe Jelena, honey we'll take you back, as long as Dr. Simms promises to do a quick physical and then cut ya loose? Okay?" Kate pleaded with the two of them.

"Fine," Bruce said bluntly. "But you ARE going back!" he mouthed at her.

"Yeah, okay," agreed Jelena. "NOT YET!" she mouthed back at him.

"Now… our biggest problem is Vladomir Khishchnik," Kate started. "We know he's in Moscow, probably having a lil' Moscow Mule of his own, celebratin' that he put your ass in an early grave…"

"Yeah… but that's what **he** thinks, Kate… He doesn't **know** that I'm still alive right?" Jelena asked with the gears in her head turning full force.

"So, what if we spread a rumor... you know... a rumor that I died... *really* turning me into a ghost. Then make sure that rumor is heard over every chatter line in the world... spread that shit like Cheesewhiz on a Ritz... I mean... Vladomir and his KGB buddies will hear it and believe it. Since Vladomir put me in that hole himself, he would have no reason not to believe it... and then when we strike, it'll be like the ghost of Christmas past coming back to pay homage."

"I hate to say it, but I think that would work," Bruce admitted. "Alright, smartass, so then what?"

"Well... we need some intel on where he is and what he's been up to there in Moscow. Put some heavy surveillance on him, to, you know... track him a little bit. Maybe tap his phone line. This way, we get to find the pattern in his activities and behaviors, and then we'll be able to come up with the perfect strike plan," she explained.

"Alright, fine," said Bruce. "I'll go get that set up, and we'll see where that leads."

"Okay, Jelena," Kate began sweetly, "now that we've done come up with the first part of the plan, it's time to get you back to the hospital before we give sweet old Dr. Simms a bloody heart attack."

Jelena reluctantly got up from her chair and chugged the rest of her cooler. She chucked the glass bottle into the trash bin and walked herself right into the house.

"NOT the plan, Kate..." Bruce started through gritted teeth, sounding more and more irritated.

"I know… she'll come out," Kate sang. "Bruce, you gotta trust this one… she's a good asset."

"Yeah… But…" he started but stopped when he saw Jelena come back out of the house with a small overnight bag in her hands and start heading to the car.

Reluctantly, Jelena hopped into the backseat. She was extremely unimpressed with the notion of going back to the hospital. Kate and Bruce looked at her as they got into the car themselves.

"Well, I wasn't going to go without any clothes or stuff this time. So… let's go… let's get this over with," Jelena scoffed.

Three days later, Bruce finally got the intel they had been waiting for and went back to the hospital to tell Kate and Jelena.

"BRUCE!" Jelena yelled as she threw her cards down on the bed where she and Kate had been playing Gin Rummy. "BRUCE! THIS WAS SUPPOSED TO BE A QUICK PHYSICAL! I HAVE BEEN IN THIS FUCKING PIT FOR THREE DAYS… THREE GODDAMNED DAYS! I AM DONE! GET ME THE FUCK OUTTA HERE BEFORE I GO FIND THAT CAR BATTERY OF YOURS AND SHOVE IT RIGHT UP YOUR FUCKING COCKSUCKING ASS!"

"Well… hello to you too, Jelena," he quipped back at her demands.

"BRUCE! I am NOT kidding!" she pressed.

"But I have to tell you—" he began, only to be cut off by Jelena's fury.

"Listen... carefully... I will try to use small words so that even **you**... can understand. I don't give a flying rat fuck what you have to say. Not a single, itty bitty, teeny tiny, rat fuck. GO find Dr. Simms and get this fixed, or the next time I slip away, you will NEVER find me... GOT IT? NOW GO!" she yelled.

Bruce looked at Kate, sitting on the edge of the bed all tightlipped, just shaking her head, showing him that she would not get involved this time and he was on his own. Without another word, Bruce turned back and left the room to find Dr. Simms and request Jelena's discharge. When he returned, Jelena merely held up her hand, as if she was not interested in anything he was selling, until she saw Dr. Simms follow him into her room.

"Dr. Simms... with all due respect, sir... I need to go... now..." Jelena pressed him from the start.

"Okay, settle down, tiger... I was just coming in here with your discharge papers. You are fit as a fiddle, however in the hell that happened. You're free to go," Dr. Simms said with a smile as he shook Bruce's hand and left the room.

"Ugghhh FINALLY!" Jelena exclaimed. "Come'on, Kate! Let's blow this popsicle stand!"

Jelena grabbed her bag and stormed out of the room. Kate gathered up the cards, looked at Bruce, and said in a very 'was that necessary' tone, "Three days was a bit much, Bruce. I talked to Dr. Simms, and he said that she could'a left after twenty-four more hours... not seventy-two... he said that was all your doin'."

"Come on, Kate... I just wanted to make sure that she was okay. I can't have some half-cocked asset who's not at one hundred percent out in the field. Just a formality," he defended.

"Formality, my ass. If you keep on pokin' that dadgum bear, she's gonna string you up. This isn't one of your little chippies there, Bruce," Kate warned as she left the room.

The three of them left the hospital and drove to Vanover Park, where there were some picnic tables, a little creek, and lots of ducks. Unbeknownst to the ladies, Bruce had packed a little picnic basket with snacky finger foods to munch on and a four-pack of wine coolers. Being there alone, they had their pick of the best table right next to the creek. Bruce pulled out a little black box, turned it on, and sat it on the edge of the table.

"What is that?" asked Jelena.

"Oh, just a lil' something that the R&D team was workin' on and gave to me?" Bruce replied sarcastically in a high-pitched tone and accent, mocking Kate, who was less than amused.

"Okay... what?? Is that supposed to be me y'all? Fun-ny," Kate said as she rolled her eyes at the pair of them.

"Seriously, it's a jammer. I turn that thing on, and it emits some kind of buzzing sound that we can't hear, but that interferes with any kind of recording equipment... so our conversation is completely private," he explained in his regular voice.

"Okay," said Jelena. "What's with the basket?"

"Just something to celebrate that you are back at one hundred percent," he replied.

He opened the basket and spread out some food items onto the table. He handed Jelena one of her favorite wine coolers and offered a toast.

"Here is to Jelena... my finest and most skilled protégé. I am proud to call you a fully operational asset. To you... Cheers," Bruce toasted.

Jelena raised her bottle and clinked it with his and Kate's, and took a big delicious sip.

"Alright... enough of the squishy crap... what's the deal with Vladomir?" Jelena asked, back to business.

"Here's what we know. We've had surveillance on him for the past three days. It appears that good old Vladomir is double-dippin'. He is doing some side work for the Russian Mafia. We put that rumor about your death out over the wire, and so far, we believe that they took it, hook, line, and sinker. We also heard some other interesting information from one of Vladomir's phone lines that we tapped. He has an appointment to help the Mafia with a little interrogation project. He is going to be at this warehouse, right here." He pointed as he showed the girls his pocket-sized map of Moscow. "He has scheduled two days to be there next week... Thursday and Friday. It was also reported that he has this thing for a little bakery not far from the warehouse. He has gone there every morning, that we've been watching, at around 9:00 AM and stays there until about 10:20 AM when a black sedan comes to pick him up to take him to his sister's house on the outskirts. He must be staying there while he is in town doing the Mob Boss' dirty work. So, that's what we know in a nutshell. What do you think?" Bruce concluded.

"That's great!" Jelena started. "Okay... here's what we can do..." she continued as she outlined the whos, whats, whens, wheres, and whys to Bruce and Kate.

After their time at the park, Bruce dropped Jelena off at home. He got out of the car and walked her to the door.

"I'm okay, Bruce. I really don't need an escort," she said politely.

"I know that. I just want to make sure you get in okay. I am only protecting the agency's asset," he said as Jelena unlocked her door.

"Okay... well, I'm in... thanks," she said as she began to close the door.

At the last second, Bruce grabbed the door and said, "Oh wait! I forgot, your new phone." He pulled a new burner phone out of his pocket and handed it to her. "Do you still remember my number? And maybe Kate's too?" he asked.

"In the vault..." she said, pointing to her head and beginning to close the door again.

Bruce stopped the door from closing, again and Jelena opened it back up with a confused look on her face and said, "Yessss??"

"I ummm, well I ummm..." Bruce started, "I umm just wanted to say how grateful that I am that you're okay."

"I **am** okay, Bruce," Jelena reassured, looking at this man who in the beginning had eyes filled with hate but now, he looked awkward and unsure as he stood at her door with his hands crammed down into his denim pockets and his eyes focused on the threshold.

"And ummm... you know... if you need anything... anything at all... just umm... just call me, and I'll be here. Okay?" he said without a single note of confidence in his voice, just as a teenager would on a first date.

"Okay... Will do. See ya tomorrow, Bruce," she said as she was finally able to close the door with more questions than answers about his very strange behavior.

Damn! she thought. *Maybe Kate* **was** *right... again... Maybe he* **is** *in love with me... Now, now, now Jelena... look who's feeling all full of herself... hhhmmm Brucie is in looovveee with me.* She continued to think while mocking her own ideations. *Snap out of it, Jelena... someone higher up must have grabbed him by the short hairs to make sure that I stay tip-top so that I can keep doing this spy shit without ending up in another fuckin' box.*

Jelena went to bed that night, and even in the comfort of her own soft and cushy bed, she still didn't manage to have a peaceful night's sleep. She kept having the same nightmare... one minute, Bruce was electrocuting her, and then the next minute, he was kissing her passionately. She shot straight up out of bed, drenched in sweat.

"What in the flippin' frog nuts, man? I gotta deal with this guy all fuckin day and then see him all fuckin night! I should'a ripped his tongue out when I had the chance. I need some sleeeeep," she exclaimed as she thrust herself back down on her bed and pulled the pillow over her face.

On the other side of town, Bruce was also in a dream-filled state. He dreamed of Jelena... holding her... kissing her... making passionate love to her... His dream played out in his mind like a romance novel. He imagined her walking down the aisle to marry him, and then he dreamed of their children playing in the yard as she leaned over, mouthed the words, 'I love you too' and kissed him deeply, which shot him straight up out of bed as well.

"WHY IN THE FUCK CAN'T I STOP IT? STOP IT, MAN!" he said, yelling and smacking himself in the head. "I can't have her... I don't want her! I do not want that woman... I gotta keep saying it until I believe it. This is just a little crush. NO BIG DEAL! I do **not** want that woman!" he repeated, thrusting himself back onto his bed and pulling the pillow over his face.

They all met up at the conference room the next day to continue ironing out all the details pertaining to the plan they had come up with, to find and kill Vladomir Khishchnic.

Kate was looking like her fabulous self, as usual. She was in a super cute pair of blue jeans with a short-sleeved, blue and white, plaid shirt with poofy ruffled sleeves and a pair of denim-covered mule sliders. Her hair was wrapped up in an messy bun that elaborated just how long her elegant ivory neck was.

Bruce and Jelena, on the other hand, were looking rather rugged that morning, and they must have had the same idea. For once, Bruce was wearing a plain pair of jeans with a plain white T-shirt and running shoes, and Jelena nearly looked to match, wearing her own blue jeans, a white tank top, and some running shoes. Both wore dark sunglasses as they walked into the room, and both were carrying a large cup of coffee from the same coffee-shop chain.

"Well, I'll be damned," Kate began. "What are we both twinzies today? What's with the matchy-matchy shit? And more to the point, why do the two of you look like somethin' my neighbor's dog threw up?"

Jelena stopped in her tracks, looked at herself, and then looked at Bruce. She started shaking her head as she took a gulp of her coffee. She put her sunglasses on the top of her head and said, "I had a rough night, alright? I had some nightmares... that's all... I just didn't get much sleep."

"Nightmares?" Bruce asked. "Do you need to go see mental health?"

"NO... I don't need to go see mental health. I just had some bad dreams. I can make them go away on my own... thank YOU very much," she snapped back at him.

"Hey!" Kate hollered. "Cranky people! We don't have time for that shit now, y'all. This is our last day to finalize our plans. We still have to get with Lucy to get all of our shit straight before we do this. So, y'all need to leave your crap at the door. I mean, really... we're leavin' in two days, so pull it together!"

They both apologized to Kate and sat down to begin finalizing the plan. They knew exactly where Vladomir was and tracked him. They had a general plan on how to get into the target building, and the R&D guys gave them each some gadgets that may come in handy.

Jelena decided that she needed to see Lucy first, to get her fake identification, papers, passport, cash, credit cards, and some random costume items to help her change her appearance. She hated waiting until the last minute to take care of things that could be taken care of now. After making her arrangements with Lucy, she went to the armory guys and got a few items that she thought may be necessary for this walk to go smoothly. By the end of the day, she decided that even though they had all agreed to a rather specific plan, it may be best to make a few secret alterations.

The next morning Kate and Bruce were standing outside the Administration Office, waiting for Lucy to come in that day. They were also waiting for Jelena, who was supposed to be there, with them, to meet with Lucy.

Lucy came in and unlocked the office door. "Hey there, Lima Bean! How you been?" Lucy said as she greeted them. "You too, Kate… it's been ages since I seen your purdy face! Y'all here to get your travel all set up?"

"Yes, ma'am, Lucy. We're just waiting for one more," Bruce explained.

"Who? Jelena?" Lucy asked.

"Yeah… why?" he responded.

"Oh, honey, Jelena's done been here and gone already," Lucy said as she slipped into the office.

"Kate… CALL HER NOW!!!" Bruce demanded, angrier than ever, as he followed Lucy inside to clarify what 'done been here and gone already' meant exactly.

"Hi, Kate!" Jelena answered happily.

"Jelena… darlin'… did you forget? We're supposed to be meetin' this mornin' over at Lucy's. Bruce is a little cranky that you're not here. Where are you, honey?" Kate asked.

Jelena answered, as cool as a cucumber, "In Moscow."

CHAPTER 19: MOSCOW

"You're WHERE?" Kate began. "Ohhh, honey... Bruce ain't gonna like this one bit..." she said as she heard Bruce yell, "KAAAATE!" from inside the Administration Office.

"Darlin', I gotta go. I think Bruce's head's gonna explode. I'll call you right back," Kate said, and no sooner than she had closed her phone, Bruce came storming out of the office.

Bruce looked at Kate and motioned to her to follow him. Kate followed him out of the building and into the courtyard, where he proceeded to have a ginormous meltdown.

"Did you know about this?" he snapped.

"Whaat... umm nooo. I just found out when you found out," Kate defended.

"This fucking bitch! What is she... some Goddamned rogue or something? She thinks that she can just do whatever the fuck she wants to do? I'm about ready to drag her ass right back to the dark side of the moon to teach her some manners and respect!" he snapped. "I can't fucking **believe** this, Kate! She is going to ruin the entire fucking plan! GODDAMN IT!" he continued.

"Bruce, honey," Kate started softly but was cut off by Bruce beginning another rant.

"DON'T YOU 'BRUCE HONEY' ME! SHE HAS CROSSED THE FUCKING LINE THIS TIME! I SHOULD'A BEAT HER ASS HARDER... KILLED HER A FEW MORE TIMES... TAKE HER DOWN A FEW LIVES UNTIL SHE WISED UP!" he screamed as he paced back and forth in the courtyard.

Kate looked at him, totally unimpressed by his tantrum, and said, "You about done now? Because your actin' like a three-year-old who didn't get his way. Now I'm gonna stand here and let you vent and kick and scream for a minute... then I'm gonna walk away... and when you're about done... you tell me, and then we'll figure out the next step that we need to take."

After about a minute, Kate began to walk away when Bruce called out. "Wait, Kate... I'm done," he said, walking over to her. "I'm sorry, Kate. She just gets under my skin. This kinda shit makes me want to kill her myself," he explained.

"Well, hell, Bruce... that's just because you're too damned attached to her. Is it *really* that you're mad about a plan... or are you bent because she done went off and left without ya?" Kate asked. "We need to call her and talk to her to see what the hell is goin' on and what we need to do now that the plan's changed. Christ Bruce... you know as well as I do that plans change a lot in this business. If Jelena changed the plan, then she must'a had a reason. Let's take a breath and call her to figure this shit out... You can't keep treatin' her like she's your damn prom date... she's not some dainty little girl... she is a fully operational asset... a decorated combat Marine... she's smarter than the rest of us, so maybe she thought'a somethin' that we didn't and jumped on it... we just gotta call her, Bruce, and see what's up."

"Yeah... You're right, Kate," he agreed, running his hand through his hair again as they walked over to a bench to sit down.

Kate pulled out her phone and dialed the number, put it on speakerphone, and when she heard the line pick-up, she said, "Howdy, Jane? This is Mrs. Applebie. Do you have a minute to chat?"

"Oh, hi! Sure do. I decided to take a jog out to the countryside here, and man oh man, it... is... gorgeous Kate... ohhh I mean Mrs. Applebie. No one's around. So yeah, I can chat. Is Bruce... I mean Cainen really mad?" Jelena asked, not knowing that Kate had it on speaker.

"YES, I AM," Bruce said sternly. "But *weee* figured that you must've had a reason for changing the plan, so *weeeee* were calling to see what's up and how we need to adjust."

"Well, here's the thing, you guys... I figured that it would look awful fishy if the three of us arrived on the same day at the same time and with the same backstory. So, I went to Lucy, and I got my new ID and stuff... ohh, by the way, you are now talking to Ivana Popovich, and she also gave me some costume thingies, so I hardly look like myself. But anyways, since I am the only one that speaks perfect Russian, it made sense for me to come alone, just like any other Russian traveler. I can blend in easier. I reached out to some of our local guys and asked them to keep even closer tabs on Vladomir while I'm here getting a basic lay of the land. I figured it couldn't hurt," she explained.

"Uh-huh..." Bruce said.

She continued, "Listen, Cainen, I don't want you to think that I am just going rogue or anything like that. The plan we came up with is still the same... only the travel plans changed a bit. I am just trying to use my skills and my time as effectively as possible."

"See now there, Cainen," Kate started. "I told ya she had a reason and a good one too."

"So, you're okay?" Bruce asked. "Do you think anyone suspects you?"

"Yes, Cainen. I'm okay, and no way does anyone suspect me. I was checking into the hotel and got asked out on a date already by some turd in the lobby. I am positive that they think I'm just a traveler from St. Petersburg. I was even able to master the slight dialect accent on the plane. So, we're all good here, guys. You're still leaving this afternoon, right?"

"Yes, ma'am," Kate replied. "Just dottin' our I's and crossin' our T's, and maybe slappin' a little salve on Cainen's bruised ego before we hit the road."

"Okay, well I'm staying in the Hotel Moscow, Marriott Grand on Tverskaya Street. Room four-twelve. Call me when you arrive, and I'll find a way to meet up with you. Okay?" Jelena asked.

"You got it, darlin'! We'll be in touch," Kate said as she closed her phone.

"Now Bruce, we gotta get back to Lucy and get ourselves squared away," she pressed. "Are you gonna be okay now that you got all that outta your system? Showin' your ass ain't gonna help anything."

"I'm fine. Thank you... and yes, I am all good. Shall we?" he said as he extended his arm, motioning for her to go first.

In a small unoccupied cubicle, Bruce and Kate changed their cover looks. Kate could easily pull off damn near any look that she put on her perfect lanky body. She was dawning another pair of cute tight, high waisted, blue jeans, a tight white T-shirt with 'I'm with him' written across the chest, and a pair of white and leather sandals.

Bruce, on the other hand, had to step so far out of his comfort zone that he was not without protest.

"Is this a fucking joke? I feel ridiculous," he said, stepping out of the cubicle. He was wearing longer jean shorts that cut him around the knee, a black nylon fanny pack, a larger white T-shirt with 'I ♥ RUSSIA' written across the chest, and white socks with orange-colored running shoes.

"AWWW!" Lucy exclaimed excitedly. "Don't you two just look DARLIN'! Like the perfect little couple."

"This is all we have? Come on, Lucy... Is obnoxious American tourist really the best way to go to remain inconspicuous?" Bruce begged.

"Now Bruce..." Kate began. "You know that I don't speak no Russian, and you barely speak enough to find the damned toilet. You also know that you'll have an easier time showing a southern accent than I will, not doin' one. I can't just up and go changin' how I talk. So, we need to make it work. We are Hurly and Bev Rinestone from Dallas, Texas. We're travelin' the world and markin' Moscow off the list. What are you bitchin' about? You did a southern accent before..." she finished.

"Yeah...but I was a swarthy rich Texan in the oil business... business suits... not fanny packs. That was different," he whined.

"Ohhh, shut up and let's go! We got a plane to catch!" Kate insisted.

About thirteen hours later, Bruce and Kate were getting settled in their hotel room at the Marriott Grand. As Kate was going through her bag and Bruce was still pouting over their cover story, they both jumped up when there was a loud unexpected knock on their door.

Bruce pulled his gun out of his fanny pack and pointed it at the door, as a voice on the outside said, "Domovodstvo?"

He whispered to Kate, "I think it's the maid service. Go ahead and open it. We don't want to seem suspicious," he said, as he carefully tucked his gun into his pocket, making sure that his T-shirt covered the bulging shape.

Kate opened the door to find one of the hotel's maids standing there. She had bright red hair pulled back into a neat bun at the base of her neck. She wore a tidy black dress with a white apron. She had the cleaning cart with her and had two crisp white fluffy towels in her hands, offering them to Kate as she said, "Dobryy den'. Tebyeah nuzhny polotentsa?"

"Ohhh, I'm sorry, darlin'. I don't speaky any Ruski... eennggllisshh," Kate responded, making sure to stay in character.

"Beverly, you idiot! She's asking you if you need any towels," Bruce snipped at Kate as he continued to the girl, "Da ee blagodaryu vas," he said as he took the towels from her, catching a whiff of a familiar scent that he couldn't quite place.

Bruce began to close the door gently when the maid stuck her foot in, preventing it from closing. The next several moments played out as if they were happening in slow motion. The maid violently shoved the door, pushing both Bruce and Kate back. She came through the door like gangbusters, with a gun in each hand. As the door was quickly closing behind her, Kate and Bruce were still scrambling around on the floor trying to get up but just couldn't react quite quick enough. In a split second, they found themselves standing there, staring down the barrels of something awful ugly.

The maid set one of her guns on top of the small table next to the door, tapped her temple with her index finger, and in a very familiar voice, she said, "In the vault..."

"Jelena?!" Kate whispered in disbelief.

She let out a giggle, pulled off her red wig, and whispered loudly, "It's Ivana and I totally got you guys!"

Jelena gave Kate a big hug as she said, "It's about time you got here."

Jelena then walked up to Bruce, giving him an up and down look. "Well, hey there, Satan... Is that a gun in your pocket, or are ya just happy to see me?" she said sarcastically as she grabbed the gun still stuck in his pocket in a provocative manner, making him jump back a bit.

"You… you… you don't even look like you…" Bruce said as he was studying Jelena's face.

"Oh… that's because of the fake nose… you like it? Lucy gave it to me and showed me how to put it on. I can't believe that I fooled you guys."

"You're lucky your dumb ass didn't get shot!" Kate snarked. "Where'd you get that outfit from anyways? I didn't see anything that convincin' in Lucy's collection."

"Oh, I swiped it from a locker in the basement. So, did you guys sleep on the plane? I don't think we are gonna have much time. Khishchnik's been on the move. After I talked to you guys yesterday, he changed his patterns, so we may have to do more on the fly than we thought," Jelena said.

Bruce walked past Jelena to get a beer out of the mini-fridge and once again caught a whiff of the scent that he couldn't quite place. He quickly tried to dismiss it just to have a second to relax. Jelena explained the plan modifications and went through the rough play-by-play that dissected exactly what each of them would be doing in less than eight hours.

"Okay, you guys… well, I am gonna get my stuff for tomorrow all squared away and leave you two love birds alone," Jelena said as she walked past them to the interior door that connected into the next room.

"What are you doin'?" Kate asked in a tone that implied that Jelena had lost her mind.

"Goin' to *my* room," Jelena chirped. "I'm right next door... remember room four-twelve... so no crazy monkey sex... I need my beauty sleep."

"Jelena... GET OUT!" Kate hollered as she threw one of her sandals at the door as it closed.

In the middle of the night, Bruce found himself, once more, passionately dreaming of Jelena. Images of him kissing her neck and running his hands over the length of her curvaceous body flashed through his mind. He was holding her naked frame, pulling her tightly into himself as he kissed her long and deep.

WHACK!

Bruce was instantly pulled back into reality as he opened his eyes and woke up staring into the mortified eyes of Kate, who just knocked the shit out of him.

"Now I don't know what in the sam hell that lil' ole' squirrel that runs your brain is thinkin', but I'll tell ya this... you have about two seconds to get'on up off'a me or you're gonna be missin' somethin' really important... So get!" Kate yelled.

Bruce was stunned, and his eyes were as wide as saucers. He was not yet awake enough to have Kate's protests register in his mind. Even worse, he couldn't believe that he was acting out his fantasies of Jelena unconsciously on Kate.

"Damn it, Bruce... I said GET UP OFF'A ME!" she squealed again.

Bruce sat up on his side of the bed, still trying to tame his 'excitement.' "Oh My God, Kate!! I am sooo sorry! I was dreaming... I... I... I didn't mean to... did we do anything?" he stammered.

"Hell no! we didn't do anything... other than you stickin' your tongue down my throat and grabbin' up on me with that one-eyed stallion of yours bangin' on my barn door!"

"Oh, Kate... I am so very sorry. I am so embarrassed!" he said.

"If you're dreamin' of Jelena, then you need to put that doggoned horse down. I'm sorry, Bruce, but we don't have time to divide the blood flow between your two heads... You're gonna have to get one head in the game... and we're gonna run with the one upstairs. Now, if you can't keep your damn hands to yourself, then I suggest that you sleep on the floor like any other dog!" Kate fussed.

Bruce decided to grab the extra blanket and sleep on the floor next to the bed. He really had no control over his dreams of Jelena, but he certainly didn't want to hurt Kate in the process.

"And another thing there, Mister McGrabby," Kate continued snippily, "if you can't manage to stay focused, keepin' your hands to yourself, and you just can't stop dreamin' of her like the way you ARE OBVIOUSLY dreamin' of her, then perhaps y'all shouldn't work together after this."

The early morning came along faster than Kate or Bruce wanted. Jelena was up and singing and dancing around in her room. She knocked on the interior door and said, "Y'all decent?"

"Yes, ma'am, we most certainly are," Kate answered. "Come on in, darlin'. I gotta talk to you."

"Sure, what's up?" she said, as she came into the room. Jelena was dressed in her standard go to of a long sleeve, button-down green plaid shirt, some nicer blue jeans and some comfortable tan lace-up boots. Since she was just another Russian traveler, she was grateful that she didn't have to have some fancy costume.

"Hurry, Bruce is in the shower, and I don't want him to know that I told you…" Kate said, patting the spot on the bed next to her for Jelena to sit down.

"Tell me what?" Jelena asked.

"Well last night… Bruce was dreamin' of you… you know… callin' your name and all that… but was crawlin' up on me… if ya catch my drift…" Kate began. "Listen, I like Bruce… but I don't need his tongue down my throat or him umm you know, trying to park his Chevy in my levy. He's got it bad for you, honey… maybe after this, it might best for y'all to not work together. He just can't seem to help himself."

"Holy shit, Kate! Did you guys do it?" Jelena asked.

"Hell NO! We didn't do it. But that's not the damn point. He is so lost in you that he is losin' his edge, darlin'. That's how we all end up dead. You just think about what I'm tellin' ya, okay? I mean, I've shared beds and hotel rooms with this man on over one hundred different walks, and nothin' like this has *ever* happened. His feelin's aren't goin' away Jelena… his feelin's are gettin' bigger and deeper for ya… y'all need some distance after this," Kate explained. "Y'all just can't work together. His wild-eyed stallion is gonna get us all killed."

"Damn Kate! I really don't understand any of this. This man has tried to kill me several times. I haven't done anything to try to make him like me at all. How do I make it stop?" Jelena asked.

"Well, honey, you don't. He can't help it. Sometimes feelin's just grow where they grow. There is somethin' about you that he is just drawn to. Hell, I don't even think he understands why. This man, he doesn't allow himself to have feelin's, or at least he never used to. You have brought somethin' out in him that has been dormant or sleepin' forever. I can say that he was truly embarrassed that he came up on me last night. So, I really don't think that he's doin' it on purpose. I don't think he's a bad operative, and I don't think he's a bad guy either. I just don't think that either of you can make this kind of thing go away and work together at the same time. I do think that y'all need some distance so that he can get his head back in the game," Kate explained as gently as possible.

"So, you don't think that Bruce has his head in the game?" Jelena asked.

"Oh, he has *a* head in the game, but as long as your around, honey, he has the **wrong** head in the game. You see, Jelena, Bruce is a very effective operative... as long as he ain't busy feelin' things. Hell, most of us didn't even know that boy was capable of havin' feelin's. He was like a machine. Orders received... jobs get done... management is happy, and everyone on our side stays alive. Bruce's instincts in situations have saved lives. God knows he's saved mine plenty of times. He doesn't really think or feel anything about what has to get done. He just follows his gut... methodical. I have never seen him act the way he has acted since you came into the picture. So, like it or not, it's just not safe for you two to be workin' together," Kate continued.

"Oh. I see. What should I do, Kate?" Jelena asked quietly as she looked down.

"Darlin', I have no idea. I have to tell management that I don't think you two should work together. I won't tell them the real reason, but I'll come up with something to tell them. The only issue is that management usually keeps the new asset with their primary trainer for the first year, and I just don't know how that is gonna work out?" Kate explained.

"If you told the truth, would Bruce get into trouble? Like would we get into trouble for dreaming about each other?" Jelena asked innocently.

Kate froze in her spot, and as the words processed in her brain, her eyes got large and wide and her thick lashes blinked like she was trying to fan out a fire. "Well... hold on a dang moment here...what do you mean '*we*?'" Kate asked with great concern. "Have *you* had dreams about him?"

"More like nightmares..." Jelena confessed. "Like one minute he is electrocuting me, and then the next minute he is kissing me passionately. I wake up in a horrible sweat, just mortified."

"Holy fucking God Almighty!" Kate exclaimed. "Y'all need to keep your mouths shut! You both probably *would* get into trouble, so I'll figure out something to tell management in my report. Y'all need to get some distance in between you both, before the two of you are stuck smushed together tighter than a pair of M&Ms in my jeans pocket."

"GOD, KATE! GROSS!" Jelena snarked back as she rolled her eyes. "Mine was a nightmare… night… mare…"

"Nightmare or not," Kate began, "your little squirrel brain is thinkin' about him, and his little squirrel brain is thinkin' about you. But what we all need to be thinkin' about is how to find and end Vladomir and how to stay alive while doin' it. We won't mention this conversation. Got it?"

"In the vault!" Jelena replied.

CHAPTER 20: WILD HORSES

Bruce walked out of a steam-filled bathroom, wrapped in a towel with water droplets still glistening on every single olive-toned muscle present in his upper torso. "Good morning, ladies," he said, trying to be as charming as possible.

"Satan…" Jelena responded, rolling her eyes at him as she walked to the room service cart.

Bruce walked over and crouched down next to Kate and whispered, "Fuck! Did you tell her about last night?"

"Noooo… but you need to… and then y'all need some distance… at least until you get that horse o'yours under control," Kate snipped.

"Awww geez…" Jelena moaned. "The grown-ups are at it again."

Jelena continued as she grabbed a bagel off the cart, "Well, I'm going to take off and head to the warehouse. We only have until noon before Vladomir is expected to show up there. So, you two finish doing whatever it is that you're doing and then leave here in about thirty minutes."

"Hey… Wait up, Jelena… we'll go with you," Bruce said.

"It's Ivana… Ivana Popovich… and it's really not a good idea to be seen leaving together. Give me a thirty-minute head start and then leave. Ohhh, and don't forget to get on the wrong bus, you want to appear like you are just lost American tourists… nothin' else."

Jelena shut the door, and they could hear her leaving her room.

Upon her departure, Bruce just kinda stood there for a moment, almost looking like a sad puppy.

SMACK

"SNAP OUT OF IT, BRUCE!" Kate hollered as she smacked him in the back of his head.

"Fuck… Right… I got it… pants… I need pants," he said, chiming back into real life. "Damn, Kate… you're right. I'll put the paperwork through when we get back to have her assigned to another handler. You're absolutely right. We need some distance for a bit. I have no idea what's fucking wrong with me!" he said as he hopped into his blue jeans and zipped them up.

"Well, **that's** the first dadgum smart thing that you've said in weeks. I know what's wrong with you, honey… You're love-struck! You just can't admit it to yourself, Bruce," Kate snipped.

"Love-struck? Hmmmph," he snorted back at her. "Don't be ridiculous, Kate! The people I loved are either dead or in a mental hospital… and my love died with them. I don't do feelings, Kate! I don't do romance… I don't do love… If an itch comes along, I'm attractive enough to find myself a one-night stand and get in, get off and get out before dawn. That feelings shit… it's just more bullshit that bogs down my brain."

"Bruce, think about it…" Kate urged. "How many times have we shared a bed or a hotel room? You know… work-related stuff?"

"Shit, Kate, I don't know… hundreds of times, I guess," he replied, as he pulled his 'Everything's BIGGER in Texas' T-shirt over his head and straightened it out.

"Exactly!" Kate replied. "Now, I may not speak any fancy languages, but most would say that I, my dear, am quite the dish myself. I mean, look at me... tall, blonde, thin, cute... sweet... nice... most of the time. Hell, I could probably have any man that I damn well please, right? Wait, don't answer that. But anyways, when, out of those hundreds of times, have you come up on me like that, unintentionally, like not faking it for work stuff? When Bruce?"

"Well... never. I mean... yeah, you are all those things, and yeah, you're hot, so yes, you could have any man you wanted... but me? I guess I just never looked at you like that. I mean... I might have had a little infatuation with you when we first got assigned together all those years ago, but it was nothing that I couldn't control, and after a while, I just didn't see you like that anymore. I saw you more like a sister... with a big mouth... but still a sister, not a lover!" he explained as he brushed his thick dark hair and put on some deodorant.

"So, tell me, Bruce, what's so different about Jelena? It's damned obvious that you see *her* like a lover... so why?" Kate persisted. "Why can't you see her like a sister too? Better yet, why can't you see her for what she is... a fully competent, combat-proficient CIA operative? Bruce... she's a killin' machine. Just like you... just like me... just like the rest of us. Why are you romanticizing her inside your little pea brain? You're smart enough to know that that bullshit ain't gonna end well... for either of ya."

"Kate, I know! Alright? I fucking already know! I already know that it ain't gonna end well. Everything and everyone that I love turns to shit or dies on me. I know, okay! I don't know why she's different... she just is. She's got some kind of fuckin' hold over me! I don't know why or how! All I do know is that if there is the slightest chance that she is in danger, my little 'pea brain' just shuts the fuck down, and I can't think at all," Bruce confessed as he roughly sat himself down on the bed and put his head in his hands. "I just wish it would go away, Kate... before somebody really does get killed because of me. Maybe I need a real vacation... you know, just to get my head on straight. I haven't had one for what? Nine or ten years now? I just need her out of my head."

Kate sat next to Bruce, put her arm around his shoulders, and tried to soothe him a bit, "Awww, Bruce, honey... I am so sorry that you're goin' through this... but—"

"Don't start that shit with me again! I don't need your pity! I don't need your sorries either!" he snapped as he pulled away from her. "I need that bitch out of my head, and I need you to fucking drop it! Kate! I'm serious! Drop this fuckin' topic right now. I don't want to hear another word."

"Damnnnn alright... I'll drop it, but first what I was *gonna* say before I was so rudely interrupted, was... BUTTT, if you ever rub your woody up against me again, you might as well start callin' me George Washington, 'cause I'm gonna chop that cherry tree right the fuck down... mmmmkay, sweetie?" Kate said as sweet as pie with a smile on her face and a glimmer in her eye. "Now quit your bitchin' and grab your shit! We got the wrong bus to catch."

Bruce and Kate were just about to leave the hotel room when his phone rang…"She's gonna do WHAT?" he yelled. "Okay, we're on it. Thanks!"

"Bruce, I hate to ask a dumb question, but what is *she* gonna do? What's happening?" Kate asked. "I assume that was about Jelena, and I also assume that has to do with some cockamamie scheme she concocted? Am I close?"

"Hit the nail on the head. It's Jelena. When the fuck is she *not* in trouble? We don't have time for this shit. No buses… we'll ummm you know… borrow a car for a minute," he said, as he looked over at Kate, grabbed his stuff, and continued, "Thirty minutes my ass Kate, we're going right now… before she gets herself killed… again."

They raced to the warehouse across town, and on the way, Bruce explained to Kate that the phone call came from one of the surveillance boys who was watching not only Vladomir but Jelena as well. He saw that she had bypassed the plan and had headed straight over to the warehouse via a completely different and much shorter route. Why she wanted to be there for so long without backup was baffling to both Bruce and Kate.

"Damn it, Kate… why does she do this shit? Why does she feel like she has to do it all alone? I just don't get it," Bruce asked quietly as he shook his head.

"Maybe she's just as stubborn as you are?" Kate replied as Bruce shot her a cross look, and Kate responded with a little shoulder shrug.

Once they arrived at the warehouse, they ran around the building and slipped into one of the side doors. When they came in, they immediately heard a struggle. They followed the sounds through the dimly lit halls of the warehouse building. As the sounds got louder and louder, they knew they were close by, and of course, they knew that Jelena was somehow involved.

They came around a huge corner comprised of shelves and large boxes and found Jelena engaged in hand-to-hand combat with a man at least three times her size. They quickly ran to try and intervene when the man got her in a reverse chokehold. Jelena saw them approaching, and with the little air she had, she managed to scream out at them, "NO! THIS IS MY FIGHT!" All they could do was watch as she wiggled to free herself before stepping back and flipping the man clean over her shoulder onto his back. She jumped around and found a suitable grappling position where she could apply a sleeper hold until the man passed out unconscious.

Once she felt the tension in his body go limp, she crawled out from under him and stood up and brushed herself off.

Kate looked around and noticed four other men passed out on the floor. She gently smacked Bruce in the chest and pointed to bring it to his attention that Jelena had defeated five men... by herself.

"Why do you feel that you have to fight this war alone?" Bruce asked her in a tone that was quite calmer than she had expected him to be.

"Were you in the box with me there, Bruce? Were you there when they put me in that hole to die? Were you there when he used a lit cigar to put a hole in my neck? Were you, Bruce?" Jelena asked, still slightly out of breath.

"No... I wasn't... I'm sorry about that," he replied.

"I don't give a fuck about your sorries," she snarked at him, which of course, made Kate's eyebrows go up, and she bit her lip to keep from smiling as she was looking at Bruce.

Kate mouthed the words back to him, "She doesn't give a fuck about your sorries," and shrugged her shoulders once again.

Jelena continued, "**He** made this personal Bruce... **He** made this personal when they put me in that hole to die. This is MY fight!" she insisted.

"Hey... I got news for you, lady... lots of people are gonna try to put you in a hole... lots of them are gonna try to kill you... that's their job, Jelena. Is it **them** who made it personal? Or **you**?" Bruce asked.

Jelena stood there for a second, processing what he just said and thinking to herself that maybe it *was* her who was making it personal. After all, she was the one who killed Svetlana, and killing is exceptionally personal. She ran her hands over her hair, straightening up her ponytail and pushing back all of the little whispy chocolate strands.

"Yeah... okay... so then what? We all scrap with these assholes? Is that your plan, Bruce?" Jelena asked him.

"Yes... that's how we get to the next step. This is *your* show Jelena... we are just here to support you. They have extra fists, and now so do you," he said encouragingly.

"Yeah... they're down about ten, though." She chuckled.

"We are all in it to win it... together!" Bruce continued.

"Alright... but Vladomir is mine. Got it? No interference!" she insisted.

"Okay... Alright... Vladomir is all yours," Bruce agreed.

Jelena approached the unknown man hanging by his wrists from the ceiling with thick chains. She couldn't help but think of Mel Titan... and Adam. She released the crank that held tension on the chain a little at a time until there was enough slack for the unknown man to collapse onto himself like a pile of bricks. His breathing was rough, and he had taken a hell of a pounding, but he was still alive.

Jelena began slapping him gently on the cheek to bring him around. "Hey... Hey..." she said, trying to rouse him.

"Hey... Tebya nuzhno bezhat'...Heyyy...but' svoboden...seychas BEGI!" she said to the man in Russian.

Kate looked at Bruce and asked, "What did she say to him?"

"That he needed to run away, be free..." he explained.

The man slowly got up and looked around, still a bit dazed. To speed up the process of getting him the hell out of there, as not to ruin the rest of their plan, Bruce approached him. Bruce pulled out his gun and pointed it at the man, and yelled, "SEYCHAS BEGI! RUN NOW!"

The man scrambled to his feet and took off straight out of the building.

"Follow him, Kate. Make sure that he finds his way out. We don't need any other liabilities," Bruce requested.

"On it," Kate chirped.

"Alright, Bruce, what time is it?" Jelena asked.

"11:49 AM," he responded. "Shit! Vladomir will be here any minute," he remembered.

"Yep… so once I'm up here hanging, your job will be to keep the other bugs off me until he gets here. But right now, I need you to help me get situated in these chains," she explained.

"You sure that you want to do this?" Bruce asked her.

"MY fight Bruce! This will all be over soon," she responded. "Now, give me a leg up."

Bruce helped Jelena twist the chains around her wrists in such a way that as long as she kept her hands in a certain position, the chains would be able to hold her weight and keep her dangling like the last guy until she was ready to release and drop down. She had Bruce put one of the bags over her head so that it would not be immediately obvious to Vladomir that it was her.

"Eguuggg! This thing stinks!" Jelena scoffed.

"Kinda like the good old days," Bruce taunted. "Now, shut up and hang there quietly, like a good girl…"

Kate and Bruce hung back in the shadows and waited for Jelena's show to begin. Vladomir was walking in with two other men. They quickly saw that something had happened to the men standing guard at the warehouse. They saw Jelena hanging there but didn't realize it was her and paid her no mind.

"GO!" Vladomir yelled with an accent all too familiar to Jelena. "Search everywhere! I will talk to little friend here to see if he saw ghost who did this."

Jelena hung there perfectly motionless, just waiting for Vladomir to make his move. He calmly walked over to the table and picked up a wooden bat before approaching Jelena.

"So… little friend… what you see? Did you see ghost who come in?"

Jelena remained still and silent, like a lioness waiting for the perfect time to strike.

"No speak? Nothing to say? Oh… I think you will speak…" Vladomir said as he cocked the bat back and, with great force, swung it, cracking it against Jelena's ribs.

"The last one who no speak… died in hole… in cow shit…" he taunted.

Bruce almost bolted from his hidden position, but Kate grabbed his shoulders hard, holding him back. "This is her fight, Bruce. She has to do it... this is her walk... her walk... remember?" Kate whispered.

Bruce looked at Kate and whispered back, "We should go take out those other guys before they come back. If Jelena is outnumbered, this could be a problem."

Kate nodded, and the two of them slipped through the darkness, searching for the last two men. Even as Bruce was snapping the neck of the one man he had found, he kept hearing the blows that Jelena was taking and knew that he needed to get back in case things got out of hand.

On his way back to the main area where Jelena was hanging, he bumped back into Kate and whispered, "You get him?" Kate nodded to indicate that she had, and they both crept back to the little shadowy nook that they were hiding in, ready to pounce should Jelena need help.

"Let's see your face, friend," Vladomir began. "Maybe this too easy on you, eh? Maybe you ghost, eh? Are you ghost, friend?"

Vladomir grabbed the bag on Jelena's head and began to pull it off and toss it to the side. When he refocused his sight on her, Jelena lifted her head, and with a sick twisted smile, she said, "BOO!"

Vladomir backed way up, yelling out, "NOOO... not possible... NO! I KILLED YOU! I PUT YOU IN HOLE... I BROKE YOU, AND I BURIED YOU! YOU'RE DEAD!!! HOW?? YOU'RE DEAD?"

"Think again, Vladomir..." Jelena sang at him. "I told you to be careful what you wish for... you wanted tougher spies... and here I am... a ghost from **your** past."

"NOOOOO... I KILLED YOU!" he insisted.

"Hmmm, you're wrong there too. You see Vlad... I just don't die. It's the damnest thing," Jelena said, smiling and taunting Vladomir.

"NOOO! You bitch! You killed Svetlana! I will kill you with my own bare hands this time," he said.

"You want me? Come and get me, Grandpa!" she scoffed back at him.

Instantly, Vladomir pulled out a long filet knife and ran toward Jelena, screaming, "I WILL CUT YOUR FUCKING HEART OUT!"

Jelena pulled herself up into the chains, kicked the knife out of his hand and swung around, until she got him in a chokehold around his neck with her legs. She held him there for a minute until he went slightly limp. She jumped out of the chains and landed on her feet right before him. However, she didn't quite realize that old Vlad had been trained by the best of the KGB. He may have been a bit dazed, but he was definitely not out of the fight. As Jelena was jumping down, Vlad was regaining his balance and had locked his focus on her every move.

Perhaps suffering from a little too much cocky arrogance, she missed a step and didn't catch him doing a sweep on her to get her on the ground. She landed with a thud, but that didn't keep her down for long. Every time he would knock her to the ground, she would get right back up.

She spun around and caught Vlad in the mouth with a backward flying hammer fist strike, splitting his lower lip wide open. The taste of blood in his own mouth dazed the seasoned Russian for a moment.

"You hit hard… for girl," he said, as he spit blood onto the floor and wiped the rest off his chin.

"I am **not** your typical girl, there Vlad. It's a whole different experience now that I'm… uhh.. not all tied up, isn't it?" she said, taunting him through her own bloody smile.

"You hit like man, but still… I BREAK you!" he insisted, as his left jab made contact with Jelena's cheek.

"Ohhh Vlad… I really wouldn't get your hopes up buddy," she began, "Many men have been **very…. very….** disappointed after trying to break me… unsuccessfully."

The two of them continued to trade blows until Vladomir was tired and frustrated enough to grab a gun he had hidden close by. As he grabbed it up, he whipped it around and pointed it straight at her… a mere two inches from her nose.

Out of breath from their tussle, Vladomir said, "You like wild horse… but even the wildest horse can be broken. I will find a way to break you!"

Bruce flinched in his position, and with everything he had, he fought to restrain himself, looking at Kate with pleading eyes… just begging to have her permission to jump in and help.

Jelena remembered a fighting tactic that she learned from some Israelis about disarming an opponent. Jelena raised her hands as if she were to surrender, and in a split second, she grabbed the gun with one hand and shoved Vladomir's elbow in the wrong direction with the other, snapping the gun out of his grasp and sending him to the floor bellowing in pain.

Jelena pointed the gun at Vladomir's face, now a mere two inches from **his** nose, and said, "I told you... You will NEVER break me... EVER!"

"PLEASE!" Vladomir begged, holding his broken arm in pain. "Please... do it! PLEASE... kill me."

Jelena was stunned by his request but was not foolish enough to put the gun down.

"What? Why?" she asked.

With the same pain in his eyes that she saw before, he said, "I miss her. I want to be with Svetlana. The pain without her is too much... please." He whimpered. "Please just kill me... please."

Keeping the gun on him, Jelena crouched down to the level of the old, sobbing man and said softly and gently, "Vladomir, I *am* sorry that I killed Svetlana. People always say that it's nothing personal, but you and I... we know different, don't we? We know that killing is always personal. In the end, she was doing her job, and I was doing mine. I understand pain. I understand torture. I understand death. We don't have many choices in these matters most of the time. Today I have a choice Vladomir. Today, I think you are worth more to us alive than dead, so, today... right at this moment... I choose to keep you alive. I am not going to kill you today Vladomir... maybe some other time."

CHAPTER 21: WIN, LOSE OR DRAW

Jelena rose to her feet, looked down at the broken Russian, and then looked over at Bruce and Kate. "Secure him," she instructed. "He's coming with us."

"NOOOO!" Vladomir wailed from his knees. "PLEASE! Pozholusta!"

As Kate helped Bruce tie some telephone cords around Vladomir's wrists and helped him to his feet, she asked, "And why again is he coming with us?" Kate had a confused look on her face as she looked back and forth between Bruce and Jelena.

"Because he knows the plan," Jelena replied quietly as she flipped the gun's safety on and stuck it in her waistband.

"Plan?" Kate said softly. "What plan?"

"We were so caught up in other things, Kate, that we missed it. Svetlana's place may have only given us a fake drive with a goose chase on it, but this man right here... this man, he knows the real plan. Don't you, Vlad? He knows exactly what attack the KGB is planning on our intel site out there. He knows the players, the dates and times, and the endgame... and so, we are gonna take him back home, and I am going to help him write it all down for us so that we can intervene and do our little part to protect what's ours. That's why," Jelena explained very matter of fact.

Bruce looked at Kate and then down in disbelief. He ran his hand through his hair as he realized that all this time, he was so busy feeling up Kate, with his head in the clouds dreaming about Jelena, that he missed the bigger picture. His feelings for Jelena had not only clouded his judgment but also blinded him from what the real objective was.

It wasn't 'Jelena vs. the Russians,'

It wasn't 'Let's keep Jelena alive.'

It wasn't 'Right feelings vs. Wrong feelings.'

His fucking feelings really didn't matter at all, but because of them, he lost his edge and nearly failed his team. The objective was to obtain the plans that the KGB had to attack the CIA's classified intel site in the remote area on the outskirts of Moscow… to probably steal whatever intelligence was there and torture and kill any one of our people on site who may know something. THAT was the plan. THAT was the objective.

Bruce had never had something like this happen before. He knew that Kate was right on the money and that he and Jelena could not work safely together. Now he just had to figure out a way to get Jelena a new handler without anyone getting in trouble over it. He just couldn't believe that he missed it… all because, as Kate said, he was thinking with the wrong head.

Kate also looked a little bit disappointed in herself for missing it. She was so busy trying to convince Bruce to accept his feelings and confess them to Jelena that she didn't have her head in the game either. She also found herself attached to Jelena, although in a more sisterly manner but, still… attachments are never a good investment where spy work is concerned. This whole time, Jelena thought that she was the one to let Kate down, when in reality… right at this moment… Kate was positive that it was the other way around. As her mentor, Kate felt that she had failed Jelena, and if Jelena weren't as Goddamned good as she was, they all would have died for nothing.

In the end, Jelena knew she was there for a reason, even if that reason wasn't entirely clear from the start. First off, she didn't even know what Bruce was feeling, other than what Kate reported back to her. On the plane heading into Moscow, she thought about why she was going. What she was there to do, and for a bit, even *she* didn't see it. The only thing she saw at that point was red blinding rage. She wanted sheer revenge and only revenge. She wanted to put a bullet right between the swollen eyes of one Vladomir Khishchnik, right after she gave him the same royal brass knuckle treatment that he gave to her. Payback for throwing her in that hole to die... and not to mention, costing her fourteen days of her life that she will never get back. Jelena wanted that payback, and she wanted it bad.

It wasn't until Vladomir begged Jelena to kill him that she thought about the situation and the true end goal. Could a killer and a brute like Vladomir be capable of love? Did he truly love Svetlana? Or did he just want to die to protect the information in his head? Did he love her just enough to make sure that she kept the plans safe? Or did he love her so much that the plans didn't matter at all anymore? Only time in interrogation would solve that mystery. If he truly loved Svetlana as much as he claimed, then he should have no problem at all spilling the beans, especially if offered a timely reunion with his beloved, as soon as his intel checks out. Spies didn't usually get a peaceful ending... so that was a valuable bargaining chip.

Maybe all this talk about Bruce and love and dumb-ass feelings did help Jelena to see that it was far more important to keep Vladomir alive to finally know the detailed plans of Russian Intelligence and protect our people out there. Logic over emotion... Intel over vengeance... but she still couldn't help but wonder if Bruce was the same? She considered him a killer and a brute. In her opinion, those words didn't even do him justice. No matter how she looked at it, she still couldn't make any sense of it. A man who tortured her mercilessly... who beat her... who electrocuted her repeatedly... who stood by while the others tried to drown her.

Was Kate right? Did he really have feelings of love for her? Or was it just another ploy to use Jelena and get her to perform like a lion in a circus? Did he genuinely care? Is *he* even capable? Jelena had all these questions in her head, just floating around waiting for answers. For now, all she knew was that she still didn't trust him, and there was no way in hell that she could fall in love with a man she didn't trust.

Jelena took Vladomir by the arm and sat with him in the back seat of the 'borrowed' car as Bruce drove them back to the airstrip where their black flight awaited them. They bypassed the hotel as Kate had called earlier for a team to come in and collect what they had left behind. Sometimes in these situations, it is best to get the hell out of Dodge before anyone has realized what has happened.

Bruce left the equivalent of $100 in the front visor as a little inconvenience fee for borrowing their car. He took Vladomir by the arm, walked him out onto the strip, and got him secured into the plane, which was headed to Langley Airforce Base. Jelena and Kate were not far behind them, but both ladies just walked in silence. It was a long ride to Langley.

Jelena had not felt so incredibly free in a very long time. As she sat in the CIA transport plane, she had time to think about how her world had changed so much, so quickly. How she had started as a Marine, one of millions... a warrior assigned to defend a nation. Nothing special... Nothing unique... Just another in a long line... All wearing the same uniform and all with the same mission.

Once again, she thought about Bruce. She remembered the first time she had seen him in that tiny room on base. Telling her that this was just another mission... just another boot camp. She remembered how she hated him and remembered quite vividly, planning his death from her dark little hole. She still didn't understand how he could go from adversary to ally... and even more, how could he even remotely develop romantic feelings toward her, according to Kate, after everything he had done? Was he really her ally, or was he just another trickster monster that her father had warned her of, just playing the part? Who in the hell was he? How did he fit in? So many 'whys' with that one... so many whys.

And, of course, there was Kate. Sickly sweet vanilla ice cream, just as smooth as silk, Kate. She remembered how beautiful Kate was, both on the inside and outside. She remembered, when this crazy adventure began, how she wondered exactly how this dainty blonde was going to teach her anything. At first, she feared Kate's judgment, but now in retrospect, she realized that she was judging her too, and probably more harshly. Thinking that Kate was way too prissy to teach her anything about being a spy, let alone combat. She remembered how Kate always seemed to know just what to say... or what to do... and how she taught her what it truly meant to conduct herself with grace and virtue. She was amazed to see how that 'blonde' was indeed a bombshell.

She thought about all the people she had met and learned something from. Mel Titan, for instance. She didn't have much time with Mel, but he left her a huge legacy filled with secrets that she knew would be extremely valuable someday. She remembered how he was just hanging there and how much pain and suffering he endured. How kind his eyes were. How things happen so fast. One minute you're here, and the next minute you can be gone... in a flash.

Her thoughts would frequently travel to Adam. A friend... kind and caring. While enduring his own torturous pain, he took time and love to care for a stranger, Jelena. She felt denied closure, and maybe that's what she craved... closure. At first, she was determined to find him, but now, she couldn't help but ask herself if that was really a good idea. Kate was right. Emotions... attachments... these are vulnerabilities... and vulnerabilities line the path to an early grave. Maybe it was best for Adam to stay hidden in the darkness, away from harm. She didn't like that notion, but she accepted it... for now.

Her mind shifted in a different direction. She remembered her interactions with Svetlana and couldn't help but feel a loss. Looking back, she could clearly see how Svetlana wasn't threatened at all by her presence, how Jelena's trickery flowed so smoothly that it charmed Svetlana into a false sense of security. She remembered feeling so naïve when Kate told her to put the poison into her cup, not understanding the CIAs most finite end game... and her frenzied panic when Svetlana died right there in front of her. Kate said it was all part of the job, but Jelena didn't feel it was a win at all. She never thought that she would be capable of killing in cold blood. She finally figured out that killing Svetlana did cause a loss. It caused Jelena to lose part of her soul and believe that she was also, in fact, one of the monsters her father told her about. Could she ever go back to just being normal? Or would she remain a monster for all time? Like a pet? Belonging to the CIA...

She thought about Vladomir Khishchnik. She remembered seeing how happy he was in Mel Titan's surveillance photos. Just smiling and happily walking into Svetlana's arms, with the flowers he brought her each week. She remembered the pain and agony that echoed in his eyes. She had to accept that she caused it, and regardless of reason, the blood of Vladomir's suffering was on her hands. Even worse yet, was that that suffering hadn't even begun. Vladomir was in for weeks or months of interrogation to pull every last detail of the KGB's plans out of his head.

She thought about how she won against Vladomir, but was it really a win? She asked herself if she really showed mercy by keeping him alive... or did she condemn him to a fate worse than death.

She knew that Vladomir would be sent to a containment facility for the rest of his life. She knew that she would rather be dead herself than have a similar fate. Being in that pit, constantly questioned... in a place where you never have the right answer. She'd been there already and barely got out with only a thread of her dignity and sanity left intact.

Jelena realized that this new life was not without cost, repercussion, or loss. Was it better to focus on winning, whatever that means, or was the better angle to just be grateful that she was alive to fight another day? For now, the latter would have to do. Despite the wins, losses, and even the draws, Jelena felt like she had finally found her place in this world. She knew that she had changed a lot, although she wasn't always certain if that change was for the better or worse. Regardless, this was her new world. It wasn't always clean… it wasn't always messy… but as Bruce had said in the beginning, there was no out now. She was in it, and she chose to accept it.

Two weeks later, Kate and Jelena got together over coffee at one of the local shops. They giggled and laughed, and the two of them seemed to be in a world beyond reality.

"Girl!" Kate sang. "I just can't believe you did that! You just pulled that stunt like you'd been doin' it all your life. It was the damnest thing I'd ever seen."

"Well… you know, you were busy yickety-yackin' with the old broad up front, so I just thought I would move things along. Hey… there were no rules in the book about breaking and entering not being allowed." Jelena chuckled.

"Have you heard from Bruce?" Kate asked, slightly raising one eyebrow.

"Hey! You keep that nasty eyebrow right in line with the other one," Jelena said jokingly. "Not really. He didn't say a word to me the whole way back. Then like a day or two later, I was transferred and never heard another word from him. Anyways, I was transferred to some douche canoe named, ummm, Treesman... Dick Treesman... short... stubby... personality of a wet mop... ever heard of him?"

"Yeah, Dick ain't a bad fella... but you should know... he ain't much for sarcasm," Kate replied.

"Hmmm, we should get along ggrrrrreeeeeaaaaattttt then," she moaned sarcastically.

"Now honey, you gotta give him a chance. It really *is* for the best," Kate reassured. "When I told Bruce that I thought that he was in love with you... He didn't say that he wasn't. I just know that he can't help feelin' the way he's feelin'. I've just never seen *him* feel anything ever. So, you MUST have some sorta Bruce charmin' magical powers there girly!"

"Well, I wish that I knew how to use those magical powers back at the farm when he was kicking the shit out of me. Didn't work back then... but I get what you're saying Kate, I know... no attachments..." Jelena started. "But this is *really* Bruce's problem since that attachment is quite one-sided."

"But you said that you dreamed of him too?" Kate said softly as she sipped her tea. "I know that you said it was a nightmare, but Bruce is a handsome guy, and he is a good guy. Are you sure that it is entirely one-sided?"

Jelena looked around and took a moment to sip her own tea as she figured out how to honestly explain her feelings, "Look, Kate, I just don't think that I'll ever be able to forgive him for what he put me through. I don't think I can ever trust him, and I know myself well enough to know that I can't love a man I don't trust. I just don't know how to get past that... how to forgive him... the look in his eye Kate, when he was electrocuting me, he enjoyed every time he hurt me. That look in his eye was scarier than actually being hit or electrocuted. I know that he was just doing his job... blah, blah, blah... training me to take as much as possible, but I can't see it ever being anything more than one-sided... on his end. It's sad, though, that he just can't be a teammate. I still don't understand why that psycho thought I would feel the same? He never even talked to me about any of it. I don't know... maybe if he did, things might be different. I just don't let myself think about him much anymore."

"Darlin', I am pretty positive that he knew damn well that you didn't feel the same way, and that's probably why he didn't talk to you about it. I don't even think that he could talk to himself about it, to be quite honest," Kate replied. "As I said, I ain't never seen **him** feel anything about anyone ever... but, girl, you done got right up underneath that boy's skin. Hell, maybe he does have a heart after all."

"Eh... Whatever... But you're right, Kate. Distance is a good thing right now. I still got so much to learn... ya know?" Jelena continued.

"Honey, I sure do!" Kate giggled. "Hell, I'm still learnin', and I've been at it for over seven years now."

"Alright, lady... it's been so great to see you," Jelena said as she stood up and gave Kate a huge hug. "I gotta get back to work, or this Treesman guy will have my ass. We gotta do this more, that's for sure."

"Oooohh, okay, darlin'!" Kate said. "You take care of yourself now... and call me this weekend," she continued as she walked over to her maroon-colored sedan and dug the keys out of her purse.

Jelena began to walk in the other direction and briefly turned around to wave at Kate. "You bet, Mama! Margarita's on me!" Jelena hollered out, and as she turned back around...

BOOOOM

Within thirty seconds of turning her back and parting ways with Kate, Jelena heard a loud explosion. She whipped around just in time to see Kate's car explode and Kate fly back and land on the ground motionless. Jelena ran to her and crouched down beside Kate's body. Kate was bleeding from the eyes, nose, and ears. She didn't appear to be breathing. Jelena looked around the area, trying to see if anyone was just suspiciously standing nearby and watching.

She reached down to feel for a pulse in Kate's neck, "FUCK!"

To Be Continued....

www.ingramcontent.com/pod-product-compliance
Lightning Source LLC
Chambersburg PA
CBHW062020170626
46813CB00001B/231